T0107524

Daughters of Zion

Daughters of Zion

Alma Ettore

authorHOUSE®

AuthorHouse™
1663 Liberty Drive
Bloomington, IN 47403
www.authorhouse.com
Phone: 1-800-839-8640

© 2011 by Alma Ettore. All rights reserved.

No part of this book may be reproduced, stored in a retrieval system, or transmitted by any means
without the written permission of the author.

First published by AuthorHouse   11/29/2011

ISBN: 978-1-4670-0748-1 (sc)
ISBN: 978-1-4670-0749-8 (ebk)

Printed in the United States of America

Any people depicted in stock imagery provided by Thinkstock are models, and such images are being
used for illustrative purposes only.
Certain stock imagery © Thinkstock.

This book is printed on acid-free paper.

Because of the dynamic nature of the Internet, any web addresses or links contained in this book may
have changed since publication and may no longer be valid. The views expressed in this work are
solely those of the author and do not necessarily reflect the views of the publisher, and the publisher
hereby disclaims any responsibility for them.

For Martin

Author's Note

Writing this book was an emotional rollercoaster for me. I did feel very sad and at times physically ill when I had to imagine the suffering of my people and visit some of the places in my mind, but it has to be done; the story has to be told. Today I feel much relieved and I am at peace because I am not afraid anymore to say things which are considered a taboo to speak about. I started by looking at the events of the war in a more objective way. This is why I wanted to share this knowledge with people around the world.

Those People who think that they know me well may be surprised to learn about my family tree. Writing this book has made me think of the different tribes that made me; something which I took for granted in the past and did not even think much about.

My father was a pure Zande from Western Equatoria State. My mother's father was half Zande of Western Bahr El-Ghazal State and half Baggara of North Western Sudan. My mother's mother was half Dinka from Gogrial in East Bahr El-Ghazal State and half Lugbara of Uganda. This is why I always refer to the Dinka as "my uncles". I feel very proud of all the tribes from the different areas of North Sudan and the Republic of South Sudan that produced me. Many people in the Republic of South Sudan are like me; rich history and varied ancestors. I mentioned this fact just to show that we are different tribes but are one people. If we can find it possible in ourselves to recognise and respect each other and give space to each other then The Republic of South Sudan will be one of the best places to live in.

My Great grandmother, the Baggara lady, was called "Um El Kheir". She was a Muslim. She was a great lady, with a strong character. She was the only great grandparent who lived long enough to see me. Whenever I went to visit her house with my mother, I felt nothing but glowing warmth and love. She died when I was five. Her husband my great grandfather was a Zande. He was most probably an animist who converted to Islam but their son, my grandfather embraced Christianity when he joined the missionary school. Religion was more of a personal choice, a relationship between an individual and God. No one stoned or condemned anybody. This is why the Sudan was so peaceful in those times.

The book is written hopefully to help us South Sudanese, find peace and closure after the terrible events we suffered over two decades of civil war. If our children do not know the truth behind their history then they will repeat the same mistakes that we did.

It is easy to bury our heads in the sand and "forget" our mistakes, troubles and pain. We seem to find it very difficult to sit down after events and analyse our performance especially after such a long and messy war. Burying our heads in the sand is the same like brushing dirt under the carpet; the dirt might not be seen but *it is surely there and will remain there until physically moved by someone!*

I was going through a lot of emotional turmoil during the Referendum campaign of November 2010, the voting and finally the achieved freedom of South Sudan in July 2011). I began thinking about the similarities of our story and that of the "chosen people of God. The two nations have been so much hated and derided by the same people who happen to be their "neighbours" or so called "brothers". Thanks to the Lord Almighty who has listened to our cries of anguish and distress. We are a free nation at last.

We are a nation deeply rooted in the shackles of slavery constantly looking for Zion, that Promised Land, the land of freedom, peace and happiness. Constantly entreating with our Maker . . .

Solomon's Song of Songs mentioned in this book is not mere sweet words to describe love between two lovers but go far deeper. I hope that the readers will understand and enjoy this synopsis about a land defiled; a woman equally defiled, scorned and later loved as an unblemished virgin: Zion.

The SPLA is an army that fought voluntarily for the freedom of South Sudan. Many of our family members were recruited in this force. My father, God the Almighty rest his soul in Eternal Peace, was a high ranking officer in the SPLA, and so were some of my brothers. They worked without salaries; they had no proper or regular food supplies and other equipment to help them with their struggle. Where will they get their food and all the creature "comforts" that goes with it? Who is to blame?

In this book some criticism was levelled at the SPLA, because many innocent civilians were badly hurt by the actions of "some elements in the SPLA". The message is: Yes the SPLA was fighting for the rights of the South Sudanese people but not all of them have observed the law which has been clearly set out by the United Nations General Assembly. In that respect one may conclude that some of them did not share the same vision as the late Dr. John Garang de Mabior, founder of the SPLA /M. That law was set in order to uphold Human Rights in armed conflict. Anyone who breaks the law will have to answer to the International Criminal Court of Justice. There is no excuse whatsoever for murdering, raping and taxing innocent civilians by armed forces.

This book gives us the chance to think about the good and the bad things which were carried out by our armed forces: rebels, militia and the Sudan Government Armed Forces. We will then have to build on and improve the good things they did. It is also our duty as a nation to create ways and means to correct, stop or prevent in the future, the many mistakes they committed.

When reading the story many people might wonder as to why Dinka land was so much devastated during the war while other places in Equatoria such as Yambio seemed to have fared much better.

If you happen to travel hundreds of miles in a southerly route from Aweil, in North Bahr El-Ghazal, you will find yourself in Zande land or Western Equatoria after crossing part of the *Fertit* land. People who lived in Zande land at that time were perhaps more lucky mainly because of their geographical location.The Zande land is far away from the *El Niño* and the *Baggara* and their neighbours. The Azande and the *Fertit* are mainly farmers. They have equatorial climate and very dense forests. The land is rich in edible fruits and game. They did not experience drought and hunger. Their terrain helped them at times to hide from approaching enemies. The indigenous people of the Democratic Republic of Congo (DRC) and Central Africa who live on the borders with the Zande are mainly Azande themselves. When war broke out in South of Sudan, the Azande people fled across the borders to their *families* thus escaping a lot of the suffering which was inflicted on their brothers the Dinka.

These are the main reasons why the Equatoria regions and Western Bahr El-Ghazal (where the Fertit live) have fared better than the other areas inhabited mainly by the Dinka tribe during those dark times.

All the characters mentioned in this story are purely fictional, based on true story of the civil war in South Sudan. Although the names of the individuals mentioned are real names, they were not used to directly or indirectly refer to any real person. The exceptions are the late Dr. John Garang de Mabior, President Omar Hassan El Bashir, the late Field Marshall Gaafar Mohammad Nimeri and retired Lieutenant General Joseph Lagu Yanga.

Many verses from the bible were used to refer to or give an essence to certain events. I feel that you do not have to be a Christian or religious in any way to understand or appreciate the meaning of the verses and make a connection. These verses are purely used for illustrative purposes.

Daughters Of Zion

Sudan, 1987-93

Map of States of the Republic of South Sudan 2011

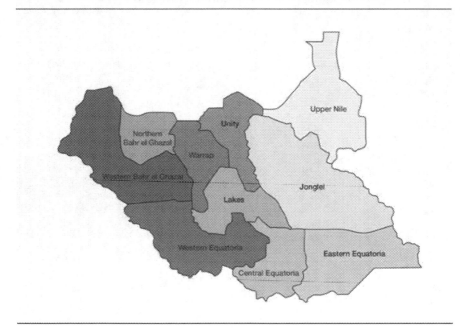

Glossary of terms and abbreviations:

Abeed   Plural of 'Abd' meaning slave. (Origin: Arabic)

Acholi   An African Luo people living in East Equatoria State.

Ajous   Old (Origin: Arabic)

Aliwara   Second hand clothes.

Allah   God (Origin: Arabic)

Ambororo   Cattle keepers from Chad similar to "Baggara" of Sudan.

Andaya   A Public house or a drinking place.

Anyanya   Deadly snake venom. A name of a South Sudanese rebel group. (Origin: Madi)

Aragi   An alcoholic drink made from fermented fruits, mostly dates (Origin: Arabic)

Avukaya   An African, non-Nilotic people living in West Equatoria State.

Avungara   A clan of the ruling nobles or chiefs of the Azande people.

Baggara   Arabised cattle-owning nomad tribe of western Sudan, including the Misseriya of southern Kordofan and Rizeigat of southern Darfur. Their name is derived from the Arabic word "bagar" meaning cow.

Baka   An African, non Nilotic people living in West Equatoria State.

Balanda   (See Fertit)

Banda   (See Fertit)

Bangara   A mild and sweet alcoholic drink made from fermented sorghum. It is a native drink of the Azande people (Origin: Zande)

Bongo   (See Fertit)

Conjur   A fortune teller or a witch doctor.

Dar   House (Origin: Arabic)

Dinka   An African Nilotic people living in Bahr El Ghazal and Upper Nile in the Republic of South Sudan. They are the largest ethnic group in the Republic of South Sudan.

Dous   Push (Origin: Arabic)

El Huda   Providence or gift (Origin: Arabic).

El Niño   A climatic pattern that occurs across the tropical Pacific Ocean. This climatic change occurs roughly every five years. It causes extremes of weather such as flooding and drought. (Origin: Spanish)

El Salam   Peace (Origin: Arabic).

ET   Extra terrestrial being.

Fallata	A name given to West Africans, mostly Muslims who settled in Sudan, often in transit to or from Mecca.
Fertit	A name given to many small tribes (non-nilotic) including Kreish, Banda, Bongo, Ndogo, Golo, Balanda and Forge, all of African Bantu origin who live in West Bahr El Ghazal State. Are mostly non-Muslims and non-Arabic speakers.
Gbudwe	A great King of the Azande Kingdom from the Avungara clan. He went into history as one the greatest warrior kings of Africa.
Golo	(see Fertit)
Haram	Forbidden or illegitimate. (Origin: Arabic)
Hai	Area (Origin: Arabic)
Henna	A red dye made of natural herb or shrub. Its colour can turn to black which is the colour favoured by Sudanese women to make artistic and decorative tattoos on their hands and feet. The colour wears off after a period of time. (Origin: Arabic)
Hilla	Area (Origin: Arabic)
ICC	International Criminal Court of Justice.
Itisalat	Internet café. (Origin: Arabic)
Jenge	A derogatory term used in reference to Dinka and other Nilotics by non-Nilotic tribes.
Jur	An African Luo people living south and south east of West Bahr El Ghazal State. They are non-Muslims and non-Arabic speakers.

Kafir/Kuffar A non-believer in God. Kuffar is the plural of Kafir. (Origin: Arabic)

Khawaja A white person. (Origin: Arabic)

Kisra A wafer thin food made of maize or dura (type of grain). It is used as bread in Sudan usually eaten with stews, salads etc.

Kreish (see Fertit)

Kubri Bridge (Origin: Arabic)

Kuku An African, non-Muslim people living in East Equatoria State.

LRA Lord Resistance Army

Lugbara An African people living in East Equatoria State and North Uganda.

Madi An African, non-Muslim people living in East Equatoria State and North Uganda.

Mara Woman or female. (Origin: Arabic—Imra-*at*).

MSF Medecins Sans Frontiers. An international emergency medical nongovernmental organisation often working in war zones

Mundu An African, non Muslim people living in West Equatoria State.

Mundukuru A name given to the North Arabs of Sudan by the South Sudanese.

Muraheleen A Messeryia word for "travelers". It is a name used in reference to Baggara tribal Arabs of southern Darfur and Kordofan who have been incorporated as a government militia under army jurisdiction to fight the Dinka in Bahr El Ghazal.

Muru An African, non-Muslim people living in West Equatoria State. They are the second largest group.

Mutu Kali sandals or slippers made locally from car tyres.

Muslim A follower of Islam which is a religion based on the word of Allah (God) as revealed to Muhammed the prophet, during the 7th century.

Naeem Heaven (Origin: Arabic)

Naziheen A wonderer or a person who takes aimless walks outside his/her territory or place of residence. (Origin: Arabic)

Ndogo (See Fertit)

Neem Tree A tree native to Asia and sub Saharan Africa. It is a tall evergreen tree. Its bark, resin and seed oil have medicinal properties.

Nuer An African Nilotic people living in Upper Nile and Unity States, Republic of South Sudan.

OLS Operation Lifeline Sudan. A United Nations emergency relief operation for Sudan which began operations in 1989, serving territory controlled by the government and by the SPLA.

Pazande Zande language

Rabbaba A musical instrument (Origin: Arabic)

Rakuba Lean to, made of beams of wood with a roof of grass or other flimsy materials to lend a shade for people to sit under.

Rizeigat   (see Baggara)

Sharia Law   Islamic Law based on the teachings of Mohammed the Prophet.

SPLA/M   Sudan People's Liberation Army/Movement. The political organization and army of Sudanese rebels formed in 1983, of which Dr. John Garang De Mabior was chairman and commander in chief.

Suk   Market. (Origin: Arabic)

Tob   A transparent piece of long cloth worn by Sudanese women over a dress, covering the whole body. (Origin: Arabic)

Tonura   A short underskirt worn by African women.

Walad   Son, boy (Origin: Arabic)

Yuma   Mother or an elderly aunt. (Origin: Arabic)

Zande   Azande (plural) are the third largest tribe in the Republic of South Sudan. They are found in West Equatoria State and West Bahr El Ghazal State (after remnants of Gbudwe who was a great King of the Azande, went on rampage in the area during the eighteenth century). The Azande are also found in the Democratic Republic of Congo and Central African Republic. These were areas which originally constituted part of the great Azande Kingdom destroyed by the Belgian, French, Mahdist and finally the British in the European scramble for colonization and domination of Africa.

Zion   Hebrew word transliterated (Tzion or Tsion). It is a term used to refer to Jerusalem or metaphorically to the Biblical land of Israel. In the bible it refers to a certain mountain where King Solomon built the famous Temple in Jerusalem, the City of David.

History tells us about the captivity and enslavement of the Jewish people by the Babylonians. Their longing for Zion was mentioned in many parts of the Bible. The Black, impoverished, embattled and enslaved people of South Sudan have also identified their homeland as "Zion"; the land of freedom, peace and equality.

"Your land is a desolation; your cities are burned with fire.
Your ground—right in front of you strangers are eating it up,
and the desolation is like an overthrow by strangers.
And the daughter of Zion has been left remaining like booth in a vineyard,
like a lookout hut in a field of cucumbers, like a blockaded city."

Isaiah 1:7-8

Prologue

"Mummy, please do not leave me. Please mummy, take me with you. I will be a good boy".

His mum turned away, tears choking her, unable to answer.

"Mummy, why are you taking Kwal and leaving me? Who shall I play with?"

She started to move away quickly from the small hut, shutting the door securely to prevent hyenas from entering. She was shaking; she nearly fell with the load in her arms. She took two steps and then went back, picked a stone from the ground and pushed it against the door to make it more secure.

She had to leave now.

Now; and never look back.

"Mummy I am scared, please come and take me with you". He was weeping and in distress and fear, letting out feeble, whimpering noises.

Silence.

All what he could hear was the howling of the wind, followed by the sound of silence.

Lual, covered with flies and lying in his own urine and excrement was begging his mum to save him and comfort him.

Aweil became a ghost town, reduced to rubble. It was a no man's land. Everywhere was bare and dry. Lual could not remember when he had his last meal. He was now only skin and bones. He wanted to muster his very last ounce of strength to get up and run after his mum as he used to do but alas, he could not even lift an arm . . . or a finger. He knew that his mum will never come back. He was scared of ants, scared of mice and hyenas . . .

Alwel, Lual's mum was a skeleton walking. She was carrying Kwal her three year old son. Kwal looked as if he was less than a year old. His eyes were shut and he was nothing but a bag of bones. She had to run with Kwal to a place, to find food. She had to be strong. She was told to go to the outskirts of the town where she will see a crossroad. There she will find many people leaving Aweil. She will have to go with them to safety; to save Kwal. She has to shut her mind on Lual; He was gone. She is unable to carry both of them. May the Lord Almighty be kind to Lual. May the Lord Almighty forgive her.

"How will I know that I am on the right tract?" she asked someone.

"Just follow the trail of bones. The bones are visible near the sides of the road. These bones belong to those who could not make it. They are now used as a beacon. They will lead you to Safaha."

A few weeks later . . .

"Remember us when we had to travel miles on foot, without water and food, many dying on the way. We had to close our feeble eyes on sisters, brothers, aging fathers, and babies. No time to dig a grave. There was no one to dig a grave. Our bodies were a feast for the birds of the air and the hyenas of the night.

Remember us, having to choose which of our children to save and which to leave behind to die . . . Remember us when we had to *sell* our children to aliens who deride us in order for them to live. Can you imagine selling your little beautiful son or daughter for fifty pounds so that they can survive and you can eat one last meal before you die?

How can the world around us not know of our suffering?

How can the world around us ignore our pain? How can we say that The Lord God is ruling the world?

Where are the World Leaders?

Where are the men of good will?

As we lay dying with our children, we became abused by evil men who showed no compassion and no mercy. Men who claimed they were following a *clean* religion, full of compassion.

They came and finished us off.

They humiliated and degraded us while our dying children were snatched away from our breasts and thrown away like bags of rubbish. How can you forget us? How can you forget our babies? How can anyone deny the truth?" Alwel Deng Akech. Deceased in Safaha, Western Sudan on June 17th 1998.

"I hope that one day there will be comfort for the South Sudanese people. I hope that one day there will be justice and peace for the South Sudanese people. The world watched and ignored.

I have a message for you, daughters of Zion: God loves you. One day we will bring you all back from captivity and enslavement.

We will bring every flesh, skin and bone. Every single one of you will be brought back to Zion and that and that only will be your final resting place." This is a message from a daughter of Zion.

That was what was happening in many places to people from the Dinka land. It was a story which happened to many women and children and old men who could not fight. Helpless, bewildered, dispossessed and disoriented people. It happened in a land that is supposed to flow milk and honey! Where is the milk and where is the honey? Who was the cause of all this suffering?

One

Across the azure clear skies you can see the rays of sunshine. The tall mango trees swaying in the gentle breeze, flirting with the taller palm trees and intertwining with long grasses and shrubs. On the other side of the hill you can see acres upon acres of rich luscious foliage beneath. The chirping birds darting from tree to tree in clusters of ten, fifty or even more are almost unnoticed. They are always there; part of the landscape. That their noise is pure bliss which completes the sleepy almost perfect scenery is a gift from the Creator which most of us take for granted.

The meandering dusty road was as red as the afternoon sun itself. The different shades of green contrast beautifully giving the soft vibrant foliage a silky tender and shimmering "feeling". The smell in the air is so pure it can take your breath away and give you a new beginning. This is virgin Africa. This is South Sudan—a land more than half untouched by humans.

This is Yambio.

This is *Home*.

This is the land of the great and mighty. It is a land of powerful chiefdoms and proud self sufficient subjects. The great chiefs used to sit under the huge mahogany trees to organise their village affairs, ranging from births, deaths, and funerals. They used to preside over marriages and resolve intimate problems in the homes. They formulated their own socio-political set up to foster security, stability and prosperity. They have continued to do this up to this day. These were customs, traditions and

1

culture which were handed from generation to generation. People kept it sacred and upheld it however high or low their position in the society is. The core customs entreated each to respect their mother, father and elders and forbade killing and stealing. It also does not allow anyone to bear false witness nor covet a neighbour's "property" which mainly means wife and children. They also believed that there is a higher presence in the universe which is there to protect them. They usually refer to them as the "souls of their ancestors". They did everything based on commonsense, wisdom and experience. They used to come together and consult with each other. No one was of lesser importance. There was respect for others and the elders. Men used to care for their wives and children. Widows used to be looked after by their family and the community. Orphans used to be taken care of as if their parents were alive. Those were the times and those were the good days.

"Nora, where is Nadi?" muttered Mama Maria.

"She is in the hospital with her son. Mathew is very ill, suffering from malaria. Last night we all went to visit them. The boy who used to be so chubby and bubbly is now reduced to skin and bones in a matter of days following vomiting and diarrhoea".

"Oh my Lord, let us pray that our little Mathew will recover soon."

"If something happens to that child, I do not know what we will do."

"Spit it from your mouth woman!" shouted Mamma Maria. "Hope for the best and pray. Illness will not kill you; your *time* will".

Mama Maria went away bent double with age uttering prayers and blessings to protect little Mathew. The cool afternoon breeze flapping her gleaming white pleated dress against her thin wrinkled ankles. She looked frail and weak but the respect and love she commanded from everyone in the community was immense. Yes she was frail in body but she was one of the *powerful* women in town.

Before the old woman reached the corner of her small hut, a young boy about fifteen years of age came pedalling a bicycle in such haste that he sent a big cloud of dust as he braked sharply under the mango tree. He was breathing heavily from the effort, with rivers of sweat and what Nora thought were tears streaming down his face.

He just stared at Nora as he dropped his bike against the tree. The group under the tree, all waiting to be served Nora's favourite tea suddenly and collectively held their breaths. In that instant, everyone just knew; something terrible . . . God, please no . . . Nora started to shake.

She just knew . . .

She cradled the boy in her chest and sobbed and sobbed . . .

Mathew's tiny body was carefully bathed by Auntie Tabitha and Mama Maria, who always looked calm and collected and tackled any unforeseen situation with self reassurance and wisdom. Later on Mathew was dressed in his favourite "gentleman's suit "as he used to call it. It was a full three piece suit of little sleek black trousers, white shirt and a little cute vest. Auntie Susan, Norah's sister who used to live in Juba sent it as a birthday present for Mathew when he was two. She sent the suit all the way from England where she is now living. At first it was too big but Mathew wanted to wear it even then. He would cry and scream "I want my gentleman's suit". His mum used to fold the trousers' ends up as they were too long. As Mathew grew and was nearly three, the trousers fitted him perfectly. He wore it only on Sundays and other occasions such as birthdays. Lying there on the bed which was covered with a white embroidered sheet, he looked so *alive* you would think he would suddenly open his beautiful eyes with the strangely long lashes and wink at you.

Nadi, sitting close to Mathew's head knew that he was not going to open those lovely smiley eyes ever again. The room was full of people but Nadi was not aware of anyone. Her mum held her as she looked as if she was going to faint. Her tears were flowing and her voice and her thin frame were shaking.

"Oh my son; my joy; my gift . . . Why have you left me?" lamented Nadi. "Where is your smile? Who will ever call me mamma again? Who will make me laugh and be happy? Where are you Mathew? Why don't you wake up?"

The priest, Father Gabriel Limbo was praying and telling everyone that Mathew is now in heaven with the angels and saints where there is no death, no illness, no tears and no pain.

But Nadi was not in heaven, she was in hell. Her life has just been shattered. Her child has been snatched from her and nothing will ever be the same again. Does the man know the real meaning of pain? Did he ever bury a child? Did he see his future snatched and thrown into the unknown?

It was only people like her, Nadi who know the real meaning of pain. Pain not of the body but of the spirit, and of the soul . . .

Nadi was Norah's eldest child. Nadi was followed by Madelena, Gloria, and Taban, the boy who broke the bad news to Norah.

Nadi was lying on her bed three days after her son was buried. She closed her eyes but could not sleep. Her short life started to unfold in front of her like a film . . .

It started from the time when they were very young. She was only eight years. Madelena, known as Mado was six. Gloria was three and Mama had just had baby Taban. Those were very happy days. Their father was Baba but others called him Nathana. Baba used to work in the hospital. He liked wearing white clothes. He was handsome and tall and always looked happy as he smiled all the time showing a set of lovely white teeth. He used to look awesome and Nadi used to brag to the girls in school about how good looking and important her "Baba" was.

One day Baba came from work complaining of a strong headache. At this point her memory started to blur and move quickly. Up to this day she does not know exactly what killed her father. She remembered the large number of people flocking to the house crying and wailing and falling on the ground and rolling about. It was a shocking and bewildering experience. No one took the time to explain to her and her little sisters and brother what was happening. People seemed to be oblivious of them and the focus of attention was their mum who was surrounded by the big aunties and other people they have never seen before. Some aunties were taking care of them but not talking much.

"Go away. I want my Mama. I want my Baba. Where is he? Where have you taken him? I want to see him. I want to see him. I want to see him . . ."

Then years later, there was Paul. After school, he used to stand there against the tree, pretending that he was not waiting for her. He was every girl's dream of a boyfriend. He was a real heart throb and was interested in no one but her, Nadi. Tall, handsome and cool was he. Nothing seemed to ruffle him. They were both seventeen and were both sitting the Sudan School Certificate Examinations and hoped to pass and go on to the University. Paul wanted to join Khartoum University and study Law. Nadi wanted to go to Cairo University. Her cousin Viola was in Cairo University. Nadi saw how Viola changed from looking "ok-ish" to looking really fabulous with the latest hair styles, shoes and clothes that were every girl's envy. Viola looked so hot that every boy in town wanted to court her, except her Paul of course.

Nadi's memory then rolled on and the faint smile she had was wiped away by pain and anguish. She remembered how when they finished their exams, she travelled with a group of five girls, all friends to visit Juba which is the biggest city in South Sudan. She has never been in Juba and was eagerly looking forward to going there for the first time to stay in Auntie Susan's house. They were told that the journey might take two to three days as the roads were quite bad and that they will be relatively safe on the journey. That was 1992 and at that time they heard that the "rebels" or SPLA were on the offensive on some of the roads.

Nadi remembered how happy and innocent and full of life all of them were as they said their goodbyes to everyone. Auntie Rita gave her some peanut butter mixed with honey in a small container. Uncle Alfred gave her two small succulent pineapples. People brought all sorts of gifts and her mum gave her a jar of her favourite red jam, six hardboiled eggs, roasted meat and bread for the journey. She smiled as she remembered all the four brand new dresses which were made for her in the newest fashion, similar to Viola's by the best taylor in town; Mr Bazambaco. Wasn't she lucky that Bazambaco happened to be her uncle? Yes, her mothers' half brother's third cousin! She did not know exactly who was related to who but did it matter? What was important was Bazambaco was her uncle and he made her dresses although he was a very busy man! Nothing too much for flesh and blood!

Then she remembered how the Land Rover they were travelling in started to slow down due to pot holes in the road. There was a small slope and the road took a bend this way and that and suddenly there was chaos, shouting, gunfire, screaming and the car screeched to a stop. Before the car stopped properly, all the doors were swung open and everybody was pulled out by some savage and strong muscular arms. The driver and Mr Aguillo the owner of the car were sitting in the front. Auntie Miriam an elderly lady and two young girls of around eighteen were sitting in the middle seat. Nadi and two others all ranging between seventeen and eighteen sat in the third seat. She remembered how mean looking, rough and utterly wild the men were. They were wearing old torn clothes and some were in shabby army uniforms. Two wore hats or helmets with foliage pinned to them. What scared her most were their eyes. She shut her eyes tight but she could not banish their foul smell. Oh Lord!

"Why did we have to be punished like that? What did we do? Did our forefathers commit a crime against The Almighty Lord?" thought Nadi.

Nadi tried to blot the nightmare by shutting her eyes tightly but she could not stop the images of the film that kept rolling in her mind. She remembered how the two men, the driver and Mr Aguillo, were separated from them and taken further in the bushes. The rebels gave them a dressing down in the local Arabic dialect as to how they were sucking up to the Arabs. How could they eat and drink and sleep in comfortable beds with whores and girlfriends, while they the SPLA are suffering in the bushes to free South Sudan and defend "dogs" like them? Poor Mr Aguillo tried to tell the rebels that he did not like or work with the Arabs and had many brothers in the SPLA but he wasn't given the chance to explain. He was hit across the face and told that he was nothing but a "woman" and will be made to pay for his cooperation with the oppressors. Mr Aguillo was shaking so much that even his face started to tremble. He knelt down to remonstrate but was struck again and again until his head was cut wide open, with blood spurting everywhere. As for Nadi she remembered that out of fear, she wet herself without realising. They were all shaking like leaves in the wind. The driver was also struck until he was bleeding and hit again and again with the butt of a rifle.

The two men's hands were then tied behind their backs and were led deep into the forest by two rebels. There were about seventeen to twenty rebels; Nadi couldn't recall the exact number. They then heard four distinct shots after which the SPLA men shouted their triumph signal and raised up their guns and shook them. The other two joined the rest and ransacked the Land Rover. The girls could see the clothes that Mr Aguillo was wearing including his shoes and that of the driver being divided and worn by the rebels. At that point all the girls thought that they were as good as dead and some started to cry and beg for their lives. Then Nadi remembered vividly how each of them was gang raped by the, smelly, dirty and wicked men. It was the most horrific experience she thought she will ever have, even if she lived to reach a hundred. Did anyone see Hell, Satan and all the Seven Deadly sins rolled in one? That time the manifestation was very real. Nadi had to dissociate her mind from her body to survive the brutal and horrific assault. She had to go far away with her mind into the woods, valleys and the hills . . . go to a cool brook where she would kneel down and cleanse herself of the nightmare. In order to cope she tried to think that 'that body' that was being abused was not hers at all but belonged to some alien and that whatever was done to the body had nothing to do with her . . . her spirit was safe; no one could touch it.

The old woman Miriam was spared but every night she heard the screams of the helpless girls as they were raped. She wept because she could not help them. The girls were very young and innocent. She later revealed that she used to kneel down the whole night and stick her fingers deep in her ears and rock herself like a caged animal to block the screams. She said that ever since she started having recurrent nightmares of the girls screams, which were like that of people being slaughtered. Miriam was sure that death was better for all of them than that terrible experience. She lost faith in the Lord. She knew that after enduring all this misery they were going to be killed anyway. After spending a week in this nightmare, she asked God to take her soul. There was no meaning to life; dignity and humanity were lost . . .

Then she heard a loud and clear voice saying to her "Miriam, since you are kneeling down every night and crying why don't you cry out to your Lord to deliver you and those poor girls? Why have you stopped believing in your Creator? Why are you condemning Him?"

"How can I pray when these terrible things are happening? Is The Lord deaf? Can't He hear our screams? Is He blind? Can't He see our suffering, our humiliation and our degradation? How can we protect ourselves against an army? How can we save ourselves when our tormentors have guns and strength on their side?"

"Miriam, you can pray even when you are face to face with the Devil. These people do not know what they are doing. The Devil has taken hold of their souls".

Miriam then knelt down for the first time in seven days to bless The Almighty's name. She thanked Him for the girls' courage and resilience. Above all she asked Him to forgive those men their sins. She asked Him to intervene and deliver them from this terrible vice in which they were sucked through no fault of theirs. She could see that some of the rebels were as young as thirteen or fourteen. They were mere boys playing men.

Early the next day, the rebels received a radio message. The message seemed to have ruffled the rebel's feathers and changed their attitude and demeanour. They became tense and whispered a great deal, sitting in small and big groups. Their leader then called Auntie Miriam and said he wanted to speak to her privately. Auntie Miriam was so frightened she nearly fainted. She thought they were going to be killed or separated or something even worse . . .

"I want to thank you *Yuma,* for being so good to us all this time that we spent together. Thank you for fetching us water to drink and the good food you and the girls cooked. We are very happy with all of you because none of you tried to escape or give us trouble while we lived together." He had no idea.

"I am sorry for the things which happened to the girls but this is war" He continued, as if this was an excuse for them to abuse girls that they were claiming to protect and liberate! "Wolves in sheep's clothing" thought Auntie Miriam bitterly.

"In this war a lot of bad things are happening to all of us. We are going to a different location and we will not take you with us. I will give you two people to escort you to the nearest village where you will get help to proceed to Juba".

Up to this day Miriam is not sure. Was it a coincidence or was it Divine intervention that they have lived to tell the tale?

Nadi remembered how instead of proceeding to Juba as planned, they went back to Yambio; battered, delirious and utterly traumatised. Nearly all the town went to meet them at the junction leading to Yambio. Word travelled fast that they were on their way back to Yambio. They saw the shock on people's faces.

Is this the happy group of girls that set off only ten days ago? The crying and the wailing of the girl's parents and relatives and friends were deafening. Nadi thought that perhaps they were brought in coffins and that they were *dead*. For Nadi, her friends and family, the mourning and the nightmare had just begun . . .

She used to wake up nearly every night screaming and sweating because of the horrible recurrent nightmares she used to have. She discovered that although her mother knew she was raped, she never wanted to hear Nadi talk about it. Her mother said that the best way was to forget that she ever met these bad men. Her mother just didn't understand. Parents don't understand, do they? No one knew how traumatised and broken Nadi was inside and out. She used to be the envy of all her friends. Her skin used to shine without needing extra cream or special oils to enhance it. Her hair which was soft and thick reached up to her shoulders, when plaited. Her eyes, large and dreamy, would smile at you before her lips did. She used to work hard in school, always achieving top grades. She was exemplary in nearly everything. She also worked hard at home, helping her mother to clean the house, wash and cook the food and look after her younger siblings. The Azande people have a big obsession: cleanliness. Everything has to be clean. You have to wash your hands *clean* whenever you want to come near food or drink or do *anything*. No fowling of humans or animals is allowed anywhere except in the designated place. Fowling in the streets is considered a taboo. If caught, the punishment can be quite costly: You might lose face completely in the community or worse still you can be branded a "witch doctor" or a "sorcerer". Nobody wants such a name!

Nadi's mother worked as the Headmistress of the local Primary school. Financially they were fine because of additional money coming in from her dear father's pension. The only problem they had was bad luck.

"Look at Nadi. Everything seemed to go right for her. Now she is unable to lift her head from the pillow. She has grown thin and cannot stop screaming at night. What am I going to do?" Norah kept thinking.

When Nadi arrived from the ill fated journey, Paul her boyfriend came only once to see her. He never came back again. One day she heard that he has travelled to Khartoum which is the capital city of Sudan in the North of the country. Nadi was distraught but Paul's sister Sarah who was Nadi's friend said that Paul was giving Nadi time to recover because he knew that she was suffering from the bad experience with the rebels.

"When he comes back from Khartoum you will always be together as you have ever been." Sarah reassured her frequently. Nadi believed her. She later heard that Paul managed to get admission in Cairo University in Egypt and will be studying Law. Nadi was happy for him and wrote him a letter. He promptly answered her letter. Unfortunately Nadi with all her abilities, failed to make the grades. She decided to join her mother in the teaching profession and easily got a job in her mother's school. When Paul came for the first time during the holidays, it was clear that he had moved on. It was his last holiday in Yambio. There was nothing to come for. He did not love Nadi anymore. Later on Nadi heard rumours that Paul's parents did not want him to befriend a girl who was raped by savages. What if she had AIDS? Nadi challenged Sarah one day and said that she thought of them as 'shallow and totally ignorant'.

Then there was Mazindo, Mathew's dad. Mazindo went to join the SPLA and did not know at that time that Nadi was pregnant. They never heard from him again. Some people came with stories that they had seen him in

Torit, others said that they saw him around Malakal etc but so far no word from him. That was her luck and she was only twenty three. How can she have so much grief in her life in just twenty three years? Even Mamma Maria the oldest person in town did not have half her experience!

At the same time in a small village near Aweil, a government Antonov aircraft was shelling villagers. Men, women and children were running in all direction trying to take cover. Some women, with children on their backs, were fetching water a minute earlier. Some were grinding millet for their evening meal. Young boys watching as their cattle were grazing in the sparse vegetation. Some men were playing domino under the tree. Another group in the chief's court was listening attentively to some judgments on domestic issues. People were going with their normal business. They were normal unarmed people. These were people who had no clue if asked "who is the President of Sudan?" These were people who were already suffering the effects of hunger due to the unprecedented drought in the surrounding areas. They were forcefully sharing too much with the new rebels. Pressed from all sides and forgotten, they were a people finding themselves between a rock and a hard place!

A loud bang was suddenly heard, followed by several others and in a big swoop the silver shape of the *bird of death* deposited its load and flew away!

The cries of people . . . body parts flying . . . blood, blood and more blood everywhere; death and devastation.

A woman who has gone to fetch water ran towards what was left of her house. There was nothing; no husband, no family. She sat in the middle of the destruction wailing. She took the debris covered in minced flesh and blood and mangled metal and heaped it on her head. Slowly everything started to trickle down her face, mingled with her tears and ran down her neck, her shoulders and her naked, shrunken breasts. She kept pouring on her head. No one came to comfort her because, like her, no one came to comfort them either.

Her eyes which were bloodshot were filled with insanity. She looked up howling like a wounded wolf, her bony frame looking like a corpse moved by invisible hands. She looked up at the sky and cried

"Oh you being up there, where are you?

Oh you who call yourself God, where are you?

I went to fetch water, I entrusted my sons to you,

Where are you?

I told you they are young, where are you?

I told you to take care of them, where are you?

You up there, where are you?

Where are you?"

Let me say to God my Rock,
"Why do you forget me?
Why must I walk so mournfully
oppressed by the enemy?"

The Psalms 42:9

Two

Susan become increasingly worried about the stories she has been hearing. Yes, scary, frightening stories about people getting ambushed by the rebels called the SPLA, while travelling from one town or village to another. You would be lucky if they eventually let you free. There were stories of murder, rape and terrible deeds—stories that will make your hair stand on end. The SPLA had a radio station and they were broadcasting to people in Juba to move out of town to avoid getting hurt in the crossfire. They wanted the citizens of Juba to move out so that they can go into Juba and take it over from the Sudanese Army (mainly from the North and Western Sudan). Where were they going to go? The citizens in Juba were suffering harassment and lynching daily by the Sudanese Army, why is it that their own people, the South Sudanese of the SPLA harassing them as well?

Susan is Norah's younger sister. She has come to live in Juba after she got married to Luka. Luka worked as a civil servant in the Ministry of Public Service. They had two daughters Sarah and Mary and two sons Musa and Bindi. Marianna, Luka's sister's daughter who used to live with them got pregnant last year when she was only seventeen. Marianna had to live with the boy's parents. There was a lot of anger and friction between the two families over the whole thing. Marianna gave birth to a daughter whom she called Gloria. A traditional marriage will take place between Marianna and *that boy* very soon. Some of Marianna's family called her husband-to-be "that boy" as a derogatory term because of his dependence on his parents. *That boy* is hardly older than Marianna and was still in school. They met in school. That was what annoyed and upset everyone, including his family. How can he provide for Marianna and the baby, being a dependent himself? "Well", thought Susan, "if *that boy* knew that he was young then he shouldn't make other people's daughters pregnant! *That boy* is not only reckless but also stupid. What will that make Marianna? More stupid and troublesome than the boy himself!"

Marianna's parents wrote a long insulting letter to Susan and her husband, blaming them for everything. They said that if Marianna was well looked after by Susan, she would never have got pregnant in the first place. Arrgh . . . She felt like screaming and boxing someone. Everything that goes wrong is always her fault, isn't it? Did she tell Marianna to go and sleep with *that boy*? Isn't Marianna the laziest girl in town? Send her to the market and she will come back after sunset. Ask her to make you a cup of tea and you would think she has gone to fetch the water from the River Nile!

"Why didn't God create me a man so I don't have to deal with all this nonsense"? Thought Susan with annoyance.

Lucinda, Susan's younger sister lived in the same house. Boy, oh boy isn't she different from lazy Marianna? Didn't Lucinda do much more work in the house than lazy Marianna?

Susan's mind came back to the most recent events; the most painful event in the history of her family. She was trying her best to forget but the more she did the more her mind seemed to drift on its own to what she wanted to shut out.

Oh my Lord, when she received the news about what happened to Nadi, her goddaughter and niece, she felt completely numb. She could not tell exactly which would have been less painful for her to bear; if Nadi had died or the things that happened to her at the hands of the rebels. Southerners like themselves, who are claiming to fight to free them from the bad Arabs.

Why Lord, why? Why did it have to be their lovely Nadi? Why did it have to be the Bakata family? She closed her eyes as if to erase the ugly scenes which kept playing in her anguished mind.

The Sudan, before the secession of the Southern States, used to be the largest country in Africa. The political divide was the predominantly Muslim and Arab North; and the Christian and animists African proper of the South. Now this racial and cultural differences is something that will certainly guarantee an explosion if put in any container of whatever shape or size! However, the British Administrators governing on behalf of the Anglo-Egyptian Condominium ignored the impediment. In 1946 the two regions which were administered separately were then merged as part of the strategy of Britain in the Middle East. This action was taken without consultation with the Southerners who felt disadvantaged by the political power of the larger and much affluent North. In the Juba Conference of 1947 they expressed the desire to remain under British tutelage until they were ready to stand shoulder to shoulder with the Northerners. In the beginning of 1953 an agreement was signed by Great Britain and Egypt to grant independence to the unified Sudan. Tension and distrust between the Northern and Southern Sudanese started to build up. Matters reached a climax in August 1955 before full Independence of the Sudan on 1st January 1956, when the first Sudanese Government came to power. To allay the fears of the Southerners, the Northerners promised they would consider the Federation of the South if the Southerners voted for Independence. "A Federal Government? What Federal Government?" they later on retorted. "We, the Northerners are in charge and we will do as we want!"

In August 1955, members of the Sudan Defence Force Corps mutinied in Torit, Juba, Yei and Maridi. The mutinies were quickly suppressed by the might of the outgoing colonials. The resultant survivors fled to the bushes and began an uncoordinated insurgency mainly in the rural areas. Being poorly armed, they stood very little threat to the new Sudanese Government. From 1955 up to 1962 the insurgents led guerrilla warfare of survival. What kept the movement going was a handful of trained former Army officers and a small number of warrant and non-commissioned officers. Later on around 1963 the disorganized insurgents gradually developed into a secessionist movement composed of the 1955 insurgents and the Southern students. The *AnyaNya* guerrilla army was formed under the leadership of retired Lieutenant General Joseph Lagu Yanga. *"AnyaNya"* is a corruption of the Madi word "Inyanya" for poison usually extracted from snakes. The *AnyaNya* movement spread like wild fire from Equatoria to Bahr el Ghazal and Upper Nile Provinces. However, the Movement had an Achilles heel which was ethnic divisions. The ruling Government had a weakness as well and that was the divisions between Socialist Ideologues and religious sectarian factions in the form of Mahdists, Khatimiyya-ists and Muslim Brotherhood. The first new Government was quickly replaced by coalition of various conservative groups. That did not last long as it was toppled in a coup d'état in 1958. People in the North resented the military government which led to wave after wave of popular protests. Between 1966 and 1969 a series of sectarian Islamist dominated administrations were not successful in dealing with the multi pronged issues of racial identification, economic depression and secessionist movement in the South.

On 25ᵗʰ May 1969 a military coup d'état was staged by a group of young Free Officers and socialist politicians. Their leader was Field Marshall Gaafar Muhammad Nimeri. They immediately suspended the Constitution, outlawed all political parties and ruled by decrees. In July 1971 an internal rift led to an unsuccessful three-day coup by the hardliner Communists which was brutally quashed. Meanwhile in the South, that same year, former guerrilla bands under Southern Sudan Liberation Movement (SSLM) gathered momentum. A unified command structure to fulfil the objectives and aspirations of the secession was established. It paved the way in the formation of the State of South Sudan today. The SSLM under the leadership of Joseph Lagu became a formidable and organized force which can play havoc with the governance of the Sudan. After many years of negotiations and mediation between the World Council of Churches (WCC) and the All Africa Conference of Churches (AACC) the two opposing groups, Nimeri and Lagu, reached an agreement rectified in Addis Ababa in 1972. The peace Agreement granting Regional Autonomy to the South did not hold long. The Southerners accused the National Government in the North of interfering with the Governance of the South economic starvation. In 1977 a military unit rebelled in Akobo and *AnyaNya II* was born but attempts to crush it led to relocation of its Headquarters to the borders of Ethiopia. Similar to the events which led to the Torit mutiny in 1955, orders for troop movement without their equipment saw an outbreak in Bor Garrison which became the SPLA movement in 1983.

Susan worked in one of the offices in the Ministry of Public Service as a clerk. Life in Juba was getting harder and harder every day. The moment you open your eyes in the morning you want to shut them again. Getting water was a struggle. Finding money to buy sugar for tea was a struggle. Going to work was a struggle. Getting food was the biggest struggle of all. "Till when Lord . . . till when are you going to shut your ears to our prayers?"

"Are you there? If so can't you see our suffering? Why are you ignoring us? You said 'Ask and you will be given'. We are asking but you are not giving. We are asking but you are not helping."

Susan suddenly came to herself and started to shake her head violently. She is blaspheming. She is blaming The Creator and that was wrong.

She then knelt down and prayed . . . "Please forgive me Lord my Creator. Please Lord help me, please . . ."

"Woman, what are you doing kneeling down and praying as if someone has died? Christ in heaven; did you receive bad news again?"

Susan opened her eyes and stared into a round shiny face full of concern and eyes full of compassion and dread.

That was Ju'Ndogo known to everyone as Ju. She was one of Susan's neighbours and a friend from across the road. Ju was younger than Susan but being overweight and riddled with arthritis she looked older.

"No you silly woman. Everything you think about is bad news, funeral and death. Why are you in such fear of death? I am just praying so that The Lord will help us."

"Really??!! I have stopped going to church a long time ago. Where was God when Everesto left me with six children, running away with that tart Suna?"

"Was it the Lord's fault?"

Ju'Ndogo swung her ample frame and sat easily on the mat near Susan. They were in the compound under a shady big Neem tree.

"Then whose fault is it?"

Bindi, wearing a school uniform came towards them riding a small bike. He nearly landed on Ju'Ndogo's fat legs. In a quick movement she swung them out of harm's way.

"E,e,e . . . Bindi, do you want to break my legs? These are the only good assets I have"

"Sorry auntie it was going to be an accident"

Susan and her friend started to laugh.

"Then you have planned to break my leg, eh?"

"What he meant was: *if* he breaks your legs then it will be an accident" explained Bindi's mum still laughing.

"Well Bindi" said Susan, "after having so much luck as not to break *someone's* leg, go inside and get your food. It is the one covered with the white plate."

"Yes mummy" said Bindi running inside.

"Susan, you have such good kids. Mine take after their dad; rowdy, stupid and obstinate".

"Ju, most kids are the same. Your problem is that you shout too much at them. Children need to be talked to quietly so that they can understand what you want them to do. I know that you are now left on your own to deal with six children but you get a lot of help from your mother and sisters. I personally think that your children are not worse than the average children in this town."

"Thank you Susan, you have made my day. I will try hard not to shout so much, but sometimes it is difficult."

"I know. Well here is Musa at last. Musa, why are you late today?"

"I had to do some of my homework in school"

"Bindi is already inside, eating. Yours is the one covered with the flowery plate"

After a few minutes, there was a lot of commotion and screaming coming from the house. The two women ran inside to see what was happening. They found the two boys rolling on the floor. Musa's hand was on his brother's throat. The food was all over the place. One of the plates was broken.

"So you ate mine by accident, didn't you?" shouted Musa angrily at his brother who managed to wriggle free and dashed to hide himself under Ju's ample wing.

"Well, well" muttered Ju'Ndogo to herself as she went back to her house. "They are exactly like mine after all. The only thing is that Susan never seems to get mad at them or shout. Well, at least *lucky Susan's* husband, Luka, is always there to help with the boys not like that stupid good-for-nothing rat that used to be my husband."

As Ju'Ndogo was entering her house, Lucinda was arriving in a small white car with Peter her fiancé.

Have you daughters? Take care of their bodies,
But do not be over-indulgent.
Marry a daughter off, and you have finished a great work;
But give her to a man of sense.

Ecclesiastics 7: 24-27

Three

L ucinda was the youngest of the Bakata family. She was living with her older sister Susan as is the custom of the South Sudanese people. Usually when a girl is married one or two of her younger sisters will be given permission by the parents to live in the bride's house. The reason behind this is to give the bride company as her bridegroom goes out to work. The girl will help with light household chores and later on help with babysitting when babies come along. Usually such a girl is chosen by the father from among many daughters. Such a companion would usually be between six and eight years old, obedient and healthy so as not to give trouble to her sister who might be quite young herself. This arrangement is made so that the bride will not feel homesick or lonely, especially if she has to live far with her husband or among strangers or in-laws. Once this arrangement takes place the young girl will have a special status. Her newly married sister and her husband will promise in front of the family to look after her and cherish her exactly like their daughter. She will be respected by everyone including the in-laws as a special person in the house however young she might be. She will also have the privilege to be a member of two different households at the same time. In other words, in her parents' house, her room and belongings should be kept as if she is still residing there so that when she calls, she will not feel as if she is a mere visitor.

Lucinda was such a lucky girl. She remembered when Susan was married. Although she was quite young she still remembered the event as if it happened yesterday. It seemed that the singing, dancing and partying would never stop. People came as far as Ezo, Tambura and Wau. There was a big number from Yei, Juba and Maridi where Susan's husband comes from. Lucinda remembered how proud she used to feel that she was

Susan's little sister and how being young she was able to sit and listen to the women and also run and listen to what the group of men were saying under the big mango tree. She remembered how beautiful and shy Susan looked when she stood in the All Saints' Church dressed in a long flowing bridal dress. The church was full of people she knew and didn't know or recognised. She could see how proud their parents were and ever since, she always wished to have a wedding like Susan's. Luka, Susan's husband was looking very dashing in black trousers, a very shinny pair of shoes and a snow white brand new shirt. The only problem was: He looked very skinny as if he has been starving for days. He kept smiling throughout the service though.

A few months after arriving in Juba with her bridegroom, Susan wrote to her parents to say that they were well settled in their new home. She also told them that she was working in the same place as her husband. Her only concern was that she has just discovered that she was pregnant and could do with her parents sending one of the girls to keep her company and help her. She referred to "the girls" because there were at least five girls in her father's house besides Lucinda. Those girls were part of their extended family—mainly children who were staying to attend local schools because their parents either lived far away, have died, divorced or were too poor to look after them. Lucinda knew in her heart that Susan would love to nominate her. She would love to go to see Juba and live with Susan and Luka. Luka seemed to be rich because people who were coming from Juba were saying that Susan looked very well and happy and they lived in a big house and had a car! Oh, she would love to have a ride in that car with her sister Susan and Luka. Luka was very kind. He gave everyone loads of presents. He gave her a white doll with yellow shinny hair and a pink ribbon. She used to put her doll in the shoe box and her mamma helped her make nice clothes for the doll. Her doll's name was Amelia. Amelia was her pride and joy. No one had such a lovely thing to play with in the whole of Yambio except that stuck up girl "Nana" with her older sister who had not one, not two but four dolls including a black one which she would love to have. Their dad was the Governor, whatever that is and their house is massive. Anyway, her Susan is also rich and has a big house.

Lucinda remembered how her mother cried when she was getting into the Land Rover Station to join Susan in Juba. For a moment Lucinda's excitement was dampened at the sight of her mum's unhappiness. Her mother tried to convince her that she was crying because she was happy for her! Lucinda was not entirely convinced but accepted what her mama said and sat down holding tightly to her dad's hands in the Land Rover. Her dad was a medical assistant and on the verge of retiring. He was travelling in order to attend a seminar in Juba Teaching Hospital. It was a good chance for him to take Lucinda to Susan.

Lucinda remembered her first day in school. She did not know any of the girls. The school was massive and the classes were many. She could easily get lost and she would not know how to find her class! When the bell rang, two girls came from the other side of the class and stared at her. She looked at them and they all started to smile, one showing a big gap in some goofy teeth.

"You are called Lucinda, right? I heard Sitt Nybol call you". Sitt is an Arabic word for "Miss".

"Yes"

"Well, mine is Clara and my friend is called Anna".

Later on she came to know that Anna is Sitt Nybol's niece.

"Have you got some lunch? We can go and buy roast groundnuts, doughnuts or ice lollies from those women sitting under the tree" said Anna.

"I have some packed lunch in my bag and some money for an ice lolly".

"That sounds good".

These three became good friends and continued so until they left school.

Lucinda had nieces and nephews, Norah's children; Nadi, Mado, Gloria and Taban. Nadi is about four years younger than her. She never felt that she was old enough to play the role of the "aunt" with Nadi but now Susan's child will be her "proper" niece or nephew. She will be able to carry, feed and wash the baby. She remembered how much she anticipated and prayed everyday for the baby's safe arrival and how proud and happy she would be!

She remembered how she helped Susan prepare her little bag of baby clothes to take to the hospital. Lucinda was in charge of that bag. She used to fold every little garment, towel, tiny vests and count them every day. She remembered all the nice smelling soaps, oils and powder. When bored she used to sneak into Susan's room and open the small bag and take every item out and run her fingers through them again and again.

"My baby's things are going to look dirty and old with you taking them in and out the way you do."

"Oh when are you going to have the baby? I can't wait" Lucinda would reply.

Susan's feet started to swell when she was in her last few weeks of pregnancy. She liked foot massage.

Lucinda used to massage her feet with nice fragrant oil made of a mixture of sweet smelling spices and perfumes.

"If I tickle your feet, will that make the baby laugh?"

"Maybe. What I know is that whatever happens to me happens to the baby".

Lucinda made sure that she brought Susan anything she liked to eat so that the baby can taste it as well.

Susan used to help Lucinda with her school work but Lucinda did not like to count or do any writing. She found school work hard and boring. What she liked about school was playing with her two friends Anna and Clara.

Sarah, her little cuddly and beautiful niece, when she eventually arrived was the other source of Lucinda's joy. As soon as Lucinda woke up, the first thing she would do was to dash into Susan's room and pick Sarah from her cot, even when she was still sleeping. She did not mind Susan's half hearted protests.

When Lucinda finished primary school at the age of twelve, she joined the junior school and later High school known as Juba Day. She started to grow into a lovely and smart girl. She was obedient and helpful in the house, making life much easier for Susan and Luka. Every year they used to go to Yambio to see the family. Rutha and Bakata, Susan and Lucinda's parents were satisfied that their daughter was in good hands. Looking healthy and smart and doing well in one of Juba's best schools. They had nothing to complain about except give their son in-law Luka and Susan their daughter all the credit. They also hoped that Lucinda will be a lucky girl and later marry well. These days the girls are given too much freedom; going out with boys here and there and then guess what? Getting pregnant! Now whose fault would it be? They are sure that Susan and Luka will not allow their daughter to run around with boys!

"Lucinda, do you go to church on Sundays?"

"Of course father. Luka takes us all to church, every Sunday"

"That is very good".

Bakata was introduced to Christianity at the age of fifteen when he joined school. His parents were farmers living in the remote countryside. One day a white man riding a bike and wearing some funny clothes came to their village and talked about the church and school. The local priest, as he later came to be known was called Father Remigio. He explained to Bakata and his parents how their son will learn about the new religion, called Christianity. He will also be able to read and write just like Mr Gambiri the local clerk working in the Judge's Court who has made it to prosperity.

That rainy evening, Bakata and his father talked until late at night. In the morning, Bakata said good bye to his parents and brothers and travelled in a lorry to Bussere near Wau to join school and the church. Ever since, he never looked back. He was brilliant in school and was nearly ordained to become a priest himself if it wasn't for his mother's intervention. His mum put her foot down and said that there was no way her son will not marry and have children. Bakata has now realised that he was not cut out to become a priest after all, seeing the way he fell for his wife to be. He came to believe that his mum's intervention was by the power of The Divine One!

As Peter opened the car door for Lucinda to step out he realised what a lucky man he was. Lucinda was a girl that every man would do his best to take as a bride. She was beautiful, well educated, came from a good family and a believer in God. The only little problem was that she did not belong to his tribe. To him it was no problem at all. Unfortunately to his parents it was a major one. Initially his parents were not happy when he told them that he wanted to marry this girl from a different tribe. They were careful not to upset him but disappointed.

What if she does not accept and respect his family including the wider extended family?

What if she does not produce children as she looks so old??!!

Why? Because they do not know her age!

Can't anyone just ask her about her age???

What makes her look old? I know the answer: Prejudice.

What if she is a greedy cow?

What if? What if?

"Mama, Baba I am going to marry the girl I love, not a monster" said Peter frustrated. "I need your support. Look at many of the men who married from our tribe. I do not want to name names but many are either divorced, died prematurely because of family strife or are on the brink of splitting up or even contemplating suicide. Maybe the Lord is taking me further away to save me."

"But there are many very nice and well brought up girls from our tribe that we want you to marry. Look at Keziah the daughter of Alfonso and Lucy the daughter of Marino"

"No way! These are like my sisters. I do not love either of them. If I marry at all it will have to be Lucinda."

And indeed it will be Lucinda . . .

Yes, Yahweh says this:
You were sold for nothing and you will be redeemed without money.
Yahweh bares his holy arm
In the sight of all the nations,
And all the ends of the earth shall see
the salvation of our God.

Isaiah 52:3, 10

Four

There are striking similarities between Dr John Garang De Mabior and Moses, one of the greatest leaders who led the sons of Israel from Egypt thousands of years ago to save them from slavery. John Garang, as he was widely known to the Sudanese people, was one of the greatest leaders of South Sudan. He led the SPLA/M civil war from 1983 until 2005. In 2005 he signed a Peace Agreement with President Omar Hassan Ahmed El Bashir, the incumbent President of the Sudan. The agreement, commonly called the CPA or Comprehensive Peace Agreement later brought about the birth of the Independent South Sudan.

The two men lost both their parents at an early stage, which meant that each had to utilize their survival tactics at a stage when most of us would be clinging to our mother's apron strings. This has in effect sharpened their senses and made them physically and mentally resilient. The absence of parents at an early stage also made them patient, good judges of situations and character. At a glance they knew when they were in danger and would try to avert it. This led them to develop into good leaders. Besides, they became brave, because they had to face the whole world on their own and take initiatives in whatever situation. So no wonder both leaders were very courageous, taking difficult decisions and going through life threatening situations with all guns blazing.

According to the bible Moses had a close encounter with death immediately when he was born. Moses was born to a Jewish couple and at that time Pharaoh ordered the killing of all male Jewish children. Pharaoh was worried because the Jewish people were growing in number and strength and could swallow them and take over their land. Moses however survived because his clever mother hid him in a small basket made of reeds and put him in the path of a soft hearted Egyptian Princess who later found him and brought him up as her own.

Moses grew up in Pharaoh's palace and lived like a prince without Pharaoh's knowledge until much later. Brought up as one of the Palace's noblemen Moses learnt the skills of fighting and all the secrets of the Egyptian army, weaponry, warfare tactics etc. This was not by chance. It was God's preparation of a leader for his people. God needed a fearless, hard, charismatic person, full of self confidence and belief. He needed a fearless soldier, a nobleman who had high credentials, and a man who could stand in front of the Pharaoh and not feel intimidated. He needed a man who will stand in front of the arrogant and pompous Pharaoh and make him quake with fear. This is because the Pharaoh was aware that Moses knew everything about him including his palace, army and people and can inflict damage to Egypt and the Pharaoh himself if he so wanted.

John Garang on the other hand was born in South Sudan to a poor family. He was orphaned at the age of ten. He was then adopted by a relative who helped him with his education. The first Sudanese Civil war gained momentum around 1962. By then he was adjudged too young to join the AnyaNya movement. Being a bright and intelligent individual, he won a scholarship to attend his secondary school in Tanzania. He was later offered a scholarship to study in the USA and worked in the Sudanese Army long enough to understand the army "system" inside out. At that stage it is fair to say that Garang, like Moses worked hard and armed himself with the highest degree of knowledge, skill and expertise within the Sudanese Army that will later help him in his mission to save the South Sudanese people from slavery.

The story about Moses went on to say that he had a fiery temperament which landed him in trouble when he killed an Egyptian overseer. He had to flee into exile as he was exposed as a "Jew" and a criminal to the Pharaoh. While he was in exile, God appeared to Moses in a vision and asked him to lead his people, the sons of Israel, out of Egypt. He gave him the wisdom, the courage and the fortitude to undertake this difficult task as he was to defy the Pharaoh as well as many other nations on their way to the Promised Land; *A land flowing milk and honey*

Garang's story was not any different. In 1983, he went on holiday to Bor his birth place in South Sudan. There he mutinied with a whole battalion and formed the Sudan People's Liberation Army / Movement. He was vilified by the Sudanese Government as nothing but a Southern rebel and an enemy of the State.

Garang had the same dilemma as Moses. He had to convince the South Sudanese people from other tribes to join his Liberation Army. He had to go as far as Equatoria which later proved to be a wise move as in the latter part of the struggle some of the other Nilotics rebelled against him and wanted to kill him and many deserted him. But he remained steadfast to his cause. With his charisma and power of persuasion he included people from Western Sudan, Southern Blue Nile and other parts of the North who were disgruntled with the Regime in Khartoum.

When Moses finally managed to get his people out of Egypt, he spent with them forty years in the wilderness, preparing them to settle in the land God chose for them. It was an indirect route from Egypt to the Promised Land.

In Garang's case he led his people initially away from the Promised Land in 1983. This was to prepare them. When he led his people away from South Sudan he was a "rebel, a criminal and a slave" as far as the Government in the North was concerned. When he re entered the Sudan in 2005 he came as a free man, triumphant, highly educated Leader. He was carrying a TRUMP card in his back pocket: The CPA which later proved to be the Arab's undoing.

As said earlier, God prepared his chosen people, the Jewish nation or the Israelites or the descendants of Jacob by taking them for forty years through a certain route to the Promised Land. During that time his chosen people went through villages and towns. They met with many different nations. Some were friendly, some unfriendly. The Israelites learnt a lot of skills, languages and cultures which strengthened them and made them unique in their capacity as a nation. They also had time to test each other. They rebelled several times against Moses and God. They lost some wars and gained many. Their decedents became healthy, strong and wealthy. The most important thing is that their faith in God never wavered, even in their darkest days.

God also prepared the South Sudanese people who rightly call themselves the chosen people of God. God has prepared his people for fifty five years. Right from the first mutiny in 1955 of the South Sudanese Soldiers. God was preparing his people who will later reside in the Land he promised them: *A land flowing milk and honey.*

During the second civil war (1983-2005) there was a massive exodus of people from South Sudan to nearly every country in the world. This was entirely for self preservation but unknown to the people this was God's master plan. The South Sudanese people started to learn the different languages of the different countries where they took asylum or refuge, including the Arabic language which is the key language; the language of the slave masters. The language spoken in North Sudan. They learnt languages from all over the globe where they settled. Their children are now professionals in every field and capacity. They learnt skills and gained experiences and expertise from all over the world.

After the exodus of the Southerners to the North of Sudan, the Southerners were forced to learn and practice some of the cultures in the North of Sudan and at the same time trading some of theirs. This brought a better understanding in the way both parties think and act. This later on proved to be a strong tool in dealing with the Sudanese Government to settle issues of Independence and Secession. One of the advantages that were gained by the Southerners in exile is that they improved immensely in the fields of education, job opportunities and better health which have boosted their numbers and presence all over the world.

God has not only prepared his people but he has also prepared the land. The land of South Sudan is rich in many minerals including gold, uranium, copper and diamond. Oil will prove one day to be one of its main resources. It is arguably one of the most fertile lands in Africa with an abundance of animal wealth. *It is indeed a Land flowing milk and honey.*

Moses died as he was looking at the Promised Land across the river. He died before he set foot in the Promised Land. Likewise Garang died as he was looking across 6 years of time to achieve his final wish: The total liberation of South Sudan from oppression by the North. That was his vision. That was his dream.

To the Israelites and likewise to the South Sudanese the untimely deaths of those leaders were the darkest and most disturbing times of their history. But it is the Lord's plan and the Lord's way: *He chose other leaders to cross the bridge to the Promised Land. He alone knows why.*

Do not underrate the talk of old men,
After all, they themselves learned it from their fathers;
From them you will learn how to think,
And the art of the timely answer.

Ecclesiasticus 8

Five

About ten men and women were walking slowly towards Susan's house. They were smartly dressed and seemed to be in a jolly good spirit. They were talking in hushed voices, every now and then letting out soft gurgles of laughter.

Meanwhile Susan was very busy in her house. There were some women and men sitting under the big *Neem* tree. There was always the option of going into the veranda if it rained. Some of the women were cooking huge quantities of meat, vegetable, rice and *kisra,* under the *rakuba*. The *rakuba* is good because it can provide a cool place during the day to sit under or cook. It is usually qualified as a woman's domain. It is usually built adjacent to the kitchen which is normally a little far away from the main house. A lot of brisk activity was taking place in and around the *rakuba* and the kitchen. The kitchen was very spacious and well stacked with shelves and cupboards. On the shelves and in the different cupboards there were numerous kitchen wares.

Today is Marianna's traditional marriage to *that boy,* Kennedy. Marianna had her baby nearly a year ago. Kennedy who was nineteen, finished school and got a job as a clerk in Juba Teaching Hospital. His mother and father helped him build a two bedroom house in a plot of land they own in "Muniki" area which was an up and coming area. They also helped him furnish the dwelling with a large wooden (teak) bed in the master bedroom and a matching four-door beautifully carved wardrobe, also made of teak which grows in abundance in South Sudan. The other bedroom had two beautifully carved single wooden beds. That was the workmanship of non other than Kennedy's uncle and godparent. Marianna and Kennedy were lucky to have so much help. The baby's cot was previously purchased by Kennedy's mum who seemed to dote on Marianna. Marianna had to pull her weight and so started to do some housework as she now realised that she cannot play the fair idle princess any more.

Luka, Susan's husband left for the United Kingdom two weeks ago after winning a scholarship. He left all the necessary instructions with his uncle and two younger brothers and their wives to help and support Susan in this very important but stressful day. He gave Susan 2000 Sudanese pounds for today's occasion and bought and updated things in the house. The three bedrooms were completely surrounded by a spacious airy veranda. All the chair coverings were newly bought. The walls were painted light blue. New light blue flowery curtains were hanging from the windows.

A good number of young women were sitting inside one of the rooms with Marianna who looked lovely with her stylishly braided hair, piled high on her head. She wore golden bracelets and a golden chain with matching earrings. An elderly lady was sitting near her carrying her baby. Marianna looked subdued and quite apprehensive.

"They are just arriving" whispered Susan to Marianna.

Marianna kept quiet.

"Who?" asked Lucinda who was painting Marianna's nails with bright red nail polish.

"The in-laws".

"They better bring the right amount of dowry stuff otherwise there will be trouble".

Marianna let out a huge sigh.

Sarah and Mary were helping with handing out tea and lemonade to the guests. They were strictly instructed not to give anything to the in-laws or "anyone who will be sitting over there". This was a special place for the bridegroom's delegates. It is the custom that when dowry issues are discussed it is always conducted in the bride's house. The delegates from the bridegroom's side are to sit in a special place assigned for them. When the two parties, from the bride and the bridegroom's finally sit down, they do so facing each other and then start discussing. Each group will have a nominated spokesperson to address the issues in order to avoid confusion and heated discussions and to conduct the solemn occasion in an orderly and dignified manner. Each group also reserves the right to move to a private place within the compound and discuss their options further and then come back and relay them to the other group. Before doing so they will have to take permission from the other group so that people are aware of such a step. The ground rule is of course: respect, respect and respect.

The bridegroom's delegates are to be given refreshments only after the dowry is settled.

In the South Sudanese culture, when a girl is married, the dowry is offered by the bridegroom's family to the bride's family. They think that a dowry should symbolise how worthy and precious a daughter is and should be far removed from a commercial deal. The "dowry" is a number of symbolic gestures and rituals which links two families and should be observed in order for the girl to leave her father's house and permanently live in her husband's household. If everyone observes the true culture of dowry, it should be affordable to every man in South Sudan. Unfortunately it is not, because people tend to break the rules and ignore their culture.

The symbolic objects used for *settling* a dowry differ largely from one tribe to another and from area to area. The cattle herders like the Dinka, Mundari, Nuer, Shilluk etc. settle dowries mainly by offering cattle. Other tribes who are mainly farmers do so using symbolic objects such as ceremonial spears which epitomise authority, bows and arrows which symbolise power, an oil lamp which brings light and happiness in the house and hoes and other tools used for cultivation to characterise productivity. Goats and sheep also constitute parts of the dowry and can symbolise fertility and wealth. In some cases an additional amount of money is also requested to replace other symbolic objects. In some cultures some of the money has to be in coins to signify stability. To a casual observer this might mean nothing but for the people concerned these are very important and sacred rituals similar to those carried out in the church e.g. the vows, the candles, the rings, the white colour, the veil and the priest's blessing. The rituals observed in the church and in a remote African village might look very different but if you look closely they are alike in many ways. Such ceremonies bring people from different sides together to witness the permanent unity of two people who love each other and want to live together and create a family.

Nowadays marriages have become quite complicated. Many people have become materialistic and want their weddings or ceremonies to be unique and remembered for years to come. People have started to spend more and more money, and weddings have become big show businesses for some people. This has in effect removed people from the real meaning of marriage. Technology has also brought people closer than ever before. With the revolution of the mobile phones, the internet and fast planes, anyone can be anywhere in the blink of an eye. People have started to adopt practices from different cultures. Consequently dowry in South Sudan is not as symbolic or as traditional anymore and therefore not as affordable as it used to be. Many people have become greedy and are doing everything they can to get their hands on extra cash. Some parents are now ready to compromise their daughter's happiness in order to get more money in the shape of a dowry. Some parents nowadays don't feel embarrassed to say to the groom's family "If you do not pay that much, then you will not marry my daughter".

It is now a matter of buying and selling which is an insult to tradition and culture. Surely a few spears and bows and arrows and hoes and an oil lamp will not cost 100,000 Sudanese Pounds?!!

After Marianna's in-laws sat down, Marianna's delegates sat down facing them. Men and women were well represented in each group.

Uncle Miskin was the spokesman for Marianna's group. Uncle Kangi was the spokesman for Kennedy's group. At this point, Marianna and Kennedy were not allowed to attend the proceedings. They will both be called at a later stage, just before the dowry was to be processed.

Uncle Miskin started the meeting with a short prayer asking God for guidance to do what is best for Marianna and Kennedy. So far so good.

Uncle Kangi stood tall and thin and introduced himself and declared the purpose for visiting that home which was to ask Marianna's hand in marriage to their son Kennedy.

Uncle Miskin said that before everybody got carried away he wanted to tell Kennedy's family about their disappointment in Kennedy. Miskin said that Kennedy has disrespected Marianna and her family by making her fall pregnant before marrying her. Everyone started to move uneasily in their seats.

"Kennedy, has disrespected us and shamed us by getting Marianna pregnant before marrying her" shouted Uncle Miskin, his eyes bulging out in anger.

"I am very sorry my brother Miskin. We have come here today to put things right and to apologise" replied Kangi.

"If Kennedy was here I will skin him alive and give his carcass to the dogs." Shouted Miskin who was clearly nursing a grievance.

"Oh my God, what is happening?" thought Kennedy's mum. "Why is the man picking a quarrel?"

"Do you think Marianna can't get a better husband?" cried uncle Miskin in a loud booming noise.

By now he was sweating profusely and it was clear that he had a few glasses of "the good stuff" even before he set foot in Luka's house.

Luka's brother Tindo said to himself

"Oh no; Uncle is drunk!"

A bright idea came to him. He went to the back of the house, after excusing himself. He sat down and pulled a chair near him. He called the elderly lady who was helping Marianna with the baby and said to her

"Go quietly and whisper to Uncle Miskin to excuse himself and say to Uncle Kangi that I am having some problems here and need Uncle Miskin to come to me at once!"

After a few minutes Uncle Miskin came to him looking very irritated.

"What is it?"

"Sit down please Uncle Miskin."

He reluctantly sat down.

"You better be quick because I have to go back now" Said Miskin.

"Are you in such a hurry to ruin Marianna's life? Why are you doing this?"

"Is this why you called me?" said Miskin getting angry and starting to get up.

"Uncle, sit down" said Tindo with such a firm and emphatic voice that Miskin sobered up momentarily.

"Uncle," continued Tindo in a level voice all the time holding his uncle's gaze. "Marianna is already living with Kennedy whether we like it or not. The fact that these people came to us from their own volition means that they respect us and want their son to marry our daughter. If we push them away Marianna will not get a second chance and she will continue to live like this with Kennedy and she will be disrespected and belittled by her in-laws. Do you agree with me uncle?"

"Yes I do but I want to show that fool Kangi who is the boss today. He has to know that I am the boss and I can make him lick my *mutu kali* ". Tindo looked at the slippers which Uncle Miskin was pointing at.

The penny suddenly dropped and Tindo now remembered a similar occasion about fifteen years ago. Kangi was the spokesman for his niece's dowry ceremony. The bridegroom was Miskin's friend's son. Kangi was quite insulting to Miskin(who was the spokesman) and to the bridegroom. He said that his niece should have done better than to want to marry a beggar's son. It should be noted that not all dowry ceremonies are that acrimonious, but usually when the girl falls pregnant before marriage, the relatives' feelings can run quite high. It usually takes one unkind or "wrong" word to let the whole volatile group explode.

Tindo then took his uncles's hand and said to him, "Uncle, I now understand completely your feelings but remember this: Marianna will suffer, not Kangi. Kennedy is not Kangi's son. If you really want to hurt Kangi, help Marianna's dowry to be settled with all the dignity and respect that this occasion warrants. As for Kangi we will invite you both in the chief's house and you can tell him about your grievance. I will not be surprised if he will be made to grovel for your forgiveness".

These words seemed to pacify poor Uncle Miskin's anger, whose feathers have been badly ruffled by that grudge fifteen years ago.

"Alright son; I will hold my peace for the time being."

"Thank you Uncle" said Tindo and hugged his uncle.

They both took a deep breath and joined the group under the tree.

Word has already travelled to Marianna and her friends that Uncle Miskin was picking a quarrel with Uncle Kangi. Marianna started to cry silently.

The girls started to cuss loudly, saying that Uncle Miskin drinks too much and was going to ruin everything.

When Uncle Miskin emerged he came straight to business.

"I was telling Kangi that our daughter fell pregnant before she was married. To us, I repeat this is a big disrespect. Before you pay the dowry we are going to fine you. The fine is 3000.00 Sudanese pounds."

After conferring briefly Kangi stood up and said

"I repeat to all that I am sorry about the mistake which our son did and we will do our best to put things right. We have 2000.00 pounds only." He unfolded a white table cloth and placed it on the coffee table in the middle of the two groups. He put the money on the white cloth.

"A fine is a fine. If you do not have 3000.00 pounds then go home" said a very stern looking Uncle Miskin.

Kennedy's mum quickly passed something to Kangi which he put on top of the money and said sheepishly

"The money is now complete!"

Everyone breathed a big sigh of relief.

Before the dowry settlement was discussed, Marianna was called in front of everyone and was asked if she wanted to go ahead with the marriage. Kennedy was asked the same question. They both consented for the marriage to go ahead. They were then asked if they know each other's parents by their proper names and about their clan and so on to establish how much they knew about each other. Marianna then withdrew and left Kennedy sitting with the rest.

The dowry was then settled satisfactorily. Kennedy's uncles produced the bows and arrows, the spears, an oil lamp, matches, five packets of cigarettes and a piece of a beautiful cloth for Marianna's mother.

Some money was offered and accepted.

The whole discussions and ceremony took about six hours. During that time Kennedy's relatives had nothing to eat and drink in that house. They had to go elsewhere to take refreshment. When the dowry was settled, Marianna and her friends heard a welcome ululation ringing from the women to express their happiness. People clapped and the party began and continued late into the night. *Now* everyone can eat and drink to their hearts desire!

Meanwhile, Tindo made sure that Uncle Miskin was at least ten meters away from Uncle Kangi throughout the night.

Your men will fall by the sword,
Your heroes in the fight,
The gates will moan and mourn;
You will sit on the ground desolate.
And seven women will fight
Over a single man that day:
"We will eat our own food,
And wear our own clothing" they will say
"Let us just have your name;
Take our disgrace away"

Isaiah 4

Six

It was around eight o'clock on a Saturday morning so most people were not at work. Susan and Lucinda sat in the veranda folding clothes which have dried in the scorching sun the day before. They were chatting about today's upcoming event. They were going to attend the christening of one of Susan's friend's baby. Everybody was very excited because that baby survived against all the odds. The baby girl was born prematurely. During that time a number of women have given birth to premature babies. Most of them either died shortly afterwards or were still born. There were no incubators or specialist care for these babies in Juba Teaching Hospital. The anguish of the bereaved mums was heart breaking.

Susan remembered a friend of her friend who was unfortunate to have a premature baby. The baby seemed fine initially but died six weeks later. That lady went into a complete decline and later suffered a full blown mental health problem.

The hospital and the authorities seemed unable to do anything to prevent the high number of neonatal and premature deaths.

Could it be due to malnutrition? Could it be due to the effects of these lethal weapons being used around Juba by the rebels and the Government forces alike?

Susan remembered how at one time there was an epidemic of a very serious and mysterious eye condition. People used to wake up in the morning with severely inflamed red eyes. The eyes would go so sticky that someone else has to wash it with warm water and force it open for you. There was a family of six who, one morning found that all of them could not open their eyes and had to shout to the neighbours to help them.

A loud bang suddenly shattered the morning silence followed by a series of other louder bangs, preceded by whistling noises which rocked the whole building and ground.

Susan stared at Lucinda. Lucinda opened her mouth and eyes wide in fear.

"What is this?" She said looking very frightened.

"It could be a plane crushing" Said Susan.

Susan was out of the house in a flash, looking for her children.

With relief she saw Mary and Sarah running towards the house. Bindi was in bed, sleeping. He suddenly woke up, running out in confusion and distress. Musa was at grandma Honoria's house in Hai Kator which was about three miles away.

Susan and Lucinda collected the children together. There was a lot of commotion in the streets. People started running in all directions.

Susan asked someone "What is happening?"

"I don't know."

Another shouted in annoyance; "Don't you know? It is the SPLA, trying to kill us".

Ju was clutching her youngest children by the hands and running while the older ones were following close at her heels.

At that instant, louder bangs were heard.

"Ju, where are you going?" cried Susan

"I am going towards the stream. What are you doing, waiting there woman? Come quickly with the children".

Susan, Lucinda and the children followed Ju who surprised everyone at the rate of speed she sprinted in spite of her heavy build. It was hard to catch her.

Then they saw the small nearly dried out stream. Many people were already lying on the scanty sand next to the stream which was surrounded by tall graceful trees with silver barks and thin long leaves. Susan was not sure about the name of the trees but to her they looked friendly and inviting as if they were extending their hands to help hide them from their terror.

At that very moment they heard a loud deafening whistle followed by a massive frightful loud bang. All of them dived on the wet marshy ground in one great sweep, looking like a group of rugby players trying to tackle each other on the ground.

If you have a bird's eye view you will see nothing but a carpet of human bodies, flat on the ground; dots of red, white blue, green and yellow.

Everyone was lying face down and closed their eyes. Yes, everyone, including the tiniest child. It was as if everyone wanted to make themselves as small, as flat and as invisible as possible to escape this murderous attack.

Susan then saw a scene which looked as if she was in a dream. People of all ages, colour, shapes, sizes and walks of life came running towards them from different directions; many, with children in tow. Some deposited themselves by the stream, some went further. They said that they were going towards the Nile bank. Someone explained to Susan that the shells and rockets fired are much less likely to detonate or explode in soft ground. They will explode mainly when they fall on hard or rocky surfaces and Juba is a very rocky place.

Susan suddenly turned on her back and looked up.

Three massive bangs sounded very close to where they were. Smoke started to rise in the distance.

The noise was not only deafening but death was coming. A silver cylinder flashed. The cylinder had things that looked like wings attached to it. Later Susan came to know that they were propellers, to help propel the tool of death and make it fall where it was intended.

Susan thought that was their last hour on earth. They were now face to face with Death.

Susan, remembering her son Musa and his grandma and not knowing or daring to think what has happened to them, started to cry and pray.

"Dear Lord. I place our souls including that of my son Musa and his Grandma Honoria in your hands. Please forgive us any sin or deed that we have committed against you. If you have to take our souls at this moment please Lord, send your angels to sit by us and comfort us".

At once a strange sense of peace and warmth engulfed her. She stopped shaking. She was not afraid anymore. She has made her peace with God before dying. They have made their peace with their God.

She was ready to die.

Bang . . . Bang . . . Bang . . .

This time the noise was not as loud, it sounded further away.

Everybody waited. Some people started to move away.

Susan, Ju and the children remained where they were.

They remained for at least two hours, too dazed and weak to go back to their homes.

Early the next day at around six in the morning, a long queue was quickly forming in front of the Sudan Airways booking office.

That night of the shelling, most people had one thing in their minds: To get out of Juba by all possible means. The SPLA's tactics was working but they invited the anger and bitterness of the residents of Juba.

People were queuing to buy air tickets to travel to Khartoum. The only planes that could carry people were cargo planes. The passenger planes stopped ages ago because the South of Sudan was deemed "unsafe" for passenger planes to travel to. Cargo plane tickets cost four or five times the cost of a seat in a passenger plane. The cost of the cargo "ticket" was not open to negotiations or regulation by anyone, even the Government! Take it or leave it. It was war time and the *Mundukuru* were here in Juba to make money!

Luckily for Susan she had some money in the house which Luka gave her before travelling for his course. Susan gave Lucinda a wad of cash to purchase five tickets to Khartoum. The tickets were for Lucinda, Sarah, Mary, Musa and Bindi. They were leaving this afternoon, at two.

When Lucinda was getting the tickets, Susan was preparing her children to travel. She had to stay back in Juba to sort things in the house before joining them.

Musa arrived early that morning with his Grandma Honoria. They all hugged and cried as if they have not seen each other for years. Later on they all knelt down and prayed to The Almighty for saving their lives and reuniting them in this very difficult time.

Susan, who was now living in the house with Honoria and some few other relatives of her husband, learnt that a woman and her three children were killed in yesterday's attack in Hai Kator, not far from Honoria's house. They said that the woman's head and her children's were cut and thrown in all directions by the shell's propellers. People who attended the scene said that the bodies were so mutilated that even the most hardened policemen and soldiers were badly shaken. Another group of three young girls walking with their father in Hai Cinema where Susan lived were another set of victims. The father and one of the girls were killed on the spot. The other two girls that survived had pieces of shrapnel imbedded all over their bodies. The shrapnel included poisoned pieces of glass, nails, other metals and debris to inflict maximum and fatal injuries to its victims.

The two girls suffered for months and later died within two days of each other.

What annoyed Susan most was what she heard when they tuned in to the SPLA radio at three that afternoon. A jubilant broadcaster started to taunt people in Juba saying

"Didn't I tell you? Didn't I tell you what will happen to you, men and women of Juba? I told you to get out and because of your hard headedness you have had it." He laughed arrogantly "Ha ha haaaaaaa. You got what you deserve and you will get much more. You have not seen anything yet!"

"How can one of us say something so abhorrent and painful and mock us when innocent children and women have died?" everyone was asking. "Are they fighting the Government Army or the innocent civilians? Do you kill people in order to free them? How? Are these people really fighting for the people of South Sudan or they are fighting for themselves? Who is their real enemy?"

People were angry mainly because none of the government soldiers or their barracks ever got hit. Everyone in Juba knew that the soldiers have deep and well built trenches and air raid shelters to protect them. They have weapons in place to defend themselves against any attacks. They also have huge stores of food. The poor citizens had nothing and were facing hunger and lack of basic necessities and no sense of security.

After two days another rocket attack was carried out on the people of Juba by the SPLA. Further reports of women and children killed, including babies and toddlers. It was gruesome. It was very painful.

The biggest pain was that the people of Juba were attacked not by mere Sudanese but by the South Sudanese themselves; by their own people.

The biggest pain of all was the taunting and the abuse they were subjected to over the radio every single day. Hardly any reference was made to the mighty Sudanese Army whose soldiers were laughing in their barracks at the "slaves who were killing each other".

What was to hurt the poor citizens of Juba more was the atrocities carried out on them systematically by the army of the Government of Sudan. The Army's main mission was to protect Juba. They received their orders from the government in Khartoum. In the eyes of the Sudanese Army what they were protecting was their interest only in Juba. This did not necessarily mean the protection of the civilians. On the contrary, the army which was run mainly by the Arabs in the North looked at the people of Juba as the helpers of the SPLA. The people of Juba are Southerners and the SPLA were mainly Southerners, so that meant they were the same people; the same rebels. To the Sudanese Army, the people of Juba were the other face of the SPLA! The people of Juba found themselves caught between the rock and a very hard place.

The exodus from Juba continued. The indigenous people of Juba started to flee to Khartoum, Kenya, Uganda, Central Africa and other parts of the world. They fled every day in large numbers.

People from the country sides who feared the SPLA started to take refuge in Juba. They felt much more secure in Juba. After a while the Sudanese Army and the Security Systems within Juba started to accuse people of colluding with the rebels. A system of detention and lynching began.

Things came to a head when the Sudanese Army received a long list of names of some indigenous citizens of Juba who were teachers, doctors, lawyers, civil servants and business men. That list claimed that the men were helping the SPLA to enter Juba and take it from the Sudanese Army.

Everyone on the list was taken to the Army barracks, interrogated, tortured and killed. Some citizens of Juba up to the present time think that it was all a murderous and filthy plot orchestrated by the SPLA. They think that the list was written by the SPLA and handed to the Sudanese Army so that these innocent people get lynched.

It was one of the darkest days in the lives of the citizens of Juba.

From the daughter of Zion
All her glory has departed.
Her leaders were like rams
That find no pasture.
Listlessly they took the road,
driven by the drover.

Lamentations 1:6

Seven

Susan followed her sister Lucinda and her four children to Khartoum, two weeks after she packed all the stuff in the house. She gave away some of the furniture to her relatives and her husband's family and some to friends. This included furniture such as beds, tables, chairs, fridge and TV. She put some of her books and her husband's in containers and gave it to some local nuns for safekeeping. Luckily Lino her brother was arriving in Juba with his family shortly to live in the house, so they kept the house in Luka's name.

The flight to Khartoum was chaotic. Cars were stopped and searched a few kilometres from the airport by the state security bureau, which had the power to prevent anyone from progressing further to the airport. Many people were taken off their cars for no apparent reason and lost their chance to travel. It was terrible. Every individual was living in total fear of being singled out and punished for doing no wrong at all.

The car Susan was travelling in was allowed to pass after the security personnel delayed them for nearly half an hour. When they were finally waved in Susan's tears were silently running down her cheeks. She thought she would never see her children again. It was rumoured that flights might soon be stopped.

As they reached the airport people were already lining up to go to the plane. Susan hurried, followed closely by her kind in-law who gave her the lift in his car. At the gate she was supposed to stop and as she was hurrying to join the group ahead she was violently pushed back by a crazy looking man in uniform. Susan fell on the floor. Everyone looked away. When her in-law moved forward to help her up, he was struck across the face by the crazy looking man, who looked as if he was going to give them the beating of their lives or even more. The man was carrying an AK-47 assault rifle.

"Stop, you stupid woman! Where do you think you are going? Do you think this is a bloody "*Andaya*?", bellowed the arrogant looking man, with tiny darting eyes that reminded Susan of a serpent.

"I am sorry Sir", said Susan after unceremoniously getting on her feet. "I am travelling in this flight"

The man cussed very loudly looking Susan up and down in derision. He was a South Sudanese in the Army. Why was he so hostile?

"Your ticket", he demanded.

Susan handed him the ticket, blood trickling slowly from a gush in her right elbow.

The man flung the ticket at her.

"Go", he spat.

Only when Susan sat on the plane did she remember that she did not even turn round to say goodbye or thank her kind in-law.

The cargo plane was full of goods. Some of the furniture and teak must have been looted by the army. Sacks of coffee beans, elephant tusks etc were staked to the roof. In spite of charging people more than five times the normal price of a passenger plane, no special seating area was prepared for the poor travellers. Each person, including children and pregnant women had to perch on a piece of unstable furniture and hold onto something else or even another human being, whichever was close during takeoff and landing!

When they landed at Khartoum airport one unfortunate women had blood running down her legs. She later fainted and miscarried the baby she was carrying. Her mother who was travelling with her started to wail at the top of her voice. Everyone was shocked. Eventually an ambulance was brought.

Susan's children and her sister Lucinda were staying in Susan's uncle's house in Khartoum in an area called Shagara. After Susan stayed there for two weeks she managed to speak to Luka who was studying for his Masters Degree in Manchester University in the UK. Luka was very relieved to hear that Susan arrived safely in Khartoum. Susan told him that she needed to rent a house. Luka did not have to send Susan money as she came with all the reserves of money in their joint bank account. That was in excess of 20,000 Sudanese pounds. They managed to rent a small two bedroom house near her uncle's house in Shagara.

One day, Susan woke up early in the morning and was about to go to the market when she heard a faint knock on the front door. When she opened the door, she saw a young South Sudanese lady whom she guessed was from the Dinka tribe. The girl was also able to know straight away that Susan was from South Sudan. She suddenly relaxed and gave Susan a beautiful smile.

"Do you want your clothes to be washed?" asked the girl.

When Susan hesitated, the girl explained

"I will wash for you for a lowered price".

Susan asked the girl to come in. The girl explained that she washes six pieces of clothing for five dinars. Susan gave her some clothes, soap, wash basin and a small stool to sit on. There was some shade so the girl started washing the clothes in the shade.

"Tell me, what is your name?" said Susan

"My name is Rebecca"

Susan said "Rebecca is a beautiful name. Mine is Susan"

"Are you from Juba?" asked Rebecca.

"No. From Yambio but I lived in Juba".

Rebecca became a regular worker for Susan. Susan would give her food for her children and other things to help her.

Rebecca's story was a very sad one. Rebecca was a Dinka from Bahr El Ghazal. She said that they used to live in Wau. She was originally from Gogrial. Two years ago there was severe drought in the Bahr El Ghazal area. At the same time there was a lot of fighting and many people died. They had to flee to the countryside around Gogrial as the Dinka men, women and children were targeted by the pro government militias and Government Army. All her uncles and cousins were either killed or ran away to join the SPLA, mainly for safety rather than to fight. The hunger in the country side was terrible. She saw many people dying, especially children. The bodies of the dead and dying people were in their thousands. They were attacked by the Baggara Arabs known as *muraheleen*. The *muraheleen* came from Western Sudan and attacked their villages burning their huts to the ground. The women and children were abducted and sold as slaves. The men were killed. Susan's jaws dropped.

"Slaves, in this day and age?"

"I swear to God, our people were taken as slaves" replied Rebecca.

"Oh my God cried Susan. Why are we suffering like this?"

Famine in South Sudan, especially in the mid nineties was estimated to affect the lives of 2.4 million people. The population of South Sudan is about 2.7 million. The main cause of the famine was the civil war and the effects of drought. South Sudan claims a third of the whole area of Sudan before the secession. It is about 2.5 million square kilometres. The areas most affected by the famine were in Bahr El Ghazal. Most of the people affected by the famine were Dinka. They are the largest tribe in South Sudan and are mainly cattle herders and live a nomadic life, trying to find grazing ground and water for their cattle. In 1998 alone at least 250,000 people died as a result of famine.

At that time the SPLA rebels were engaged in fighting against pro-government militias some of which were led by South Sudanese themselves including Dinka!! Human right abuses were carried out by both parties and of course the victims were the already beleaguered unarmed Dinka women, men and children. Famine would have been avoided if it was not for the human rights abuses carried out by both sides in the conflict.

The United Nations Operation Lifeline Sudan (OLS) was created in order to avert humanitarian catastrophe created by the famine and war but maybe it was too little too late.

The Government's counterinsurgency plan in Bahr-el-Ghazal was to attack civilians and destroy the rebel social base, displacing, killing and capturing civilians and depriving them of their meagre assets which will help them with survival in the harsh land. It would be remembered that the Dinka are nomads so they have limited skills in farming or cookery. They live mainly on milk and dairy products; hence removing their cattle is subjecting them to starvation.

One of the Government's strategies was to 'divide and rule'. By using militias from the local Southerners they guarantee that the Southerners will fight among themselves and destroy each other. Additionally, the neighbouring Baggara militias were to strengthen the government's hand in reinforcing the atrocities.

On the other hand the SPLA's strategy and tactics disproportionately affected civilians. They tended to lay sieges to force the surrender of government garrison towns such as Juba, Wau, Torit etc. and divert food supplies or relief food from starving and suffering fellow South Sudanese people to themselves. So it may be concluded that the people who lived in the mainly Dinka areas at that time were like those in Juba, pushed between the rock and a hard place.

In Upper Nile where the biggest tribe is the Nuer, the Government's strategy was slightly different. The Government helped to form two separate militias who hate each other. The reason being that the Nuer area was the place where there are the richest oilfields in the South. By skilfully forming two warring militias the Government has guaranteed that the Nuer people will slaughter themselves, while the Government silently pumps out and makes maximum use of the oil revenue by improving and rebuilding the North.

Images of the children of South Sudan covered with flies and dying, shown on TV screens round the world is a living testimony to the whole sad story. Isn't life complicated enough? How much should a nation actively complicate their own problems?

In this conflict each tribe in South Sudan thinks that they are the victims, not knowing that everyone is as much a victim as the next. No one, no area in the whole Southern region has escaped the pain.

Civilians are not legitimate military targets. This is expressly forbidden by the UN General Assembly Resolution 2444, "Respect for Human Rights in Armed Conflicts, UN resolution2444". The duty to distinguish at all times between civilians and combatants, and between civilian objects and military objects, included the duty to direct military operations only against military objectives.

Susan suddenly had a flash back of some of the suffering of the South Sudanese women in Khartoum. She remembered how one day she bumped into one of her best friends Ju'Ndogo. Ju, her parents and children fled to Khartoum like Susan and many others. They lived in a shantytown in the outskirts of Khartoum. To make ends meet, Ju started to brew a local alcoholic drink called *aragi*. The North had adopted the Islamic Sharia Law in the Nimeri regime banning any alcoholic drinks. Ju'Ndogo, like many other displaced Southern Sudanese women with no means, had to take the risk of selling *aragi*. Anybody caught selling alcohol, faces a fine, months in prison and all the utensils for making the alcohol will be confiscated and destroyed.

Ju'Ndogo told Susan how one day her house was raided by the secret police. Her utensils including all her saucepans which she bought with her savings were confiscated and she was thrown in prison. She broke down as she remembered how the prison was full of South Sudanese women who were caught selling alcohol. She said during the night, the jailors used to rape them. Many of the young women got pregnant while in jail. No one listened to their pleas and complaints. Most of the women got rid of their pregnancies. Some became infected with sexually transmitted diseases.

Ju'Ndogo said that when they went and complained to some of their Southern politicians they were told that the only way to avoid getting caught is "not to sell the stuff!" but there was no assistance offered to them or plans to speak to the government about ways to alleviate their poverty.

The other major party to compound the suffering of the people of South Sudan is the Lord's Resistance Army of Uganda, known as the LRA or Tong-tong. LRA was engaged in civil war against the Ugandan government. Their incumbent leader Joseph Kony, who succeeded Grace Lakwena similarly proclaimed himself the spokesman of God. However, the LRA has proved to be as far placed from God as Satan himself. The LRA operates in several countries including Uganda, South Sudan, Central African Republic and The Republic of Congo. The LRA is accused of widespread human rights violations, including murder and mutilation of innocent civilians. They tend to abduct, sexually enslave women and children and force children to participate in the most horrific acts of violence. Some of these Child soldiers are as young as five years old. The Ugandan Government and many others believe that the Government of North Sudan is firmly behind the longevity and survival of this rebel group by supplying them with arms, food and money in return for destabilising the South.

Another twist is that the people in Eastern and Western Equatoria think that The SPLA has dealings with the LRA and is prepared to use them as a lynching tool against other tribes.

After its inception in 1987, the LRA infiltrated Sudan around 1994-2005. Initially, they started activities in Eastern Equatoria then spread to where they are presently: Western Equatoria. They raided villages killing, maiming and abducting civilians. This has caused people from Eastern Equatoria, mainly the Madi tribe to flee to Uganda for refuge. Their displacement was compounded by the insurgency works of the SPLA who by that time were expelled from Ethiopia. The people of Eastern Equatoria found themselves faced by the LRA and the SPLA. The women and children were the main victims. The LRA helped to clean Eastern Equatoria borders from its indigenous people who are mainly the Madi, Acholi, Kuku etc. The SPLA who are predominantly Dinka and assume the movement to be theirs, moved with large herds of cattle and settled in Eastern Equatoria, mainly Nimule. When all the indigenous inhabitants of Eastern Equatoria were displaced or killed, the LRA were moved by some *invisible forces* to settle in Western Equatoria and attack and displace its indigenous people, mainly the Azande.

The International Criminal Court issued arrest warrants against the LRA leadership on 8th July 2005. They were charged with crimes against humanity and war crimes including murder of civilians, rape (male and females) and sexual slavery and using children as combatants. Those warrants were sent to the three countries where the LRA are active. They are: Uganda, Sudan and the Democratic Republic of Congo (DRC). The LRA stated that they will never surrender unless granted immunity from prosecution. This led the ICC to come to the conclusion that the insurgency will not have a negotiated end.

Interpol then issued five wanted person notices to 184 countries on behalf of the ICC which has no police of its own.

Around 2006 after the signing of The Peace Agreement between the SPLA and the Government of Sudan the LRA activities of abduction, mutilations and murder became more vicious in West Equatoria State and the areas within the borders of the DRC and Central Africa. These are areas where most of the people are Azande. The Azande people feel that a system of genocide is being carried out against them.

The New Government of South Sudan ignored the ICC and Interpol notice and chose to meet with the LRA leadership. They supplied them with cash and food under the glare of the whole world. Their meeting was televised and the images were flashed around the world! The explanation that the Government of South Sudan (mainly SPLA) gave to the International Community was that they took those steps to stop the LRA from attacking the citizens of South Sudan!!! Did the insurgency activities of the LRA stop after the generous donation? You must be joking. The Azande people who have suffered most at the hands of the LRA have the right to demand for an explanation from the Government of the Republic of South Sudan. Why did they publicly "reward" the LRA for carrying out genocide activities against them? If the Government of the Republic of South Sudan has given food and cash to the LRA to stop the LRA killing the Azande people then why didn't they come back to explain as to why the LRA have in fact increased their attacks and atrocities against the poor civilians instead? Whose money has been given to these villains and savage murderers anyway? Isn't it the Azande people's money? Why are they killed and their money given to their killers? One day someone will be brought to face Justice. No one in this world is above the law. The clock is ticking for all leaders, however omnipotent they think they are.

In 2009 an operation led by the Ugandan Army (Operation Lighting Thunder) to inflict a final military defeat on the LRA was not fully successful. The operation was supported by the US. This led to retaliatory attacks by the LRA on the people of Western Equatoria—the Zande, Muru, Baka and people along the borders of DRC and Central Africa. Over 5000 people were reported killed and maimed. The maiming was to inflict a lasting psychological damage and fear on a nation already very much under attack by other groups such as the armed group of the Ambororo nomads who have cattle and were armed to the teeth. They were said to be supported by the Government of North Sudan. The Ambororo originate in Chad and infiltrated the Sudan through the Western Sudanese border. They were also reported to kill, loot and capture women and children as slaves.

The maiming by the LRA included mutilation and cutting of limbs or sexual organs and other body parts. They would kill individuals, cut their sexual organs and place them in their mouths to instil terror and fear in the hearts of the rest of civilians. When they attacked people they would ask them if they were happy. If they say that they were "happy", the rebels will cut off all their lips thus exposing their teeth. They will then tell the individual "You said you are happy, so keep on laughing" They usually do that at the end, after beating and seriously wounding them. In most cases the poor souls will eventually bleed to death as they were usually tied to trees, sometimes head down. If they say they were "sad", the LRA will make a hole in their upper and lower lips and place a massive padlock, thus closing their mouths. They will then laugh and tell them "If you are sad there is no need for you to laugh". They will get hold of babies and children by one of their legs and kill them by hitting their heads against a tree trunk, wall or stone or against another person's head most probably the parents. If they see a pregnant woman they will ask her "Madam, are you carrying a boy or a girl?" Obviously she will reply "I do not know". They will then say "Well, it is very easy to find out". Her tummy will be slashed by a knife or a machete and they will snatch the baby from the womb of the collapsed and dying woman and say to her

"Congratulations, you have a boy or a girl!"

"Swifter than the eagles of the heavens our pursuers have proved to be.
Upon the mountains they have hotly pursued us.
In the wilderness they have lain in wait for us."

Lamentations 4:19

Eight

The real suffering of the South Sudanese people started in 1998 in Bahr El Ghazal province. The suffering started as famine which was due to natural and manmade causes. The Bahr El Ghazal famine of 1998 had one natural cause: a two-year drought caused by El Niño. This helped the natural conditions from which human violence and repression would generate one of the worst famines in human history. By that time a commander in Bahr El Ghazal Government Forces who was a Dinka by tribe and from the same area had a few years earlier defected to the SPLA. Unfortunately for the other poor unarmed and vulnerable Dinka civilians in Bahr El Ghazal the commander and his defected battalion decided to go on a rampage on their way to join the SPLA in Ethiopia. They looted and raided their own Dinka communities and the neighbouring *Fertit* communities too. The *Fertit,* a conglomerate of other smaller tribes such as the Balanda, Kresh, Golo, Ndogo, Banda, Bongo etc. are mainly farmers. They are peace loving people and the Dinka tribes throughout the history of Sudan have dominated and marginalized them, reducing them to weaker retreating people with low rate of representation in all aspects of development and opportunities up till the present day. The defecting battalion decided to take a parting shot at the *Fertit* people for a laugh, as they have always been their scapegoats and objects of contempt. They murdered *Fertit* villagers while the innocent people were sleeping. The defecting battalion, crazy with the power of weapon and as a show of strength, slashed the villager's throats saying that they "will not waste their bullets on the Fertit". The main villages affected were Mboro and Khor Shammam. That attack generated intense anger, fear and a bitter backlash from all sections of the Fertit communities. They had no other option but to go to the Government and ask for protection against the Dinka (SPLA) who have clearly targeted them for no apparent reason. The Government of Sudan which was waiting for this kind of breakthrough responded immediately. Their strategy was to kill all the "Stupid Southerners" and take their Land. Hence the opportunity presented itself on a golden plate to—fulfil the motto: *"Hit a slave with another slave"*.

They armed the Fertit up to the teeth and encouraged them to kill all the Dinka and the Jur. As the innocent Dinka civilians (Some had no connections with the SPLA) were butchered by the Fertit militia, they too started to arm themselves and hit back. The Sudanese Army, mainly from the North and West of Sudan, was in the middle, stirring the big pot and adding more fuel to the fire. In wars like this it is the women and children who get hurt most. Because the Government was siding with the Fertit militia as retaliation against the SPLA which was mainly dominated by the Dinka, the only leeway for the Dinka and Jur was to flee out of Wau into the surrounding villages. Unfortunately and by a twist of fate, the drought started kicking in. There was nothing to eat or to hide behind. In the past when the El Niño used to visit the Dinka land, they used to flee in massive numbers to the Fertit areas where they used to get food and shelter. After the massacres, the Fertit areas became a "no go area" for the Dinka. The only place for the starving Dinka is to go northwards to the hostile territories of Darfur and Kordofan. There they faced their most aggressive enemies; the Baggara. For the Dinka it was a case of:

"I have burnt all the boats behind me. Now I am standing on the shore facing my bitterest enemies."

The defecting Government Army also raided the Dinka villages and burnt them out. The remnants of the same villages were plundered and burnt by the Baggara militias coming across the borders from the North. Government Antonov planes would bomb Dinka villages thus killing and displacing them further. One of the affected towns was Aweil in Eastern Bahr El Ghazal. The people of Aweil had to run for their lives northwards towards western Sudan, mainly South Kordofan. As cattle herders The Dinka do very little subsistence farming of dura, millet, groundnuts and okra. They are nomads as they have to take their cattle to greener pastures to graze. This has caused them a lot of problems with their neighbours the Baggara tribe in South Kordofan who are also cattle herders. The

Dinka are mainly animists or Christians. The Baggara on the other hand are Muslims. They are two totally different people but share the same area. The military trains that supply Wau and Aweil government garrison towns in Bahr El Ghazal, brought *muraheleen* horsemen and troops of the Sudanese army, who rampaged the Dinka communities along the rail line. The railway served both to bring in the raiders and their horses and to remove their booty: cattle, grain, women and children who were abducted into slavery. The rural Dinka communities were also assailed by raiding and looting by the Government forces. The Government's persistent obstruction of relief in the region for many years and the SPLA's looting of relief goods and taxing of civilians greatly contributed to their starvation and death. When aid agencies started to get threatened and attacked by the SPLA for relief goods, the aid agencies deemed the area too dangerous to operate in, hence they pulled out.

As mentioned earlier, when trouble and famine broke out in Bahr El Ghazal, thousands of starving, frightened and disoriented Dinka fled to Southern Kordofan for refuge. The first point they reached was a place called Safaha. To the Dinka women Safaha is what Auschwitz was to the Jewish people. Safaha was the place where the human being showed how he or she can be the other face of Satan. Safaha was a place where the children of Zion were reduced to nothing. In Safaha, a feeding centre was set up. It was run by UN aid agencies mainly the *MSF*. However, the centre was nothing but a big lean to or a *rakuba* made of grass roof supported by wooden beams. Safaha feeding centre was where starving children were fed milk in order to stand a chance of survival. The starving Dinka children whose body weight fell below half of that of a normal child of the same age will be taken. That was the criterion. French and Belgian doctors, who lived in an adjoining hut to the feeding centre, were forbidden to go to any other place outside the feeding centre. They were also forbidden to mix with members of the public. They were closely monitored by the Government police or the Rizeigat Militia.

The women who were skin and bones, used to carry and feed their skeletal children milk prepared by the doctors in big buckets. A child was to be fed a cupful of milk every three hours to give it a chance to survive. The mother of the child had to be strong enough to feed her child. If she was too weak and unable to sit up to feed the child, then her child would definitely die. The children were too many for the doctors to help. In the centre, all you could see was a sea of skulls and bones. All you could hear was the groaning, the terrible coughing and the retching of moving skeletons. Some were unable even to shift the flies off their faces or lift their heads. Many of the children couldn't cry: they just stared in space like dummies.

Many mothers at that point would have given up hope of life. They started to sell their children to the Baggara and anyone who wanted a child to do what they wanted to do with it! The price of a child was about fifty Sudanese pounds. A mother would think that at least if her child is "sold" it will be given food and will survive, hoping that one day when things get better she will reclaim her child! Isn't "buying" a human being called "slavery"? The people of Southern Kordofan tried to cover the ugliness of the word "slavery". They called it "Pawning". What is the difference? How can people of The Holy Koran accept other human beings to be sold to them in a situation like this? How can anybody take advantage of someone including a child who is dying of hunger? They try to justify this by saying that since these people are not Muslims it was only right for them to be made slaves. However, Muslims testify that there is no any other god but the one God. Hence mankind was created by the same one God, be they Muslims or non-Muslims. What they were doing in Safaha is contrary to what their religion teaches!

In Safaha feeding centre the mothers who were reduced to skin and bones used to lie with their dying babies next to them. At night the Riziegat Militia used to come and rape them. Yes, they would rape a dying woman lying next to a dying child! It was not "lust" because the women wouldn't inspire any "lust" or any thought of sex in any "normal" human being. How can they pray and shortly afterwards sexually abuse a corpse? It is diabolical sadism.

The helpless women were raped to death. The next morning the beleaguered aid workers were left with the task of removing their dead bodies and putting them under the brambles. Some of these women would have survived but for the rape. Killing a mother was in effect killing her child. No child has survived without its mum in those camps. No burial;

no respect. There was no one to close their eyes. The smell of the decaying and dead bodies all around . . .'

> "*I fear no foe with thee at hand to bless;*
> *Ills have no weight, and tear no bitterness.*
> *Where is death's sting? Where, grave, thy victory?*
> *I triumph still, if thou abide with me.*"

"Do not yield your scepter, Lord,
to non-existent beings.
Never let men mock at our ruin.
Turn their designs against themselves,
And make an example of him who leads the attack on us.
Remember, Lord; reveal yourself
In time of our distress.

Esther 4

Nine

Norah, Susan's sister and her children like many others continued to live in Yambio, Western Equatoria., Many people from the West fled to the neighbouring countries of the Central African Republic, the Democratic Republic of Congo and Uganda which are arguably considered "safe havens".

The SPLA entered Western Equatoria in the mid nineties. Years before the LRA. The Azande and other tribes living there welcomed them and they lived quite peacefully side by side. Initially there were sporadic occurrences of murder, rape etc. Soon it died down and people lived relatively peacefully; the majority of men and women joined the rebel movement.

Norah joined the SPLA. Being a well respected individual in the Community and having the high position as the headmistress of a local School, she caught the attention of the SPLA leaders who promoted her to the rank of an officer. Norah kept calm and collected in spite of her pain at knowing that her daughter Nadi was raped by a group of the SPLA soldiers. She knew that there was nothing now that she could do to undo the past. She therefore vowed to herself to try her utmost to protect young women and children from such attacks in the future and to build good relationships between the indigenous citizens of the area and the incoming SPLA.

Norah called a meeting of all the elders of the tribes of Western Equatoria and the high ranking officials of the SPLA. This was a preliminary meeting meant to facilitate a bigger meeting to include the general public in the near future. She took out a note and addressed them:

"Dear brothers and sisters, I greet you in the name of God the Father, God the Son and the Holy Spirit. Our Land is going through a difficult time because we are now in the middle of a long war. The first thing to do is for us to ask for God's help and to unite with each other. If we do not unite then we have already lost the war. This war is for our freedom from slavery. By holding steadfast to our cause and emulating the courage and vision of our leader Dr John Garang, we will be able to get what we are fighting for.

I ask that we all live peacefully with each other, respecting the rights of each other and helping and sharing with one another. If we start fighting among ourselves, our numbers will dwindle and our guns will not fire and we will be a prey to attacks by our enemies and will be enslaved by them.

I will ask you brothers and sisters to tell everyone to obey simple rules: No looting. No murdering of innocent people. No raping of women. No abduction of women and children. No killing of animals including cattle, goats, sheep and chickens if they do not belong to you.

If we observe these simple rules and each of us encourage their groups and tribes to do likewise we should live peacefully and reserve our energies to fight an outside enemy . . ."

At the end of the speech, Norah received a warm applause and congratulations by all present, on her brave and wise speech and recommendations.

Norah was then appointed by the commander in chief to lead a committee in order to deal with public relations. When Norah went home to her children she was satisfied that she could be able to help prevent abuse of young women and children. She could also raise awareness in young people who have arms to refrain from using violence and coercion to deal with others who are defenceless. She particularly asked the chiefs to take more responsibility and report incidences promptly so that they can be dealt with straightaway before things became complicated.

People like mamma Maria, Rutha and Miriam did all what they could to protect their community. They started to visit schools and encourage boys and young men to follow the culture of respect for women and how to protect them. In order to help the elderly and poor people, they started sharing food at least once a week with disadvantaged families. They also made it their duty to visit any funeral place and help with prayers and preparation of dead bodies for burial. These women proved to be pillars of strength in their community. Their organization was impeccable. People came to realise that they do not have to have a lot of money to have a decent funeral or a better life. Everything just needed organization and dedication. Many people who live among people from Western Equatoria have come to realise how methodically organized they are.

Ten

"I have to go to the *Itisalat* in the City Centre early tomorrow morning to speak with Luka about the arrangements for your marriage" said Susan to Lucinda, plaiting her daughter Mary's hair with wavy shinny extensions. The *Itisalat* was about five miles away.

"I am very excited auntie Lucy" cried Mary "I can't believe that it is only nineteen days to your wedding!"

"I am not so excited "said Lucinda. "Things are moving too fast and I do not think that we are going to finish things on time". She looked as if she was going to burst into tears.

"What things?" said Susan irritated at her sister "I told you not to worry. You should leave everything to me. Peter has rented that house in Jebel hasn't he?"

"Yes" said Lucinda "but we need to have completed buying all the things for the house by now"

"Lucy, what have you to do with the furniture? These are supposed to be dealt with by Peter. Our only responsibility is the tablecloths, the bed sheets and curtains. I have prepared all your kitchenware. You have prepared the rest and packed them haven't you?"

"Of course I have" said Lucinda impatiently.

"Then what is the matter?"

"Peter has not prepared everything . . ."

"Then it is his problem" cried Susan rather loudly and irritably.

Lucinda kept quiet. These days Susan was becoming less patient with everyone and seemed to lose her temper quite easily.

Susan will travel soon after the wedding to join Luka in the UK. Susan would have left by now if it was not for the wedding. Lucinda was very thankful for her sister's support. She remembered how her parents wrote a letter to Susan saying ". . . Susan, we are very proud and happy to hear that our daughter is getting married. Unfortunately we are unable to attend the wedding which should have taken place here if it was not for this fighting. We ask you and Luka to take responsibility for Lucinda's wedding. Lucinda is not only your sister; she is also your daughter. You and Luka have brought her up and we thank you from the bottom of our hearts . . ."

This letter sounded like music to Susan who couldn't help but feel as proud as a peacock to be in charge of her sister's imminent wedding. She started to plan and buy things. She wanted to make sure that Lucinda had a wedding to remember. What Susan did not realise was that to plan a wedding can be very stressful.

One of the difficulties was the issue of transport. You have to start your journey early in the morning. By mid day it was a real struggle to get public transport because the number of buses and minibuses were not enough to cope with the high number of commuters. It became all too common for people to wait for hours in the relentless and blazing heat of an unforgiving sun. Dust storms were also another issue in that place.

The price of every commodity was rising every day to the frustration of Susan. She would have to speak to Peter and ask him as to what to do. Many people will be staying in the house for days during the wedding.

As for Lucinda she decided to go to her room to have a little lie-down. She needed to rest before she had her daily session of "steaming" with sweet smelling chunks of certain tree trunks. It helps to clear and tone the skin.

This is a local Sudanese beauty treatment. Susan's neighbour Hanan who lived in the house opposite became friends with Susan. Hanan was in charge of all the Sudanese bridal beauty treatment for Lucinda. She was about the same age as Susan and had three boys. Hanan and her Husband Omar were very friendly and generous. When Susan first moved in the area, Hanan and her husband brought them food and soft drinks and welcomed them in the neighbourhood. Two days later they visited Susan again and asked if she needed help with anything after learning that her husband has travelled abroad. Hanan then introduced Susan to two of her cousins who live in the next street. Susan counted herself lucky to have such nice neighbours. Whenever Susan met with any of her other neighbours, they always greeted her politely and smiled at her and told her that she was welcome in the neighbourhood. These nice, friendly people made Susan wonder whether she was just lucky. Didn't people say that the Northerners are hostile to Southerners?

Susan came to realise that it is not the common man and woman in the street that are hostile to Southerners. On the contrary, Susan came to realise that most of the Northern Sudanese are the kindest and most generous people. It was the "System" of the Government in the North of Sudan that was at odds with the Southerners. This System has been built since the Sudanese Independence and reached a peak with the introduction of the Islamic Sharia law. The Sharia was used by the System to marginalize, degrade and enslave the South Sudanese people, ignoring their religious and cultural rights. Southern Sudanese women were forced to cover their heads and wear long dresses to conform to the Islamic dictates otherwise they were lashed in public. The South Sudanese culture and religion allows them to drink provided they do not disturb others or create public disorder. However this is disregarded by defenders of the Sharia Law and everybody will be lashed in public even on allegations of intent to purchase alcohol!! Who knows what is in one's mind, except God our Creator? The funny thing is that the Northerners tend to drink as much alcohol as the Southerners but their target seemed to be the Southerners. When the Southerners complained, the answer was "If you do not like it here then go home".

"Well, this is my bloody home. I am a Sudanese, am I not?"

The worst and the most horrific punishment they used was amputating people's arms and legs if caught stealing. Many people of African origin and Southerners were the unofficial targets of this brutal punishment. They would cut the opposite limbs e.g. the right arm and the left leg. The victim will be rendered useless, unable to walk or work for the rest of his life. Some Southerners had their arms and legs amputated for mere hearsay. No indigenous Arab Northerner had such an amputation performed on them which leaves the question if punishment of the Sharia Law was confined to Southerners only. Are there no thieves in Saudi Arabia who are ruled by the Sharia Law? Why don't we hear that they are implementing this barbaric law on them? Are there no thieves in Saudi Arabia and other Muslim countries following the Sharia Law?

When people from the South were being displaced in their thousands to the North, especially Khartoum which is the capital city, the Sudanese Government did not take any steps to help these people who were mostly poor, disoriented, starving and could not speak the local language. Though in a similar situation but unlike refugees, these people were treated like lepers and left to fend for themselves. They started to build shanty towns in the outskirts of the city and many used to scavenge in the rubbish heaps for food. They had no running water and no proper toilets and hence the frequent outbreak of cholera and dysentery used to kill many of them.

A few of the Southerners who had some money used to be charged extortionate prices for house rent but the Government closed its eyes and ears to this unfair treatment. Many Southern Sudanese children were denied education in the mainstream schools. The Churches intervened and built self-help schools for these people and helped many struggling families. Aid organizations started to come into North Sudan to help the displaced citizens of South Sudan. They built health and relief centres.

The least the Government could have done was to allow relief work to help these unfortunate people. Instead the Government was very hostile to those organizations. The government did not want anyone to help the South Sudanese people. In 1988 they expelled all the organizations from Sudan accusing them of spying and other serious charges. That was when the fleeing displaced Southerners had real crises. The death toll especially among children and pregnant women rose quite high but unfortunately it was unrecorded. After a big outcry from the International Community the Sudan Government was put under a massive pressure and was forced to reinstate some of the organization for relief aid purposes only.

In spite of all these policies, the Southerners managed to survive and some even thrived.

There were NO jobs for the Southerners in the civil service therefore that meant that the Southerners faced direct discrimination. The system would prefer to give jobs to refugees from other countries rather than give it to the Southerners. If a Southerner gets a job it was either in an independent organization or in the Church schools. Southern doctors, nurses, lawyers, civil servants; all worked as teachers in those schools.

The System of the Government saw to it that Southerners should never have jobs and should scavenge in the rubbish tips like dogs. Their children should never have education and their population ratio should be kept at a minimum. This sounds like our friend the Pharaoh of Egypt, thousands of years ago! History does repeat itself!

The "System "also saw to it that the Southerners should suffer while living in the North by making it difficult for them to get proper and comfortable housing. Although the land is plenty, the Sudan being the biggest country in Africa, the Government refused to give land to the Southerners to build houses for themselves. Whenever they saw the Southerners building houses anywhere, the Government used to send bulldozers to demolish the houses and leave the poor people in the streets: pregnant women, young children, and old people, all got the same treatment. The aim was to humiliate and to deny them an existence. The land prices were unaffordable and Northerners were told not to sell their land to the Southerners. The Government plots were affordable but will never be given to a Southerner because these plots were organized by the local authorities who are the very system that are hell bent to deny Southerners a good life.

Everything became two tiered: One for the people of the land and one for the "Naziheen" or "Abeed" and the Naziheen should put up or shut up.

It was a murky, cloudy evening. It was in one of the houses in the shanty town of "Carton Kassala" in the outskirts of Khartoum. A very distinct Bonny M song was sung clearly from an old temperamental tape recorder found two months ago in the rubbish dump and worked!!! . . .

> *"By the rivers of Babylon, there we sat down;*
> *Ye-ah we wept, when we remembered Zion*
> *By the rivers of Babylon, there we sat down;*
> *Ye-ah we wept when we remembered Zion*
> *When the wicked*
> *Carried us in captivity*
> *Required from us a song-*
> *Now how shall we sing the Lord's song in a strange land?"* . . .

He does not ignore the orphan's supplication,
nor the widow's as she pours out her story.
Do the widow's tears not run down her cheeks,
as she cries out against the man who caused them?

Ecclesiasticus 35

Eleven

Marianna and Kennedy were feeling the effects of the civil war. The price of food was very high. In fact the government was unable to control the market. Everything was now in the black market. If you want to get anything in the black market, go to *Konyokonyo* market in Juba. There were three main markets in Juba. Juba market, *Konyokonyo* and *Rujal Mafi*. All these were very busy places, but *Konyokonyo* was the busiest. It thrived along a long and windy road, with rows of small shops on either side. There was also an open place used as an open market. There you will find all the goods, ranging from kitchenware to *Aliwara*. That market used to be vibrant with people of all ages, race and colour. The different noises, the smells, the bright colours and the whole atmosphere of the place would remind you that you are in the heart of Africa.

Today as you walk in this once very vibrant place you will think that you are walking in a ghost town. Only a few shops were open. There were few *Fallata* merchants selling goods in the open market. They used to sell things such as *Aliwara* and kitchenware. Some local men sold dry fish and dry vegetables. Few women could be spotted here and there selling fresh vegetables. *Konyokonyo* market was not a vibrant or a happy place anymore. It was turning into a place where you quickly go, buy what you need and run home. It was not safe to dally anywhere in Juba nowadays because you are never sure what is waiting for you round the corner. Nearly everyone has fled either to Khartoum, Kenya, Uganda or somewhere else in the world. Marianna and her husband were still living in Juba because they heard that people were suffering even more in Khartoum. They heard that the Southerners were living in very poor conditions and were verbally abused in the streets and marketplaces. Where will they go with their two young children?

Kennedy was still working in the office where he first started. He was promoted, but even so the money was not enough. To add to their misery, Kennedy's family from Yei have been displaced by the SPLA activities and were living with them. They had three different families living with them. There were seventeen people in the house as permanent residents, leave alone those who drop by. Their lives have changed so much. They had only two bedrooms, so Marianna, Kennedy and the two children slept in one room. The other bigger room which used to be their master bedroom was left for the women and the very young children. They slept on mats on the floor. The men and the boys made for themselves a large shelter made from bamboos and covered it with grass and mats. Marianna and the three women cooked separate meals and brought all the food together during mealtimes to eat together. Kennedy instructed Marianna that however bad it got, they should always try and eat together as one family. Sometimes misunderstandings happened such as children fights, gossip etc, but somehow they managed to tolerate each other and lived in relative harmony. That was not the picture Marianna had in her mind about married life. In the beginning they were so happy together. Her house used to be her pride and joy. She used to work in the local nursery. Although her salary was not high, it was enough to cover for extra things wanted in the house. Kennedy was earning enough to cover for their food and clothes. Now, they could only manage one main meal. In the morning she could only manage to make Kennedy and the babies some porridge, made of maize meal mixed with peanut butter. Sugar was not available in the open market. You have to buy sugar and powder milk from the black market at such a high price that you have to hide them in your suitcase in case they got stolen! Wasn't life just terrible? The sugar and milk were for her children. Luckily for them, they planted black eyed beans in their big garden. They also planted sweet potatoes. It was the wisest thing they did because the leaves of the black eyed beans provided them with substantial meals at a very low cost. The other fact was that the leaves of that kind of beans grow very fast and didn't need much irrigation or attention. The Lord was looking down on them!

Mariana pushed the front gate open and walked into her house. Muniki used to be a thriving suburb of Juba but now it was emptying quickly of people. Many people were feeling more and more threatened and unsafe, so they decided either to live in central Juba Town itself or travel to another country altogether if they had the means.

The men were sitting under the tree listening to SPLA radio. Nearly everyone listened to SPLA radio every afternoon. They were broadcasting that they will soon enter Juba and deal with all those who were aiding and assisting the Arabs and the North Government System and Regime. There was a lot of rhetoric and threats and promises. Many people were scared stiff.

Marianna sat down after handing her shopping basket to one of the boys to take to the kitchen. One of the women brought her some water to drink.

"You look very tired, Mama Gloria." It is the custom of the South Sudanese to call an adult by referring to their first born instead of using their name as a sign of respect. "I hope you did not meet with any problems on the road. We were worried because you took so long to come back" the woman said to her.

"There is nothing to worry about. It is just that the sun is so hot. I stopped a little at Keziah's house, on my way back. She is having a baby very soon. She showed me all the things she prepared for her baby. Very cute"

"I saw her the other day and I thought to myself: 'this woman is looking different'. I did not know that she is pregnant" said one of the women. Everyone laughed.

"You know what, you will not know if someone is pregnant until *after* they have their baby!" More laughter.

"Is there anything to eat? I am very hungry" said Marianna.

"We were waiting for you. Everything is ready. Kennedy has not come yet"

"Oh, he said they were going for a meeting after work" said Marianna. "Can you leave him some food?"

"Of course"

They all sat down to eat about thirty minutes later. The women sat in a group, the men sat in another group and the older boys in a third group. The younger children sat in a fourth group.

Before they sat down to eat their meal, one of the women stood up to pray: "Lord our Father we thank you for our lives and the lives of our children. Thank you for enabling us to provide food and shelter for our family. I ask you my Lord to bless this food in front of us. Make it nourishment for our bodies and our souls. We pray you Lord to keep us all together and protect us from all evil. We ask all this in the name of your son Jesus Christ"

"Amen".

"Naomi, Naomi, wake up"

Naomi, the oldest lady in the household jumped up, opening her sleep laden eyes. For a moment she looked surprised, but then she smiled hesitantly when she realised it was Marianna. The smile was immediately wiped from her face when she saw Marianna's face. Marianna's eyes were bloodshot and she looked frightened.

"Kennedy did not come home last night. I waited for him all night"

It was 4.00am. By now all the women were sitting up on their mats.

"It might be that their meeting has taken long and they had to spend the night where they were meeting. Do not worry my dear. They should be fine. He will soon come home. Rosa, put the kettle on." She gave her daughter a gentle pat on her shoulder to wake her up.

"Why do you want to drink tea in the middle of the night?" said Rosa irritated at her mum, who always seemed to want to drink cups of tea whenever there was "something" she was unsure of.

83

"Rosa, you seem to be getting lazy these days. Can't you hear the cocks crowing? Mamma Gloria here is not well and could do with a cup of tea."

By now all the women were up. One of them woke her husband and told him about Kennedy.

"Oh Kennedy will come home soon".

It was 9.00 AM and still Kennedy did not come home. One of the men took his bike and rode up to Juba, trying to look for him. By now Marianna was a nervous wreck. She knew something was wrong. Very wrong. Kennedy has never spent a single night elsewhere since they lived together.

Three hours later the man who went to look for Kennedy came with two others. They looked very grave. Marianna did her best not to cry openly.

"We think that Kennedy and some other people were detained by the security people last night. The meeting broke up at about eight o'clock. Also there was supposed to be a curfew from ten o'clock. We do not know what happened, but Kennedy, Androga, Lomuro and few others are missing. People think that they were taken to the army place to be interviewed" said one of the men.

Marianna was now crying and wailing. The women came and held her as she wanted to throw herself on the floor. Some of the children started to cry as well because they were confused and did not know what was happening. Marianna's two children started to cry when they saw their mum in so much distress. Their relatives held them. When Marianna saw how upset they were, she wiped her tears and held them.

About half an hour later a jeep full of uniformed soldiers entered the house and told everyone to stand against the wall without making any noise because they had an order to search the house. The frightened and shaking men, women and children lined themselves against the wall while two soldiers kept watch over them. Nothing was further explained to them.

The soldiers were from the North and West of Sudan. They looked menacing and uncompromising. Marianna thought that they were going to be killed. She pressed her two children to her breast and was so scared she could not even pray.

The soldiers started search in the main room. They could hear furniture thrown about, mattresses thrown outside. They could hear the breaking of wood and smashing of objects. The mattresses were slashed open. Books and papers were thrown on the floor, some taken outside. Two briefcases and two suitcases were taken. There was 750 Sudanese pounds, money for housekeeping which Marianna kept inside her wardrobe. She hoped they haven't taken it.

The soldiers left the house in such a mess that you would think a tornado has hit the inside and outside of it. Nothing was left untouched.

The soldiers went without a word or a backward glance at them. They took all Kennedy's briefcases, his suites, his nice shoes. They took most of his letters, important documents, radio and camera. Marianna thought that Kennedy had money in one of the brief cases, but she did not know how much. Marianna's six gold bracelets, four rings and chains including her daughter's little bangles and tiny earrings were all gone.

Marianna just sat in the middle of the rubble hugging and rocking her two daughters who stuck to her like glue. They knew they were in grave danger.

All their neighbours fled, thinking that the soldiers were going to return and destroy the whole neighbourhood. Marianna and her relatives went into hiding as well. As it was getting late they could not chance it and go to Juba by foot. They spent the night in the nearby forest. Many people hid themselves there. The next day they sneaked to the house and quickly took what they could and travelled on foot to Juba. Marianna begged everyone not to leave her, but now they were all homeless.

Marianna knew what she had to do as her in-laws, Kennedy's father and mother were in Khartoum with the rest of the family.

By now it was quite clear to everyone that Kennedy has come to some harm, either in prison or . . . ?

You just cannot even think further.

"No God, please No".

Kennedy and many other young men in Juba were held in the Army prisons. They were interrogated and tortured. Their names were in the long list of men who were accused of providing assistance including intelligence information to the SPLA to capture Juba.

To build your house on other people's money
Is like collecting stones for your own tomb.

Ecclesiastics 21:1

Twelve

Lino, Norah's, Susan's and Lucinda's brother was among those who fled from Yei to Juba with his family. His wife Salwa was pregnant and he was worried at the deteriorating condition in Juba. Juba has changed so much. All the people who he knew were not there anymore because they have either fled, disappeared or got killed. He knew very few people in Juba now. In the past when he used to walk in the streets, he knew at least half of the people or they knew him, but not anymore.

"It is very sad" He said to himself, shaking his head. "This is like the end of the world".

It was not safe at all to live in Juba nowadays. People were constantly harassed and rounded up by the security forces and accused of all sorts of things. Everyday there were reports of killings, mostly young men who risked the curfew. It was a town of terror.

Since he came to Juba he continued to work in his department as a teacher in a senior secondary school, not far from his house. Luckily for him he was transferred to work here in Juba, so he could provide for his family. His luck kept running because as they were arriving in Juba, his sister, Susan was travelling to Khartoum and was leaving her house to him and his family. Houses were always hard to find in Juba. That was extremely lucky. The house had three bedrooms and a veranda. The space was more than enough for him and his family.

He wanted to leave Juba as soon as possible, especially after hearing what happened to a large number of young men, who were 'caught' and now held indefinitely in the Army Headquarters.

He remembered how poor Marianna came to the house with some of her in-laws, looking very thin and worn out and in a terrible state of distress. Kennedy, her young and good husband was one of those who have disappeared without a trace, feared dead. To Lino, Marianna's and Kennedy's wedding was a very recent event. He remembered every single detail. He was the master of ceremony. He remembered how stunning the couple looked and how happy and proud everyone was, especially after the initial misunderstandings when Marianna got pregnant. Life is never fair. He shook his head again.

What about all these people who used to stay in her house? He had a lot of respect and admiration for Marianna and Kennedy. They were a smashing couple, but life was treating them harshly. One of the things which he, Lino will do was to help Marianna and her children as much as he could.

Marianna came with her two toddlers, the baby strapped on her back. Bruno, Kennedy's elderly uncle and three others came with them. Bruno's wife, Naomi strapped Marianna's older child on her back. They all looked tired, hungry and very distressed. Without a word, Lino and Salwa ran to meet them, relieving them of their load, hugging and kissing Marianna. They all broke into tears and it was all very sad and heart breaking.

Salwa warmed some water and washed the two children and gave them porridge to eat. The younger one seemed to come down with high temperature. She was given painkilling syrup and soon she and her sister fell into a sound sleep. Marianna and the rest were given hot water and took bath which seemed like an impossible luxury since their house in Munuki was attacked and ransacked.

Salwa had some beans and dried fish. She always kept beans in the house and firewood just in case . . . Today they came in handy. She cooked quickly by using some of the larger firewood. The tired visitors offered to help but Salwa declined with a wave of her hand as she knew how tired and hungry they all were.

After eating and drinking tea, Lino asked them to lie down and rest. Late in the evening they all went and sat in the veranda and Marianna and the rest told Lino in detail about what happened.

Lino heard that some people were arrested. He was also told that possibly Kennedy was also arrested with these people, but no one was sure. Lino was travelling to Khartoum with his family after a few days; in fact after five days. He wanted to know what has become of Kennedy so that he could advice Marianna.

An idea sprang to his mind suddenly. He might be able to transfer the rent contract to Marianna's name. The house was a Government house and it was still in Luka's name. What a bloody mess. Lino did not want to change the contract in his name because he knew he was not going to stay long in Juba. Now he wished he did. He decided to see his friend, Tito who worked in the Ministry of Housing. Tito might be able to help him.

The next morning was Monday. He was going to travel on Saturday and still there was no news about Kennedy. What they heard was just speculation and hearsay.

"Salwa, finish packing the children's clothes. Pack only the ones we decided on so that we do not have a lot of things to carry. Otherwise we will be asked to pay heavily or return them and that will be embarrassing" Lino said to his wife as he was leaving for the Ministry of Housing.

As they were talking, their youngest, a toddler, ran into the room crying. She wanted to go to school with the rest. "I will take you later when I have dressed you in your mermaid pink dress and your "tick, tock shoes" Said Salwa to her pretty chubby toddler who ran and sat on her knees.

The child's eyes became round with delight. She turned round and looked at her mum while putting her arms around her neck.

"Tick,tock. Tick,tock" said the little girl laughing.

Marianna's two toddlers joined them shyly. Lino picked them both and gave each a kiss.

"Did mummy give you milk to drink?" asked Lino kindly

Gloria, the older girl shook her head to say yes.

"Good".

Meanwhile Lino's daughter left her mum's knees and asked to be carried by her father as well.

He ended up carrying the three little girls. Salwa laughed and shook her head.

She then went out to talk to Marianna.

Lino went to see Tito in the Ministry. Lino and Tito went to High school together in Rumbek, a once highly reputable school in the Lakes State. Tito was one of Lino's best friends. They later went together to study in Zagazig University in Egypt. They shared many good memories. Whenever they met they would always remember their student life in Egypt and all the adventures that went with it. That was where Lino met Salwa, fell in love and later married her in Wad Medani (North Sudan). Her parents used to live there.

"Hello Lino" said Tito warmly as he saw Lino entering the office. They shook hands and Lino sat down. Tito's office was of medium size and furnished with two chairs besides Tito's padded, more comfortable one. Tito was working in the finance department.

"How are Salwa and the kids? Are they excited about the journey to Khartoum and beyond?" asked Tito.

"Yes they are excited" said Lino in a subdued voice.

"Did you hear about Kennedy and the rest?" continued Lino.

"That is a bad business brother" replied Tito.

"Marianna is now in my house together with some people because they are too scared to stay in Munuki. Kennedy's house was searched and ransacked by the soldiers and Marianna and the rest are all in a state of shock. This is the reason why I came here; to ask you for a favour".

"Lino, my brother; you know that I will always help you and I know that you will always help me in whatever capacity. What do you want me to do for you?"

"Please, can you help me to transfer the contract papers of the house I am living in into Marianna's name? I want her to hold the contract so that she will not be evicted when we travel to Khartoum" said Lino anxiously to his friend.

"Well, just now you looked as if you were going to ask me a million pounds. You made me nervous just then. Is this all you want; to transfer the papers in Marianna's name? That's very easy. Just leave it with me".

Lino went home very happy and reassured. Tito had asked him to return the next day and meet his boss, who will sign the papers in a flash. A form had to be filled to transfer the rental contract of the house to Marianna. After Tito's boss signs the form, then Marianna will consider herself the legal tenant.

Lino was quite pleased with himself. The clouds of doom and gloom were lifting from their heads. Marianna will not be homeless.

The next day Lino went to the boss's office which was twice as big as Tito's and had a big teak elaborate desk where the pompous boss sat. Comfortable chairs were arranged round a rectangular table in the middle of the room. A powerful fan was turning left and right very efficiently and noiselessly at one corner of the office. A row of brand new filing cabinets stood at one side next to the wall. On his desk there was a display of family pictures in wooden frames and some artificial flowers in a glass vase. Behind him there was a wall to wall bookshelf full of what-you-know books, ranging from the bible to life in the North Pole. Everything looked nice and neat and the word "Boss" was written all over the place. The man himself looked as if he has just stepped out of a grooming salon. Shinny, well groomed and wearing one of the latest designer suits! In this weather? Yes in *this* weather! His voice was cultured, smooth and very soft. He stood up and shook hands with Lino who was introduced by Tito.

"Oh, so the unfortunate lady has left her house and is to live in this address where your brother-in-law is living?" He said gently to Lino.

"Yes Sir" said Lino

"And where is your brother-in-law, Sir?"

Lino started to feel a tiny bit uncomfortable. He shifted uneasily in his seat.

"He has travelled to Khartoum, Sir".

"What about the rest of his family? Are they in Khartoum too?"

"Yes Sir" said Lino, now feeling that this interview was not going according to plan.

The man looked shrewdly at Lino and asked

"Who is living in the house then?"

"I am living there temporarily Sir. Their furniture and stuff are still in the house."

He could not look directly at Tito, who by now was sensing real danger.

Lino breathed deeply and threw caution to the wind.

"Sir I know that I should have changed the papers in my name when my brother-in-law was leaving, but because I knew I was not going to live here longer than three months, I kept the papers as they are but have been paying the rent diligently."

"Oh I see" said the Boss after leafing through all the papers. He put the buff coloured file on one side and said smoothly to Lino "Do not worry. I will later sign the papers and if you come tomorrow, you will find the file with the dispatcher's office over there".

He again shook Lino's hand very warmly and the interview was over.

"Well", said Lino as soon as they were safely in Tito's office.

"I thought I was in real trouble at one point"

"I thought so too" said Tito. "It seems you have redeemed yourself when you told him the truth".

The next day was Wednesday. When Lino went to the dispatcher's office to check the signature, he was told that the file did not reach their office. Lino spent the whole day waiting for the Boss to sign, but it seemed that the Boss was not in a hurry to sign.

The next day was Thursday and still no signature and no file was dispatched. Tito became very upset at the way his Boss was behaving. Tito has helped his Boss in so many things in the past, ranging from fetching and carrying things for him up to lending him from the office coffers from time to time. How is it that the Boss was treating his best friend like this? He told his Boss that Lino was travelling to Khartoum on Saturday. It was already Thursday closing time. Lino also had better things to do other than sit in the office waiting the whole day for days on end.

Tito by now understood exactly what will make the Boss sign on the dotted line.

He said to his friend who was sensing defeat by now.

"Tell you what Lino; I am very sorry about the whole business, which stinks". He opened a drawer and handed Lino a brown envelope. When Lino opened the envelope he saw 300 Sudanese pounds inside. Lino was surprised.

"What is this for?"

"Just hand this to the pig and tell him 'this is for all your trouble'."

"Well, I never!" said Lino that afternoon to his wife, after the trick worked a treat and the house was now legally Marianna's.

That day both Lino and his wife called all sorts of evil on the head of the greedy Boss.

"May that money bring him leprosy."

"May he get caught out and lose his job."

"May he beg in the streets."

"May he fall in his own trap."

"May his right arm which takes bribes, wither."

"May God send fire and sulphur on his house" . . .

"May he rot in hell" . . .

On and on they went. They were mad with anger. This seemed to be the practice of many big and small bosses up and down offices and Institutions in South Sudan. People have sold their souls to the devil.

What is money anyway?

When you die will you be buried with money?

Ask King Solomon. He was the richest man on earth. When he died, he did not take with him a single blade of grass. He left it all behind. When will people realise this? When they die?

Salwa said that one day that bad, horrible man will get what he deserves.

He, Lino will never forget the dealings of the dirty pig in a gentleman's clothes.

As for Tito he was also simmering underneath. Well, he had evidence of some "secret dealings" of the boss in black and white. Just wait. Just, just wait, Mr. Bossy Boots . . . You will choke on your own bribes.

My Beloved went down to his garden,
To the beds of spices,
To pasture his flock in the gardens
And gather his lilies.
I am my Beloved's and my Beloved is mine.
He pastures his flock among the lilies.

The Song of Solomon 6:1

Thirteen

When Susan, Lucinda and the children came to live in Khartoum, Peter, Lucinda's Fiancé followed shortly after. Peter stayed at a distant relative's house who he called *uncle* and diligently looked for a job. It was hard to find a job initially and he started to do odd jobs here and there. He had saved some money in addition to what he got from the sale of his car and other personal belongings in Juba. He needed every single penny. He managed to open an account in one of the banks and put nearly all his savings in the account. His uncle was happy when he initially came to live in his house. Peter was welcomed and was given one of the best rooms in the house. Peter gave his uncle 1000 Sudanese pounds for his lodgings which he thought would last him at least three months. His uncle and his wife were overjoyed. They had two young daughters. The older, around twenty years of age was called Amelia. She had a crush on Peter. When Peter realised this he became disturbed. He was very careful to avoid being alone in the house with the girl as this could land him into all sorts of trouble. He hated the position he found himself in. He wanted to find a job quickly and get himself out of there.

When the end of the second month approached, his *uncle* tried to make him aware that there was a shortage of money and that they had to pay the house rent and food and that everything was getting expensive.

Whenever Lucinda visited Peter, Amelia would get very jealous. She was quite rude to Lucinda.

"Why is Amelia behaving like this? Is she always this rude to people who visit their house?" asked Lucinda one day. Peter was walking with her to the bus stop.

"She is generally OK. She is just a silly girl" replied Peter.

"I think there is something going on between you two. Initially I thought I was imagining things but today things are much clearer".

Peter stopped short in his trucks.

"What do you mean?" he said very slowly.

"I mean that there is "something" going on between you and Amelia."

"Don't be silly!"

"Am I the one in the wrong now?" said Lucinda getting cross.

"Listen, we do not have to quarrel over that silly girl. She is nothing to me and you know it. I have been trying my hardest to get a job and get the hell out of this house. Instead of supporting me, you come and accuse me? I have chosen you above all the rest. Is this my reward?"

"I am sorry, sweetheart. It is just that she has managed to get under my skin".

"Tomorrow I am going to Fr. Yohanna and will ask him for a job and lodgings. I am ready to do any job to get out of here. By the way, you are accusing me of having a fling with Amelia, what about you and *uncle?*" Said Peter, trying to keep a straight face.

"What about him?" said Lucinda surprised.

"Well, did you see the way he was staring at you all the time?"

Lucinda gave him a playful smack across the chest.

"Get out of here! You and your dysfunctional family"

Peter chuckled softly.

They were friends again.

Meeting Fr. Yohanna the local priest a week afterwards landed Peter a fine job. He would take charge of a primary school in Jebel Awlia. The headmaster of Comboni Dar El Salam Mixed School has resigned to take another job elsewhere. Fr. Yohanna had to act fast to fill the vacancy. Not many people wanted this job as Jebel Awlia is at least seventeen miles from the Capital, Khartoum. Seventeen miles will not be much for someone who has a car, but if the individual has to commute daily by public transport, which is very unreliable, then it will be almost an impossible task. Fr. Yohanna interviewed three people and decided to offer Peter the job. What pleased Fr. Yohanna most was that Peter said he will try and rent a house there in Jebel Awlia to make life easy for everyone and also so that he will keep a close eye on the school.

He was taken on a tour of the school for the first time, in Fr. Yohanna's small Fiat car. He could not help noticing the gradual change of the state of the buildings and houses as they approached Jebel Awlia. The asphalted main road ended somewhere in the middle of Jebel Awlia where there was a thriving market. They then took a left turn and hit a dirt road. By now all what he could see was poor mud houses, extending for miles. After another turn, Fr. Yohanna pointed to the right and said: "Dar El Salam" in a big sweeping gesture as if he was showing a king the extent of his kingdom.

Dar El Salam was a slum area. Row after row of squat small mud buildings made up the whole area. Here and there you would see donkeys pulling barrels of water. This was an area without any services and no amenities. This was a Godforsaken area for the *Naziheen* from Southern and Western Sudan. When the *Naziheen* first arrived they were given that area to live in and the Government made no effort to help them. As a matter of fact they were "dumped" and forgotten. They then started to build their houses and organised their own chiefs or spokesmen. When aid organisations for refugees heard about them, they built a number of clinics to help treat those *Naziheen*. Other organizations started with food and sanitation programmes to prevent diseases and other health issues. Some organizations worked with children in schools. Things started to get better for the *Naziheen*. The only school for their children was Comboni Dar El Salam and was a mixed school for boys and girls. When people realised that the children were offered free uniforms and food by these organizations, many encouraged their children to attend the school. The school meals which acted as a magnet, was also a source of energy to enhance the children's learning. The teachers were mostly young and energetic and wanted to see good fruit at the end of their hard work. They worked nonstop to keep the school going. They formed a strong board of governors consisting of teachers, the local priest and parents. The board of governors took active role in the running of the school. At the time that Peter became the headmaster, the school was made of mud walls covered with poor thatched roofs which looked so fragile, it was pitiful. That however did not deter the children from learning or the teachers from teaching. The church provided basic but adequate teaching materials such as blackboards, chalk, books, pens, pencils and paper.

Peter was given a plot of land by the South Sudanese chiefs not far away from the school. In the meantime he rented a two bedroom house in Jebel Awlia centre where there was service and amenities. He had to take a bus daily to the school. The last bus stop was about two miles from the school. He had to walk that distance on foot. He thought of buying a bike.

Peter managed to buy nice furniture for his new house after moving. Lucinda helped him choose some of the furniture. They bought light brown, nicely padded lounge chairs and nice bedroom furniture. Lucinda bought the kitchenware. They could now choose the date for their marriage. They had to get married soon anyway because Susan, Lucinda's sister wanted to join her husband in the UK.

Wine flowing straight to my Beloved,
as it runs on the lips of those who sleep.
I am my Beloved's,
And his desire is for me.

The Songs of Songs 8:3

Fourteen

Norah had a high status in Yambio. She was a high ranking officer in the SPLA and the Head of a local school. Everyone knew Norah as *the daughter of Bakata*. Those who didn't know her personally seemed to know of her. People in Tambura, Ezo, Nzara and Maridi and Mundre knew her well. She was an iron lady with a heart of gold. She had time for everyone and did her best to help those in need.

She has just moved to her new house on a one thousand square metres piece of land. One of the local chiefs gave her the land as a gift for her invaluable work with the homeless children in Yambio.

She managed to hire about twelve local men who made and prepared red bricks for building the house. Now the house stands proudly in the centre of the land. She fenced the land and planted different vegetables in the back yard. At the side a well was dug. She secured its opening. It was a big cry from where she used to live. She also built three huts at the side of the house for relatives and other people to stay in if they had nowhere else to go. The huts were sometimes used as guest houses for people who were travelling on to other places. Each hut was well erected with two medium windows and furnished with two wooden beds. Norah had a number of servants in the house. These people do jobs ranging from cleaning the massive compound and the rooms to washing and ironing clothes. Norah and her daughter Nadi and another relative do the cooking assisted by some helpers. Norah was a woman who did not believe that servants should cook for her.

"You do not know what they will 'cook' for you! It can be anything!" she would say.

After Mathew, Nadi's son died, Nadi went back to work in the local school. She threw all her weight in her work. She decided that she was just born unlucky. Madelena, Gloria and Taban have decided to go to Uganda to study there.

Paul, her first heart-stopping boyfriend finished his studies in Egypt and was now working in Western Sudan with an Aid Organization. This information was trickled by some very rare letters to his parents as the South was now virtually cut off from the North of Sudan because of the war. Only army soldiers and officials were able to travel between the two areas. Things came to a head when a passenger plane was shot by the SPLA just as it was taking off from Malakal airport and all the passengers died. That brought a lot of untold anguish and misery to many South Sudanese families from the three regions of Southern Sudan. Many of the victims were women and very young children.

Sarah, Paul's sister fled to Uganda and from there to Kenya. She met a young man from Western Sudan, got married and later took asylum in the United States. Nadi was thinking:

"Everyone has fled from this place except me. I can't leave my mother. My grandparents are both dead. They were always ill and looked very weak and died suddenly within a short period of each other. I will have to look after my mum so that she will never have the same fate."

As much as Norah wanted Nadi to leave to any other *better* place to seek a new life, she always wished that her beloved daughter would stay by her side. They discussed this several times but Nadi was adamant she wanted to stay. Norah wished that *lady luck* will knock on Nadi's door one day. Nadi was now about twenty four. She looked healthy and beautiful.

In fact, thought Norah, looking at her daughter critically, Nadi looked better as she was maturing and always dressed smartly. Above all she was well educated. Norah hoped that her daughter will very soon meet the right man, because Mathew's dad was a waste of space.

"Why are you staring at me like that?" said Nadi to her mother

"Was I? Sorry, I did not realise. I was just thinking how lovely you look and I wish you could meet some nice young man one day" said her mum.

"Oh mum, not again. I do not want any man. Look at me. I will never have any luck in my life. Where is Mathew? I have enough pain in my heart"

Nadi's eyes filled with tears which started to roll down her cheeks.

Her mum came over and wiped her tears with her palms. She held her by her two hands and helped her to her feet so that they were both standing facing each other.

"Nadi, my daughter, my child, I can feel your pain and I know your loss but life has to continue. You must not continue to live in the past. Look at the past as a chapter full of experience. Take that experience and knowledge you acquired with so much pain and face the future. You are only at the threshold of your life. Do not look back. Always look forwards and walk steadily."

It was late and everybody was retiring to bed. The mother took her daughter's hand and together they walked into the house.

Three days later a Red Cross plane landed. Norah was there in the airport. The airport was only an air strip. The waiting room was a group of five mango trees. The only building to be seen was a small hut which served as a toilet! Although there were a few concrete buildings in Yambio, made of solid brick and mortar, the airstrip was still in its virgin state. People were hopeful that one day if John Garang the leader of the SPLA takes over charge of Sudan, the airstrip will turn into a dazzling international airport. For the time being people could do nothing but make do with this basic arrangement.

Gai Thor, a young man working with the Red Cross was among those who landed. As soon as he descended from the plane, the green lush vegetation surrounding the airstrip with its red fiery colour captured his imagination.

He was warned that Yambio was a "nothing" place. No decent place to go out, eat, or do anything. He will just have to read or listen to music or do boring things like an old person. Perhaps lie in bed when not working and get fat.

Why do people have to fight for so long? He asked himself.

Anyway, he came mentally prepared, but he just loved the feel of this place.

Few people were standing under the trees. He greeted them when he received his luggage. A driver of one of the Red Cross land rovers was there to receive him. They drove for about three miles when Gai suddenly spotted the local market. People were buying and selling. Many people looked surprisingly in good health and well dressed, many riding on bikes. This place looked so different from Malakal which was bare and grim. He then saw several big buildings and a church. The driver said that that was the Catholic Church and the residences of the Arch Bishop and priests. On the other side was where the nuns resided. All the big buildings were solar powered!

"Very nice!" Said Gai to himself. He never expected to see such substantial well kept buildings in the so called "nothing place". The driver said that most of the people fled to the surrounding countries but the few that stayed behind are trying their best to make the best of what life was offering.

"So far everything is peaceful and in good order, Doctor. There is no trouble" said the driver.

"This is very good to hear. We need a peaceful place to live and do our jobs".

They soon arrived in the Red Cross compound which was made of whitewashed one storey buildings. The Head office was in the centre and dominated the compound. At the back, a lush garden separated the Head Office from five bungalows which were the living quarters of the Red Cross staff. The compound had high whitewashed walls.

He was shown his one bedroom bungalow which was quite spacious and sparsely but pleasantly furnished. That was also a pleasant surprise. The place was spotless. In the veranda which doubled as a lounge, there was a coffee table and four armchairs. A large bed with fresh white linen was in the centre of the bedroom. Blankets were stored neatly in a teak two door wardrobe. A small chest of drawers, a chair, table and a bedside cabinet furnished the rest of the room. There was a small en suite shower room. A small kitchenette was situated in a corner, off the lounge with a well stocked fridge. The meals were eaten in the dining room which was attached to the main kitchen at the other side of the compound. A gong would sound announcing mealtimes which was usually at eight in the morning for breakfast, at one for lunch and at six in the evenings for supper. The compound was powered by a solar system. They also had generators on standby.

Gai lay on his bed after taking a quick shower and dressing. He would be joining the rest of staff in about half an hour and get introduced to everyone. He was thinking about his grandmother and uncles in Malakal. That was his destination after he came to Nairobi. He went to Nairobi from Canada. He went to see his family in Malakal who he saw only in photos. Initially he did not want to go, but his mother insisted that he does if he had the chance. She said that his grandmother, who was his father's mother, has been heartbroken when she heard that Gai's father died. Now her wish was to see Gai before she dies. Gai has joined the Red Cross after studying medicine in the University of Toronto. He heard that all was not well between the different Nuer people there in Upper Nile. Some of the leaders jumped ship and there was a lot of bloodletting. He knew enough about the politics of South Sudan but he would not be drawn in it. He came to Africa as a Canadian citizen and a doctor in a Humanitarian Organization. His ties to South Sudan are strong and he will do his best to contribute in his own way in his capacity as a doctor to help his people. Gai managed to get a ride on one of the Red Cross planes going to Malakal about four weeks ago. His mother gave him his uncle's names and as soon as he asked about them many people in the airport appeared to know them. It seemed that everybody knew everybody in this place. Initially people thought he was an Arab because of his appearance, and when he started to speak to them they were at a loss and called him a *Khawaja*. He said to them that he was neither. He was a Nuer.

"No" they replied "Nuer do not look or speak like you". They thought he was joking.

He then told them that his mother is Ethiopian and his father a Nuer and that he came from Canada.

"Now this makes sense" they replied.

So when he asked about his uncles, everybody was keen to help him. He went and met his uncles. One of them was so happy that he hugged and lifted him off the floor, tall as he was!

They took him to the area where his grandmother lived. That area which was on the outskirts of Malakal was heartbreaking for him to see. The poverty and the state of the women and children were appalling. His grandmother cried and kissed him and would not let go of his hand. She was partially sighted and had a stroke the previous year. They had to speak through an interpreter, who was one of the uncles. The bond between him and his grandmother was instantaneous and strong.

Gai was resting on his bed with his hands behind his head. He shifted uncomfortably when he thought about his grandmother and his uncles. He knew that they were all in grave danger there in Malakal from the government army and the affiliated militias. All were deadly and can be indiscriminate in choosing their victims. He heard strange stories of abductions, murder and other atrocities which seemed to be committed by everyone carrying a gun. He stayed with them three days sleeping in one of the Red Cross battered rest houses. He spent nearly all the time with his grandmother. Malakal which was once a thriving, vibrant city was turned into a ghost town. Crumbling buildings, shuttered and boarded up shops and houses was a normal sight during that unholy period.

He closed his eyes and thought about his mum in Canada. They were among the first people from South Sudan to live in Canada. His father was offered a scholarship and took his young family to Canada. At that time he was a toddler of about two years. He was the eldest of his siblings. His mother had three more children in Canada. His father who was a surgeon got a job in the local hospital and continued to do some research linked to his job. Gai's father postponed coming to Sudan as his children were still in school. He had an agreement with his wife to go back to Sudan after Gai finished High School. Unfortunately his father died suddenly in a car accident before he finished High School and his mum had to continue bringing them up on her own in Canada. She thought that if she were to go back to Sudan with the children, they might lose the chance to finish in good schools. She could not guarantee that she would have the means to keep them in private schools. The children were offered scholarships to study in Canada if they so wished when the authorities heard about their father's untimely death. They all studied in private schools.

How he missed his mother, brothers and sister. He spoke to them on the phone only once when he was in Nairobi. He is very close to his mum. They have been corresponding by letters.

"Food is ready Doctor". A teenage boy knocked timidly on his door.

"Thank you. What is your name?" said Gai with a smile.

"John".

"You seem to be young doing this job, John"

"I am thirteen years. I am just helping my father who is the cook"

"Oh, so you go to school?"

"Yes, Sir"

John and his father were very pleased to see this new doctor who looked like a Sudanese. Most of the people who work with the Red Cross were foreigners. This new doctor was tall and had dazzling white teeth. He looked like someone from the North or "something like that". They were not quite sure. If his skin was not so light, they would have thought he was from Juba, possibly a Bari or even a Dinka. The other thing was that the doctor does not speak Arabic. He might be from Kenya, but someone said he was "definitely" from Sudan.

After taking refreshments Gai was shown his office and all the facilities in the compound by the coordinator. He was briefed about the security situation in Yambio.

Gai loved his job and liked this place right from the start. He found the local people very friendly. He made friends with some of the local young men who worked in the Red Cross office.

His main job was to run and manage the clinic on a daily basis. His clinic started at seven in the morning up to three. He treated all sorts of conditions ranging from malaria to gunshot wounds. Two medical assistants and four nurses worked with him. The clinic could get very hectic and chaotic as many people came from all the surrounding villages. They developed a ticket system so that people, who miss being seen on the day, will be able to be seen first on the next day. Many also attended the local hospital but facilities and staff were in short supply. Vital drugs were nonexistent in the hospital. Local doctors have refused to work in Yambio due to its remote position. That was why the Red Cross clinic service was preferred by the locals. At least medicines were available to cure minor ailments.

One day Gai received an invitation to have dinner at one of his friend's aunt's house. His friend was one of the locals called David who also worked with the Red Cross.

Gai was given a car for his official and personal use. They went in the car as it was a hot day and the house was over two miles away from the compound.

They came to a big house in a huge compound. They were shown into a big sitting room. Some people were in the room and they were all introduced. Later on a middle aged lady came in wearing a multi coloured African dress with a matching headdress. She was introduced to him as "Norah", the lady of the house. Norah was friendly and easy to talk to. She said that she was very pleased to see one of "our sons" in such a privileged position and she wished him a good stay in Yambio.

As they finished their dinner, a girl swept into the room, wearing a peacock blue maxi dress, revealing a tiny waist. She did not tie her head.

Her luxuriant and intricately plaited hair fell to her shoulders. She went round the room, greeting everyone with a handshake as is the custom of the Sudanese, chatting to them in the local Zande dialect. When she came towards him she half smiled showing a dimple in her cheek. Her huge bright eyes were slightly slanted up at the sides and were something he thought he'd never seen before. David said something in the way of introduction. Gai remembered saying "Hi" but he did not recall hearing her say anything in reply. Later on he remembered how her eyes *smiled* at him, dazzling him. She did not sit down but went out as quickly as she came in. Gai was stunned by the girl's beauty. He waited for her to enter the room again but she never did. He wondered to himself "Does the Beauty live here or was she just visiting? What did they say her name was?" He did not quite catch her name.

That night as he drove his friend to his house, he was told that the girl was called Nadi and that she was Norah's daughter.

So a curse consumes the earth
And its inhabitants suffer the penalty,
That is why the inhabitants of the earth are burnt up
And few men are left.

Isaiah 24:6

Fifteen

Norah always remembered the birth of her daughter Nadi with mixed feelings. From the first day Nadi breezed into the world, she did so with a big bang. Norah remembered that when she was carrying Nadi, she did not feel ill or unwell at any time. Norah started to look quite healthy and happy in midterm and continued like that until just before Nadi was born.

Nathana had insisted that Norah should have the baby in the hospital. The midwife said that the baby was not in the right position so she called the doctor. The birth was very difficult during which Norah lost a lot of blood and became very weak. All the relatives and friends were outside waiting very anxiously. The birth took quite long and at one stage Nathana broke down thinking that his wife was surely dying. His mother, a very stern lady nearly gave him a slap across the face and told him to "toughen up and be a man!" She had a rosary in her hand and was praying. Nathana was not allowed in the delivery room as was the custom in those days. After a long time the midwife came out looking tired but had a big smile. Everybody clapped and was very relieved. She told them that Norah was very weak and ill as she lost a lot of blood. The baby was a breech presentation but fine and "very beautiful". Norah and the baby were kept in a side room and only Nathana and his mum and Norah's parents were allowed to visit. They were discharged home after a few days. Norah was to take iron tablets and was given advice about food and drink.

The baby was christened Caterina, after Nathana's mother. Caterina was the most gorgeous, adorable baby. She had huge bright eyes and the most beautiful complexion. In fact some people started to whisper about her complexion. Yes Norah's skin colour was like any other Zande and Nathana was very dark. How comes the baby was so fair? When will that stupid Nathana realise that the baby was not his? The whispers became louder and louder and one day Norah and her husband started to hear what people were saying. Norah remembered that some of the people who came to visit her to "see the baby" were people she never even knew. Now she came to realise the real reason behind their interest. Norah became very upset but kept everything to herself. Nathana also heard the ugly rumours but he never said anything to Norah. As far as he was concerned Caterina was his beloved little daughter. He loved her more and more every day. You just can't help loving Caterina. When she started to walk, she would walk to you and cock her head on one side and give you a smile that you will never be able not to return. Nathana used to take her everywhere and bought her the most expensive clothes and shoes.

When Caterina was about two, Nathana went to the bus stop to pick a relative of Norah's who was travelling from Wau to Juba. The relative was a man well in his seventies. He was visiting his daughter in Juba. The old man thought that it would be a good idea to travel through Yambio to visit his cousin Rutha and her husband Bakata who were Norah's parents. Nathana thought of bringing the old man to his house first to get acquainted with Norah. As they entered the compound, little Caterina came running to her dad. Her dad picked her up and swung her high in the air. She screamed with delight saying "put me down, put me down daddy. Give me sweets first!" She wanted to see what he has brought her. Where are the sweets and lollipops?

"He is going to spoil the girl" thought Norah.

Whenever daddy came, it was "Bye mummy." Maybe things will change when Caterina gets older.

The eccentric old man stood still, looking at the toddler.

"Whose child is this?"

"Here we go" said Nathana to himself. "If he tells me that the child does not look like mine, I will throw him out of my house".

"Mine" said Nathana quite defensively.

"She is *Nadi*" said the old man bending down, stroking the child's cheek gently with the back of his wrinkled hand.

"Nadi?" said Nathana completely at sea.

"Nadi" stressed the old man. He did not look at Norah who came out from the house and heard this part of the conversation.

"Crazy old man" thought Norah to herself.

As if reading her thoughts he walked sideways towards Norah, still looking at the beautiful toddler, he held out his hand, more as a gesture than a salute.

"Your daughter looks exactly like my granddaughter who we called Nadi. In fact you would think they are twins."

"So?" thought Norah irritated wanting to draw her hand away, but the old man strengthened his hold.

"My name is Fadil. I am your mother's cousin. My mother was called Nadi and your mother's mother was Cubana. Their father was the result of a mixed marriage between an Egyptian officer in the army and a Zande girl called Azziza in Deim Zubair. Their father left his wife and the girls when those colonials were all going back to Khartoum and he never returned. Cubana was taken to Wau by an aunt at the age of seven. She later got married and came to live here in Yambio with her husband and gave birth to your mother Rutha. Cubana died when your mother was being born. That was very unfortunate. She was only a teenager. Nadi my mother continued to live in Deim Zubair. All our girls look like this child; fair and beautiful. The little Egyptian blood left is more pronounced in them and they seem to have the Zande spirit; lack of fear and resilience."

He let go of Norah's hand and stroked the child's cheek again. Caterina then cocked her head on one side and dazzled everybody with her smile. Everyone laughed.

Norah's tears were overflowing by now. She knelt in front of the old man to everyone's amazement. She addressed the old man in the Zande language, although he spoke to them in Arabic.

"Oh my great uncle, where have you been all this time? My daughter and I were abused by the high and the low in this town. They called her names. They called me names. They said that she belongs to the Greek *Khawaja* who has a shop in the marketplace. They said she might be the daughter of some *Mundukuru*. My husband and I were reduced to nothing. I know that I have done nothing wrong. My husband knows I have done nothing wrong but we were made to suffer. My grandmother Cubana died young and my mother never knew the Deim Zubair side of her family. Thank you uncle for explaining to us things because we were at a loss as to why our daughter's looks are so different"

"You give birth to your ancestors. Skin colour does not matter. Blood does." Meaning DNA.

He spent the night with them and kept calling Caterina "Nadi". Whenever he called her Nadi, she responded as if it was her name. From that day everybody started calling her Nadi.

What they did not know was that Fadil was known in Deim Zubair as "Sheikh Fadil" or "Haj Fadil". As from the name, one can deduce he was a Muslim. That side of the family has always kept their Muslim religion. Haj Fadil was known by that name not because he went to Mecca but because of his "divine powers". He became Haj at the age of eight years. He learnt the Koran like every Muslim child but one day he started to "see into people's souls and minds". He explained to his mother that he was very scared because he could "see" things and he didn't want to see these things. The things he saw were true and that scared him.

"What things?" said his bewildered mother.

"I can see who is good and who is bad and what they are trying to do and those who are going to die soon".

His mum dismissed this as child's fantasy. He started to tell her things about people which have turned to be true. He started to say things to strangers that were true. People started to wonder. His father forbade him to say things so that people will not think that he had "evil spirits". In the end his parents came to realise that their son had a special gift of connecting to people's souls and that it was a gift from God.

What Norah and her husband did not know or were not told by Fadil was that little Nadi's soul was exposed to him. He saw the path of her life in a flash when he stroked her cheek. He saw a path of pain, tears and darkness. He never thought he would see so much suffering in the life of someone so young. That night he was so disturbed he could not sleep. When he stroked her cheek again to see beyond the suffering, her path closed up. He could see nothing beyond. Was she going to die prematurely? Was she going to be permanently disabled? The vibes he got was that the source of her suffering was from outside and it engulfed her body. Was it going to be a mental health problem? He felt that in the future he might advise Norah and her husband if anything happens to their lovely daughter but for now he did not want to put fear in their hearts. Also he was hoping for one thing; that what he saw and felt was not true or that it might change . . .

Norah's memory went to the days when they were young. She remembered when she went with Susan to live for a while in their Uncle Rafael's house in Wau. Uncle Rafael was a very kind man. He wanted Norah and Susan to go to the local school in the outskirts of Wau called Nazareth in order to improve their education. He spoke to his brother to send his daughters to study in Nazareth. It was a junior and senior combined *only girls'* boarding school. The standard was very high and Uncle Rafael thought that his nieces would benefit from the good school which was run by Catholic nuns.

They used to go to their uncle's house during the short vacations and she remembered the nice time they used to have there. Her uncle had three boys. They used to help clean the house and wash the dishes and nurse the youngest boy who was about a year old. At night when there was a full moon, the children used to go to the square and play "Ka-ma". Ka-ma was like line dancing. The boys would stand in a long line, facing the girls across a space of about fifteen or twenty feet. They would then sing and dance with light steps, moving towards each other. There was usually a lead singer from the boys and the girls. The others sang the chorus. What was exciting about Ka-ma was that the songs were composed on the spot about some certain boy or girl or an incident. Many people got embarrassed in Ka-ma about something they thought they did in secret and was obviously not a secret anymore as a song would expose all. The annoying thing was that you would not know who started the song. Once the song was in circulation, you need more than the wild horses of hell to stop them! Talk about cyber gossip and restraining orders. Well, these poor guys in Wau knew the effect of such machinations years and years earlier before the computers came into effect!

Norah also remembered uncle Tomazo. Tomazo was one of her fathers' many cousins. Tomazo used to live close to Uncle Rafael's house in an area called "Hilla Zande". In those days every tribe used to live together in a certain area and the spot was named after that particular tribe. Tomazo used to live about five houses away from Uncle Rafael's house. His wife was called Zereda. She was an intelligent and well spoken lady. Tomazo was thin and wiry, in his mid fifties. At that time fourty years of age was old and if you were in your fifties then you were "very old". Tomazo used to ride his bike daily to go to the "*Suk Kabir*" or "*Suk Wau*" that was down town. On the way from his house to the town centre he would travel over some green fields onto the strongest and oldest little bridge which was built by the British colonials. The bridge was called "*Kubri Hargan*" or "Hargan Bridge", which was on the main road leading to the airport. The bridge used to run over a small stream. The banks of the stream were flanked by luscious green foliage and different reeds, grasses and bamboos, topped by magnificent trees of wild berries and coconut. At night-time, the din of legions of frogs, crickets and other nocturnal insects and animals could be almost deafening. During the day, the scene was one that could inspire an artist. Immediately after going over Hargan Bridge was when Tomazo's anxiety, tension and anguish started.

That garage! As soon as he approached the garage he used to brace himself.

"*D-o-u-s*" one person would call out to him. He knew they said it to him.

"D-o-u-s" another voice would repeat.

And then a chorus would start. They were nothing but evil, good-for-nothing, lousy, dirty scoundrels. They would shout and jeer at him.

"Dous ya ajous"

"Dous ya ajous.

Guffaws and more jeering, the horrible rats!

What upset Tomazo most was that at that precise part of the road, there was a gentle incline upwards in the road, which made it hard to pedal without slowing down and pushing harder, straining his thin, spindly legs. What could he do? He was old and his bike was old. Many a time had he mended and tied together that bike which he named "Khamis" after his dead friend. His bike has become more than a bike! It was his companion and his friend. Little did these insects know. His bike was much worthy than all of them put together! These young men will one day grow old. They will feel the anger he was feeling at being laughed at the way they were laughing at him. The teasing did not stop there, people down town got wind of the way he was being teased by the good-for-nothing mechanics and started calling to him *"Dous Ya ajous"*

It did not stop there, even the little rats in Hilla Zande, where every child was taught to respect their elders started calling out to him *"Dous Ya ajous"*

Now this is too much to take from your own kin and kind.

Tomazo would put his bike down and start running after the young tormentors with a chest full of stones, cursing them and calling their mothers and fathers who were to blame for bringing dogs and illegitimate vagabonds and rascals in the world. Tomazo started to spend more and more time in negative energy, chasing naughty boys and shouting abuses at them, trying to stone them that he became a well known legend in the whole of Wau district.

All this teasing did not stop there. His wife Zereda started getting shouts of taunts as well.

"*Mara Dous*" they used to shout at her whenever the naughty unrepentant urchins got a glimpse of her.

She also would get very angry, to the utter glee of the rascals and would start chasing them. She was not a spring chicken but she used to run like one. She was also in her fifties but boy; she would put some of the gym veterans to shame! Her agility, her muscle tone, speed and technique would make you wonder if she was not one of the Seven Wonders of the World.

At that time a young girl of about eleven years of age came from Raja in Western Bahr El Ghazal to live with them in Uncle Rafael's house. She was related to Uncle Rafael's wife. The girl called "Surra" looked like a well brought up, polite girl.

One day part of the fence at the back of the house broke and fell. The house next door was vacant so sometimes Norah, Susan and Surra used to come to the house through the vacant property and the broken fence as a short cut.

Norah, Susan and their uncle's wife were busy de-shelling groundnuts in the lean to when they saw Surra run quickly like a gazelle through the broken fence and disappear into the house. They did not think much of it. Immediately afterwards Auntie Zereda followed. She stopped short when she saw the three women in the lean to. Zereda would usually wear a *tob* over her dress. Today, what was baffling everybody was that she was only wearing an old dress without a *tob* and looked very angry. Uncle Rafael's wife rose and walked towards her.

"So, is this Uncle Rafael's daughter?" Zereda used to call Rafael "Uncle Rafael" as a sign of respect. He was from her father's clan.

"I never thought that such a lousy thing would come out of this house. I am totally surprised" said Zereda.

"It is my young cousin" said Rafael's wife. "What did the girl do to you Auntie?"

"She had the audacity to call me 'Mara Dous'!" Zereda was so angry, her eyes started to pop out of her head like a frog's.

Norah, Susan and their aunt did their best to suppress their giggles. The effort was too much for Susan who pretended that she had a violent cough and ran inside to drink some water.

"I knew that my uncle's girls are well brought up and they would never insult me the way this girl has. Where is she? Call her out here so that I will give her a lesson she will never forget. I would have followed her to whatever hole she would hide in but seeing that it was my uncle's house I could not run inside and beat her there. I want her out here now!" She started to raise her voice in renewed anger.

Meanwhile Surra, also breathing like a frog, from sheer terror was hiding under the bed.

Rafael's wife put both her hands together and begged Zereda for calmness and forgiveness.

"I will beat her myself, Auntie Zereda. She now knows her mistake and she will never do this again! Do not waste your energy on someone like her. Tell you what I will warn her that I will send her back to Raja and she will never have the education she is having here. Please go home in peace. Norah my dear, take your Auntie Zereda home and see if she needs help with anything!"

That worked a treat on the angry woman. Rafael's wife quickly measured two cups of sugar and tea leaves and gave it to Norah to take it with her to auntie Zereda's house as she could not stop for a cup of tea. Auntie Zereda thanked Rafael's wife and thanked the Lord that there were still some decent people around.

Years later when Norah was married to Nathana she saw Tomazo in the market place in Yambio one Saturday morning. Tomazo was buying sweet potatoes. He looked quite well; he seemed to have put on some weight and was wearing a decent blue shirt and black trousers.

"Uncle Tomazo?" said Norah not quite sure if it was him. He turned around and looked at Norah but could not recognize her. By then Norah was married with children.

"It is me Norah. We used to live in Hilla Zande in Wau".

Slowly recognition dawned on him. He hugged Norah and called her "my daughter". He asked her to go with him to his house and say hello to her aunt Zereda. The house was just round the corner from the market. Norah went with him and discovered that his house was a well designed hut in the UN compound which was the only compound at the time for an organization. Tomazo worked as a gatekeeper there. Zereda who also looked well was very pleased to see Norah. They said that they will visit her to get acquainted with her husband and kids. They did visit them and ever since Tomazo and his wife continued to visit them from time to time. Rutha and Bakata have decided to move to a nearby village to be close to their farm.

Bind us together Lord
bind us together with cords
that cannot be broken.
Bind us together Lord
bind us together, Lord
bind us together in love.

Sixteen

Today was Lucinda's wedding in St Mathew's Cathedral near the River Nile. The house was full of people talking, laughing and cooking. Lucinda was moved to Susan's big bedroom. It was quite warm but the fan was doing a good job to cool the room. Lucinda looked at the henna on her palms; intricate and beautiful designs of flowers and geometrical shapes that showed a high level of artistic skill on the back of her hands up to the wrists. The same designs were reproduced on her feet up to just above her ankles. Today she was going to the local hairdresser that was especially booked for her from eight o'clock up to one. The hairdresser will groom her hair and her bridesmaids' and will help Lucinda to dress and prepare for the church. That was a good arrangement because it would have been almost impossible to be organized and dressed on time with so many people in the house. Susan came with them.

Susan cried with mixed emotion when she saw how beautiful Lucinda looked. He baby sister has become a lovely bride and is now leaving her father's house for good!

When they were ready at about one, Lucinda's uncle arrived. He was going to give her away in the Church. The car was decorated with flowers and ribbons. Lucinda, Susan and the uncle travelled in the bridal car and the bridesmaids including Susan's daughters travelled in a separate car.

They arrived in the church at two. Already a big number of people were in the church. The church benches were decorated with white ribbons and flowers. People were looking their very best. The air rippled with expectation. A big choir of young boys and girls was in full swing, complete with guitars, drums and tambourines. They were all wearing white shirts and navy blue skirts and trousers. The bridegroom was sitting with his best man at the front, near the altar.

As Lucinda arrived on the arm of her uncle, her long veil was pulled over her face. She carried a bouquet of pink and white roses. Her dress was white with small rows of frills from the waist all the way down. It was stunning. The congregation was asked to stand and the choir began with the hymn

"This is the day that the Lord has made . . ."

Peter was shaking. He couldn't believe that that day was the day and they will soon be husband and wife. He did his best not to turn round and stare at his slowly approaching bride.

When the veil was finally lifted from her face, he thought to himself

"Was it really my Lucinda?"

She looked different. No wonder. He hasn't seen her in ages. Those hard hearted women, including Susan prevented them seeing each other for a month.

"God, she is beautiful" He said to himself.

Lucinda kept her gaze averted and looked at him fleetingly only once. She seemed tense but later began to relax when the priest said a joke about the rings. He wanted to know that the best man who looked "nervous" did not forget the rings. There was a lot of laughter and later applause when the rings were produced.

After the service Peter held her hand and squeezed it gently and she gave him a dazzling smile. They did not kiss in the church. What a shame! It was not customary for couples to do so. They would if the priest asked them but of course kissing in public even for legally married newlyweds was not encouraged in that part of the world.

They then took many photos in the studio and along the Nile with their numerous relatives. Later on they went home for the big party. It was a street party. Two big marquis were erected after the whole street was closed off at both ends. The floor was levelled with white sand then sprinkled with water and left to dry. A big platform was built of wood planks and was covered with two big massive Persian carpets. Two gilt chairs with beautifully carved arms, crests and sides were placed on the platform, for the bride and bridegroom. The background was covered by light golden curtains which were interwoven and had fairy lights. Chairs were placed on each side for the best man the matron and bridesmaids. Artificial flowers along the edges of the platform were fixed securely. Two steps led to the platform. The DJ and his system were at the other corner. Hundreds of seats were put in rows facing the platform. The place was set. The party started when the arrival of the bride and bridegroom was announced. They sat down and the party began. People continued talking about Lucy's beautiful wedding years and years later.

Susan was to travel to England in a week. Her husband sent her the tickets via the British Council. Luka's sponsor was the British Council which offered scholarships to hundreds of people across the Sudan.

Susan's worry was Marianna. Her husband has been detained by the army and it did not look good at all. She was pleased that her brother Lino and his wife helped Marianna but she had a nasty feeling that something bad has happened to poor Kennedy. The only thing for them was to pray and hope for a miracle. She sold some of her gold and gave the money to Lucinda. She advised Lucinda to buy Marianna and her children air tickets to travel to Khartoum if Marianna decides to leave Juba.

After Susan left to the UK, Marianna insisted on staying on in Juba until her husband gets released. She said that if she was to die she will not leave her beloved Kennedy in prison and go to live in Khartoum.

Marianna used to go and meet some of the politicians and people of high offices in Juba and begged them for answers or an explanation as to where her husband was held or when he will return home. Some gave her evasive answers. Some lied. Some did not know what was going on. In the end they started to avoid her. She never gave up hope. She used to pray day and night. She could not sleep. She used to wake up every midnight and dawn, kneel on her knees and pray:

> *"Why is it that forever you forget us that you leave us for the length of days?"*

Lamentations 5:20

How beautiful you are, my love,
How beautiful you are!
Your eyes, behind your veil, are doves;
Your hair is like a flock of goats
frisking down the slopes of Gilead.
Your teeth are like a flock of shorn ewes
As they climb up from the washing.
Each one has its twin,
Not one unpaired with another.
Your lips are scarlet thread
and your words enchanting.
Your cheeks, behind your veil,
are halves of pomegranate.
Your neck is the tower of David
built as a fortress,
hung round with a thousand bucklers,
and each the shield of a hero.
Your two breasts are two fawns,
twins of a gazelle that feed among the lilies.

The Song of Songs 4:8

Seventeen

"A black girl I am, but comely, O you daughters of Jerusalem. Like the tents of Kedar. Like the tent clothes of Solomon"

(The book of Solomon 1:5)

After meeting Nadi, Gai's thoughts kept straying to her. He has seen and known many beautiful girls from different countries but he has never had a lasting attachment to any of them. He was well travelled. He went on holidays and business trips to many parts of Canada, the USA, Cuba and China. He also visited Great Britain, France, Germany and Holland and now Africa. This girl who has been born in a totally different culture and who he only met very briefly twice has captured his imagination. What does she do? How old is she? What does she like? After asking his friend about her name he did not want to ask more. He will soon find out . . .

One day his curiosity got the better of him.

"Your aunt Norah seems to be a very generous and a good lady. I would love to eat a Zande meal. Do you think she can cook for us Zande food?" Said Gai innocently.

"No problems. I will ask Nadi to cook *Gadia* and I will bring it to you here" said his friend. David had no sister. Whenever he wanted to invite his friends, he would ask Nadi to help with the cooking.

"Why do you have to trouble yourself carrying food which might spill on you? We can go and eat in their house, can't we?"

"Oh sure" said his unsuspecting friend. "Norah did mention last time that I should take you one day to her house to sample our local indigenous food. I think she will be happy to see you again"

Gai surely remembered this kind invitation very well!

David sent word to Norah that they will be dropping at her house after the Sunday prayers to eat traditional food. When they arrived, Nadi and two other girls welcomed them. They sat on beautifully hand crafted cane chairs under the big mango tree at the front of the house. The weather was very warm and the best place was to sit under a cool shade. Nadi and her friends brought them cold water and *Bangara*. Gai has never tasted an alcoholic beverage as fragrant or as good. The girls were cultured and very polite, smiling and handing them their drinks.

"Why don't you girls sit down and join us? Are you going to serve us like kings all the time?" said Gai jokingly.

"We are joining you in a minute, Doctor" replied Nadi. Her English was quite good and she had a soft, pleasant voice. His Arabic was not good. If he knew how to speak in Arabic he would have a better chance to engage her in a proper conversation. He knew that she liked speaking in Arabic and seemed reluctant to speak in English.

One of the girls remained in the kitchen to help Norah cook the meal. Nadi sat near her cousin across the table from Gai. The other girl sat next to Gai and started chatting to him. Nadi on the other hand did not bother to take part in their conversation as it was a strain for her to try and understand the doctor's "strange accent". She opened a dialogue with David, her cousin in the Zande language.

Gai was unable to take his eyes off her. He was oblivious to a question put to him by Nadi's friend. The poor girl had to tap him on the knee to get his attention. He apologised and rearranged his chair so that he remained focused on the girl beside him instead of that rude girl across the table who thought she was the Queen of Sheba! It was strange how his mind went to the Queen of Sheba to draw a comparison. Was she that queen that captivated King Solomon? He will look it up later. These days he had enough time to read everything he did not have the chance to read since he was born! Nadi later remembered her manners and apologised to Gai, reminding everybody to try and speak in English as the doctor did not understand *Pazande*!!

"Cheeky, isn't she?" smiled Gai to himself.

On the other hand Nadi was aware of Gai's interest, although she pretended not to. She noticed that his eyes were on her nearly all the time but she was not going to go down that road ever again. He can look at her as much as he wanted but that was all what he will ever get as far as she was concerned. She had enough of men and their abuse of her innocence, trust and love. She was not going to give in to "This one" who behaved like a white man. Let him eye her to the full because he will find that he is wasting his time. Let him plan his plans. She will plan hers. Men! The world would be a much better place without them.

But Gai discovered that the more she became aloof and unresponsive to him, the more he desired her.

Gai never had to chase a girl for any length of time, even when he was a bare teenager. Thinking about it, he never had to do any chasing at all. Everything was easy and simple until he met this tantalizing witch. He remembered his mother's saying "Someday every person will meet their match!" As always, she is right. He has met his match!

He remembered two days after they first met he saw Nadi coming out of the school. He was walking towards a shop in the same direction. She pretended she didn't see him. She hurried away from him and took the opposite road which led away from her house. He remembered how he pretended he did not see her either and went quickly behind the houses to waylay her. At a turning she came suddenly face to face with him and was very much startled, nearly dropping her books on the floor.

"Oh, you startled me!" She said accusingly in Arabic.

"Sorry, I did not mean to" He replied in broken Arabic but she understood him.

"Oh I remember. You are Norah's daughter!"

"Yes. You are Dr Gai. For a moment I did not recognise you".

LIAR

"I was going to my friend's house!" continued Nadi.

"Shall I come with you?"

"No" She giggled, showing perfect white teeth.

Gai smiled.

"I know, you will feel embarrassed if I am to appear with you" He said in English more to himself, thinking she will not understand

"They will start talking about us if we go together" she replied in perfect English to his amazement.

"You speak good English" he said to her.

"I find it difficult to understand you because of the way you speak. You can always teach me, can't you?" she looked the picture of innocence.

We can start right now!

Aloud he said "Sure"

"Thank you Doctor. Until we meet again".

She turned on her heels and quickly, walked away. Her well shaped derrière wiggling.

The minx!

That night he went to visit her cousin David.

"Has Nadi got a boyfriend or something?"

His friend gave him a sly smile

"Are you interested?"

Silence and a shrug of the shoulders

"I thought you were, you poor chap" said his friend.

"Why are you calling me 'poor chap?'" said Gai starting to feel slightly irritated.

"You better forget her. She had so much trouble in her life that she has ended up with some complex. It is sad and I feel angry, as her cousin, but this poor girl's life has been completely turned upside down and inside out" said his friend, his face contorting with pent up emotion and bad memories.

"Are you talking about Nadi, your cousin?"

"Yes. We never talk about it because it is so painful to remember. Her mother nearly lost her mind. For a moment we thought Nadi did. For days she refused to eat or drink or even talk. That was hell man. Hell."

Gai started to get more and more confused. What is this crazy person talking about? Nadi? Mad? She looked saner than all of them put together.

Gai's patience started to wear off.

"Are you going to tell me or not?" He said very, very softly.

"Nadi and her friends were captured by a group of SPLA for days. They were raped nearly every day. Oh God, I find it difficult to talk about it, even now after seven years." It was the first time David admitted that to a stranger. He felt slightly relieved to get it off his chest at last.

"What?" That knowledge once it sunk in made Gai feel as if he was hit by a train. Did he really hear correctly? He sat down on the nearest chair.

Nadi's cousin related all what had happened to her when she set out with her friends on that ill fated journey to Juba. He also told Gai how after she met a man and got married, he suddenly took off to join the SPLA and no one ever heard from him up till now. He left Nadi pregnant, young and vulnerable. To rub salt in the wound, Nadi lost her child to dysentery and malaria, aged three years about two years ago.

"What did you guys do?" said Gai still reeling from the shock

"What can we do? This is what the war does. When you are attacked you are not supposed to say anything, especially if you are a woman. You shouldn't complain. You should lie low and let everyone walk all over you."

What other surprises are there in store for him?

Walking slowly to his compound, he heard a man playing the *rabbaba*.

> "... *O my love in the hideaway of the green bushes; in the concealed places of the steep anthills; show me your form; let me hear your voice; for your voice is music and your form is lovely.*"

Yahweh, forever faithful,
Gives justice to those denied it,
Gives food to the hungry,
Gives liberty to prisoners

The Psalms 147:3

Eighteen

Susan and her four children, Sarah, Mary, Musa and Bindi arrived in Great Britain in the summer of 1993. Sarah was fourteen, Mary twelve, Musa nine and Bindi six years. They remembered how excited they were when the journey first started. They boarded the KLM plane at exactly 1.00 am Sudan local time and headed for Amsterdam, stopping briefly in Egypt. Susan and the two boys sat together in the middle seats. Sarah and Mary sat across from them.

Wow! There was a TV in the plane and you can even play music.

Before setting off they were advised to take jumpers and keep it with them as it will be cold in the plane. Lucinda plaited the girls' hair and attached pink beads and small ribbons at the tips of their plaits. They looked very pretty. The boys had their hair cut at the local barber's shop. They all had brand new clothes and were very happy to show them off. Lucinda and Peter saw them off at the airport. Lino and Salwa were coming from Juba two days later to proceed to Nairobi. Susan felt sad that she will not see her brother whom she has not seen for the last two years. The tears welled in her eyes but she brushed them off quickly.

"Tell my brother that if God so wishes one day we shall meet. Look at us, everyone in the opposite corner of the earth. Anyway we have to thank God that he has kept us alive."

Lucinda cried and cried. Susan was more of a mother to her than a sister. Susan's neighbour Hanan and her husband were also present. They brought sandwiches and sweets for the children.

Hanan promised Susan that she will look after her young sister Lucinda. Jokingly, she said "I will make sure that Lucy will have all the Sudanese beauty remedies so that Peter's eyes will not stray elsewhere." Susan thanked Hanan and her husband and told them that she will never forget their friendship and kindness.

The flight to Egypt was only about three hours and they did not get off the plane. Other people soon boarded and off they went. They reached Amsterdam after about five or so, she couldn't remember exactly how long. They were very tired by then and had to wait for their flight to Heathrow Airport for another two or three hours. By then the children started to think that they will never see their dad. Sarah told her sister and brothers that they might return back to Sudan! Susan tried her best to inform them about what was happening, but to them this endless ride which at first was exciting, was not so anymore.

At last they touched down in Heathrow airport. It was late afternoon. "There is daddy" said Mary very excited. She was the first to spot him in the crowd of people at the gate. They all ran to him and mobbed him, Susan standing back slightly with a big smile on her face. After disentangling himself just enough, he looked at Susan who came to him and they hugged with the children in between.

Luka, who was homesick and lonely, was not so anymore. Susan, who pined for her husband, was at last reunited with him.

When Susan joined Luka in Manchester, there were not many South Sudanese people around. In fact they were about three families and they all kept very close together and helped each other. By the year 2000, as many as twenty families were thriving in Manchester.

The South Sudanese Community formed an association to cater for their social needs as refugees. The British Government's policy is to help the refugees in general by providing for them housing and other social services so that they can be integrated in the wider community and become valued citizens. The South Sudanese association was called South Sudan Welfare Association or (SSWA). This association became quite strong with branches in Leeds and London.

Susan and the other women formed the women group which specially addressed women's issues including skill acquisition, education etc. They also formed a weekend school for improving the skills and knowledge of their children. This module of strengthening children's education has been happening with most of the South Sudanese round the world. They all seem to have formed some sort of association to bring them together from time to time. The South Sudanese people have a unique culture; the culture of keeping in touch with each other all over the world. As soon as an individual arrives in the country, the phones will be buzzing and everybody will know that there is a certain "fresh" person in the country called so and so. People will then try their best to meet that person or persons and extend help to them if needed.

Luka has been on the computer up to midnight to finalise his speech for tomorrow's general meeting. At midday he had to meet with SSWA executive Committee in order to hand over to a new Committee. There were many issues in SSWA. SSWA used to be an association to address people's social needs only. Now everything has turned political and nasty. Politics seemed to have taken over. Luka and many others were not surprised. It was difficult to remain focused when the political arena in the South was dominating every South Sudanese mind regardless of where they were. This brought about factions and divisions in the communities because whenever they met, more than three quarters of their talk was about politics. If you do not support a certain political group on the ground, then it will be difficult to be friendly or even neutral with some people. A lot of disharmony and quarrels ensued and people started to shun each other. The main unrest among the South Sudanese came about when the SPLA leadership became divided.

It was about 2.00am. Everyone was fast asleep. There was a loud ringing sound; that of the telephone. Luka and Susan had two receivers: One was downstairs and the other upstairs next to Luka, on the bedside cabinet.

Poor Luka who was tired and stressed out with the looming difficult meeting jumped up from the bed, startled by the loud piercing noise and fell forwards, banging his head against the wardrobe. Susan, whose sleep was very light, was much sharper than her husband. She recognized the sound as "Phone ringing", not like Luka who thought that a rhino had just lifted him by the horn. He let out a scream and what Susan thought a loud fart. She started to giggle.

Susan calmly walked round the bed and instead of helping him to his feet, picked up the phone.

Luka cussed loudly and started to get up.

"Hello" said Susan into the receiver.

"Hello, Is that Susan?"

Susan recognized the voice straight away. She screamed with delight. It was Lino her brother in Australia.

"Lino, how are you?"

Luka cussed again and lay down on the bed as Susan talked excitedly to her brother.

"Lino wants to speak to you" She handed the receiver to Luka.

"Lino brother, you nearly gave me a heart attack" said Luka, sounding quite cross. "Do you know what time it is here?"

"Is it morning there in the UK?" asked Lino stupidly.

"Why are you asking now? You should have asked before you phoned. It is 2.00 am."

"Well" said Lino teasingly. "It *is* morning isn't it?"

Luka just gave up. He told Lino not to ring them at certain times of the day, but Lino will always be Lino. As soon as he felt the urge to speak to them, he will just pick up the phone, at whatever time that is convenient to *him*.

After telling Lino off Luka took the phone downstairs and spoke to his brother in law for about an hour.

Politics! No wrong time to talk politics, thought Susan.

In the end Susan was the one who was more irritated than her husband. They have disturbed *her* sleep to talk about their stupid politics!

"O how she has come to sit solitary,
the city that was abundant with people.
How she has become like a widow,
she that populous among the nations.
How she that was a princess among the jurisdictional districts
has come to be for forced labour."

Lamentations 1:1

Nineteen

People were gathered in St Joseph Roman Catholic Church in Juba. Some people were standing outside; some were sitting on the steps. Many were standing against or under the trees. The church which was always full was today overflowing with people.

The occasion was not a joyous one. That day people's hearts were broken. People looked thin. Some looked ill and very miserable. Many were weeping openly. Some were hugged by relatives and friends. They were men, women and children. It was one of the darkest days in the history of Juba. That day was the day when prayers were said for the people of Juba. There should have been a funeral mass but there were no bodies. No coffins and no hearses. Not a single one. There was no funeral at all. It was a mass for the souls of the departed but was supposed to look like an ordinary mass for fear of retribution by the Government Security System. Sometimes security people were seen in churches; Arab Muslims who have no business to be in any church. They wanted to know what was being said.

People sleep at night in fear, wake up in fear and walk the streets in fear. Fear of disappearing. Fear of false accusations, fear of being tortured and killed.

Marianna, who moved to Juba town, was one of those women in the church. She tied her head and was dressed in black. Her two daughters were clinging to her. She looked left and right. There were only the neighbours and the elderly couple who moved with her from Munuki. Marianna wished Susan, Lucinda, Luka and Peter were with her to comfort her.

"Kennedy, my love, my sweetheart, will I ever see you again?

Why did you have to go so early?

The road is still long, our love is still strong.

Oh my love, my darling if you can just take a glimpse and see how much you are missed.

If you could just come along from the land beyond

You will know that forever in my heart you belong."

A flood of tears ran down Marianna's face.

Where was Marianna? Where was she? She was just like a shadow of her old self. She was now practically skin and bones. Her eyes sunken low in their sockets, her beauty dimmed, gone. Her daughters looked healthy but very subdued as if they sensed that something terrible has happened. Gloria kept asking for her daddy. She would look behind her mum and around as if her dad was going to emerge any minute, smiling and holding out his hands to lift her high up in the sky. She would giggle loudly and scream with excitement.

Marianna's nightmare came to her vividly. She remembered when the news broke out that the people who were held in the Army Headquarters were tortured and slaughtered. Marianna remembered how she did not take it in. She could not believe it. She said that she was going to the Army Headquarters to ask about the whereabouts of her husband. She had to be restrained and sedated for a while to keep her from carrying out her threats. She looked as if she was going to come to harm. Susan was already in Britain and Lucinda was pregnant and Peter will be unable to leave the school, so they suggested that she should come to Khartoum now that her husband has been killed.

Kennedy and the rest were accused of treason by the Government and had to die. They did not have access to a lawyer or even a priest to help prepare them for death. They were murdered in cold blood. Even war criminals are given more justice than these unfortunate young men. They were the best of the best. All were well educated young men and more than three quarters of them were professionals and the rest students and businessmen. They were law abiding citizens and from excellent families. These were the future of the nation. These were the lineage of the South Sudanese future generations. No one ever saw their bodies. They all vanished as if they have never been. Their families have no right to utter a word.

But they will never be forgotten; never.

One day their death will be avenged.

There is a time and a season for everything under heaven:

> *"A time for giving birth, a time for dying;*
> *a time for embracing, a time to refrain from embracing,*
> *a time for losing, a time for keeping;*
> *a time for keeping silent, a time for speaking;*
> *a time for loving, a time for hating;*
> *a time for war, a time for peace.*

Ecclesiastes 3

> *"Boy and old man have lain down on the earth of the streets.*
> *My virgins and my young men themselves have fallen by the sword.*
> *You have killed in the day of your anger. You have slaughtered. You*
> *have no compassion."*

However people have tried to hide the truth, the truth will always come out. However long it takes, things will always emerge in the open. Whatever is done in darkness will always be exposed in broad daylight.

A system of genocide was carried out secretly against the children of Zion. A system of extermination was carried out secretly against God's people. The plan was not to kill the Southerners all at once because the world will know and there will be an outcry by the International Community.

The Government Army and Militias therefore carried out silent and deadly night visits to certain individuals. A list was drawn regularly by the secret police. They had the benefit which enabled them to mingle with citizens, some being citizens themselves. The unfortunate individuals, usually outspoken, and who are seen as a potential threat were those in the hit list. They included professionals, civil servants, businessmen, teachers and students. Thousands of individuals disappeared from all the garrison towns and cities in all areas of the South. It was a professional job carried out by a deadly and organised killing machine. This genocide was cleverly orchestrated during the time people were fleeing from South Sudan in all directions. The same genocide was carried out in Khartoum and other Northern cities and towns but with much more care and stealth and cunning. It used to start with a knock on the door during the night or early morning hours and a person would disappear. Some people were followed and kidnapped in broad daylight.

When a person disappears, the police will not look for them. They know what has happened to those people. They will convince the distraught families that the individual might have either joined the SPLA or have fled to any other area or country. The probability that they were still alive and could be anywhere else was the smokescreen and fabricated reasons that the Government was feeding to people.

People came to realise that perhaps most of these young men, who kept disappearing, was because they have been kidnapped; possibly murdered but there were no bodies. No bodies meant that there were no deaths.

It emerged that Kennedy, Marianna's husband and the young men that had their names on that black list had their throats slashed or were buried alive. Some were loaded in army planes and were dropped to their deaths.

How can any nation forget this?

Will the South Sudanese people ever forgive?

Perhaps.

Will they forget?

Never!

The world has to know so that this should never happen in the history of any nation.

Leaders must take responsibility.

Marianna travelled to Khartoum with her two children. Lino also spent few weeks in Khartoum with his family and travelled straight to Nairobi in Kenya. They waited there to travel to Australia. They were lucky. Their names were drawn from a list of people who were offered asylum to live in Australia. Everyone was very relieved and happy for them. Life in Kenya was tough.

Marianna went to live with Lucinda and Peter. Peter built two bedrooms and a nice large veranda in his plot of land just after he married Lucinda. He also planted many trees in it. They then moved into their new house. Lucinda was expecting a baby quite soon. She was told that she might be carrying twins. When they heard that Marianna might be coming, Peter built a room and a small veranda in one corner of the plot for Marianna so that she will have her space and privacy. Marianna was treated like Lucinda's sister and as such Lucinda and Peter looked after her unconditionally unless she had other arrangements. Marianna's in laws were living in their daughter's house. They visited Marianna from time to time and spent days with her. Life in Khartoum was extremely difficult and transport was a killer, especially to Jebel Awlia. If Marianna was not helped by her family, she would have been homeless in Khartoum with her two young daughters. Everyone was saying to Peter how well they have done. To have a house like his in Khartoum or the neighbouring areas was a great achievement indeed.

To oppress the poor is to insult his Creator,
To be kind to the needy is to honour Him.

Proverbs 14:31

Twenty

The meeting was going to take place in Grosvenor Building in Manchester. South Sudanese people from all over the UK were going to attend.

The meeting was a special meeting, conducted in the wake of infighting and divisions between the South Sudanese community members in Britain. The divisions in the Sudanese community happened as a result of a big fall out between the SPLA Leadership operating in South Sudan. The aim of the meeting was to reconcile the members and offer them an arena to voice their concerns and criticisms so that a consensus or at least an understanding is reached. This would hopefully lead to mutual respect between individuals and create harmony within the South Sudanese Communities all over the UK. There was another group that was right from the start very vocal in its criticism of the SPLA activities in general. This group was critical of the way the SPLA forces were operating in South Sudan. They accused the SPLA of committing war crimes and crimes against humanity stemming mainly from tribalistic tendencies. The pro SPLA group in turn accused the group of colluding with the Arabs in the North. This caused a lot of bitter debates and quarrels between friends and families. At the same time Southerners living in Britain regularly received news of massacres and mass murders of innocent civilians from all areas of the Sudan. Some of the rebel factions and other militia groups started to use the international media to cover their bloody trail by accusing others of genocide. Sometimes it was difficult to know exactly what was happening, because the victim of today will be a perpetrator tomorrow and vice versa following tit for tat massacres.

Unfortunately South Sudan is such a complicated land that the South Sudanese themselves have no clue about what was actually happening. At one stage you see all the Southerners who are African Christians fighting a common enemy, The Arab Muslims, for a common cause which is liberation and freedom. Later on you find the Southerners fighting each other for nothing other than tribalism, greed and personal issues dividing them. Then you find that the ones that have broken away for a supposedly one man show and one-tribe domination of the Movement, turn and subdivide into factions. Some will start to seek the support of the alleged bad sadistic and controlling Sudan Government, making secret financial and other deals with them, while fighting their own kin. Those subdued then will turn full circle and run back to the bosom of the "original" SPLA/M, they had previously criticised as "tribalistic" and are swiftly forgiven! You may crack your brains and end up in a mental asylum if you try to understand these people's behaviour.

The end game was that the Arabs were the victors without as much as firing a single shot! They don't need to, when they can hit a slave with another slave! Yes, they would pat themselves with absolute glee and gloat mixed together saying:

"While the slaves are destroying themselves, we are building ourselves. In the end when they are worn out and weak and finished, we will inherit their Land". This is the name of the game.

The panel was assembled by three o'clock, two hours late. *Three o'clock* seems to be the magic time for things to happen in the South Sudanese Communities!

As it was not a SSWA meeting, the Community had to choose people to organize and conduct the meeting. About six community members sat in the panel to help conduct the meeting and help the Chairman to answer questions. The panel was chosen carefully to represent everyone with a different opinion. The panel's main objectives were to see to it that the meeting was conducted in an orderly and constructive manner and that it will have a good outcome.

The place was buzzing with people. Nearly every chair was occupied and people were still pouring in, both men and women.

The Chairman, Luka, Susan's husband was chosen by the mass majority of people for his long experience working as a leader of the Manchester South Sudanese Community. He was noted for his calm and no nonsense stance when dealing with rowdy people or trouble makers. Today a few potential trouble makers were present. One of them was called "Gerima". True to his name, Gerima could cause havoc in a gathering if he wanted to. He was sitting in the second row and listened attentively. He was one hundred per cent committed in the support of the SPLA/M led by Dr John Garang. If anyone dared to criticise the SPLA or its leadership, Gerima will go down on them like a ton of bricks!

Luka stood up and started the debate with a speech:

"Ladies and gentlemen I feel honoured to stand today before you with the difficult but important task of chairing this meeting. I consider this meeting a watershed to help us reconcile and gather our thoughts and energy in fighting for the cause: The liberation of our people from slavery and injustice instead of dividing our energy and resources and engaging ourselves in counterproductive activities.

Today, ladies and gentlemen, we have to put a reign on our anger and divisions and listen to each other's concerns and opinions so that we can reach a peaceful conclusion. As you all know we all differ from each other. Based on our different tribes, religion, political orientation and personal experiences and circumstances, we react differently to what is happening during this war in South of Sudan . . .

We have some ground rules which should be observed by all of us. Anyone that disrupts the meeting will be thrown out after two warnings . . ."

The general assembly then started to debate issues such as mass murder of civilians and the factors behind that. Some people were asking why the SPLA and the Government forces were both harming and killing innocent unarmed civilians. Gerima and his friends insisted that these were not innocent civilians but they were militias helping the Government forces.

Others said if that was so, didn't the SPLA hear about the Juba massacre? Was it not carried out by the government forces on innocent civilians? Were these people militia? They were killed for "colluding" with the SPLA while there was no proof that they were helping any person. They were civilians caught in the cross fire and were seen as soft targets. People argued that in the eyes of the Government of Sudan every Southerner is an SPLA. People don't have to join the SPLA to prove that they are fighting for their freedom. Innocent civilians should not be accused by the SPLA that they are colluding with the Arabs simply because they chose not to join the SPLA. Some people also noted that the factions in the SPLA who were splitting and changing sides are the most harmful element of the Movement. They have caused a lot of bloodshed and treachery amongst their own tribes and divided their own people. Some of their supporters said that that was so because John Garang was controlling and was tribalistic. Others argued that at least Garang did not run and sell himself to the Arabs like some of the SPLA warring factions. He had to deal with situations where people in the Movement rebelled against him and wanted to kill him. What will he do? Some said what goes around comes around and that Garang has been doing some bad things which some people wanted to reciprocate.

Another woman stood up and asked a question about crimes such as rape and enslavement of women and children that has been reported to have occurred in many areas in Equatoria and non Dinka areas. The perpetrators were said to be the SPLA soldiers. This prompted a heated debate.

Gerima stood up and said "This is a lie which our Equatorian people seem to level at the SPLA. Let people bring the evidence in front of us here".

Susan who was sitting at the back stood up. She started to talk before she was given permission by the panel. Luka knew very well not to stop her. Susan was shaking with emotion.

She jumped up and shouted

"Gerima, stop there" she choked with tears and anger.

"Gerima" Susan continued "Do you have a mother? Do you have a wife? Do you have a sister? Do you have a daughter?" She did not realise how loud her voice was. Gerima was silenced.

"Look at me Gerima, look at me and just cast your mind back to how your mother looks like and your sisters. I know your wife is here and you have two daughters. Focus and think about these important people in your life. How will you feel if one of them is raped by people who are supposed to look after them and defend them? How do you feel if you hear that all of your family are attacked and then murdered? Will you ask people to send you their underwear in a box in order to take it to the police to believe that they were raped? Does your mother carry a gun? Does your wife carry a gun or even know how to use one? How do you defend the indefensible? How can you stand here as a South Sudanese and defend armed men who attack defenceless women? Is raping innocent women, the war they are fighting for? Who are these people trying to fight? Are they fighting women? I tell you Gerima if women are given arms to defend themselves, no man will dare to come near them; especially people like you. Evidence? What evidence do you want? Do you want the soldiers to confess on paper or do you want to see a DNA sample of their "job"? Do you want to see your mother's skull in the post to prove to you that she was murdered? Who do you think you are to insult those innocent victims in your childish and brainless drivel?" Susan started to walk menacingly towards the front row where Gerima was sitting. The people sitting next to her restrained her.

Someone cried "Point of order!"

Everyone was silent.

Susan continued

"Gerima, today I will rip my skirt and give it to you and people like you to wear. If you think that you are the only supporter of the SPLA why are you hiding yourself underneath your wife's *tonura* here in Britain? Why don't you join the SPLA in the bush?

I, Susan I do not have to join any group to show that I love and want to free my country. I can fight my own war for my land in my own way. I do not believe in arms as a means of freeing my country. I prefer dialogue. This is me. Does this mean that I am colluding with the Arabs? Does this mean that I am against the SPLA? Do I have to keep quiet to the atrocities that some of the armed men are doing to their fellow Southerners to prove to you that I am against the things which the Government of Sudan is doing?

Some people who have accused us in the past of colluding with the Arabs are now, as we speak, sitting on the Arabs' laps in Khartoum. They have changed their names and religion and have accepted to be marked on the flesh of their backsides like animals. Some of these men were in The SPLA. Who are worse, those of us who only criticize because we want our brothers to act in a professional manner or those who have sold *our cause?*"

At this stage you can safely say that things were getting out of hand. Some of the women realising that there might be big trouble ahead, moved in order to hold Susan back. They asked her to sit down and not to let people like Gerima have the satisfaction of ruining the meeting. Gerima was hearing everything but preferred to keep quiet.

Gerima knew not to open his mouth. He saw a man beaten to a pulp and all his clothes ripped by an angry mob of women in a similar meeting in Nairobi. He must lie low. These women can damage you for life when they get angry. Men are more reasonable and calmer.

Why did they have to call these women to this meeting anyway? Most of them are illiterate and backwards. If it was men only, these hypocrites would have had a good roasting by him,Gerima. There was bound to be another day when he will lay on them and humiliate them exactly as he has been humiliated today. Luka must be behind his wife's vicious attack on him. All his friends know this but one day these "Arab lovers" will pay dearly . . .

People reached some constructive resolution in spite of the fracas between Susan and Gerima. It was concluded that the objective of the war fought by the SPLA was to liberate all Southern Sudanese people regardless of their tribe or religion. People had to accept that the SPLA was quite a big army which was spread over a massive area and therefore controlling individual soldiers can sometimes be difficult especially if they were determined to break the rules. Also some people noted that because most of these soldiers were ill equipped with irregular supply of ammunition and food, they would easily be tempted to tax civilians. This would lead to other activities such as physical and sexual attacks. Some argued that in this case when some people voice their concerns about how the SPLA treats civilians, others should listen and try and communicate these concerns so that they can be addressed by the SPLA/M leadership instead of brushing them aside and sweeping them under the carpet. If a channel like this was opened earlier, then certain tribal groups would have felt happier and would not think that they were being singled out and victimised.

Some people also voiced concerns about the victims of famine. Most people did not realise that millions of people, especially women and children in the predominantly Dinka areas were dying of hunger caused by the Government tactics. The government forces were preventing food from reaching the civilians in areas which were held by the SPLA. People concluded that the best way was to approach the media and the International community for help. Others argued that the aid agencies have filed reports that the relief supplies given to the hungry civilians were sometimes "taxed" by the SPLA and the armed militias. This also needed to be investigated further and a plea should be sent.

Everyone in the meeting realised that by opening this dialogue people seemed to have a common interest after all. Each group was coming from a different angle which in the end, when explained seemed to shed some light and make sense. People started to relax and make jokes and laugh together.

Yes, there was light at the end of the tunnel after all, even for hardliners like Gerima and Susan.

When I was a child, I used to talk like a child,
and think like a child,
and argue like a child,
but now I am a man,
all childish ways are put behind me.

Corinthians 13:11

Twenty One

Father Yohanna was the local Catholic priest. He came from South Sudan but people were not sure exactly from which part. Although it is easy to tell someone's tribe by their looks, Fr. Yohanna can be from any area of the South or even the West or Central part of Sudan. He was fluent in English and Arabic and could speak many dialects of South Sudan including, Dinka, Nuer, Bari and Zande. He said that he learnt those dialects because of his ministry in Wau, Upper Nile, Juba and Yambio. He said that he lived in Tambura as a teenager. That really made things very difficult for people to guess. You would think that it was easy to find out. Just walk to him and ask him. He will never tell you. One other thing about Fr. Yohanna was that he was very approachable. If you ask him, he will start asking *you* why you need to know: "Is it that important?" You will end up none the wiser. That was really frustrating because he does not have blood relatives among the South Sudanese in Khartoum that you can ask. It is important to know each others' tribe. In South Sudan, your tribe is as important as your name!

All sorts of rumours were circulating about him. For instance some think that he was not a South Sudanese at all but he ran away as a child from a Western Sudanese family and ended up living in the South. Some say that he was born an orphan. Others say that he was abandoned by his mother, supposedly from North Sudan for being conceived illegitimately; a Southerner perhaps being the father. All these talks and rumours have come back to him, but Fr. Yohanna was not telling anyone. He felt that that side of his life belonged to him alone and had nothing to do with his mission.

It was was Sunday and Fr. Yohanna was conducting prayers in Khartoum's biggest Cathedral, St Mathew. St Mathew can house hundreds of people. It was built more than a century ago and is the pride and joy of all Christians in Khartoum. It is situated about fifty yards or so from the banks of the great River Nile not far away from the Presidential Palace. The Cathedral boasts one of the most beautiful buildings in Khartoum. Millions of baptismal, Holy Communion and confirmation ceremonies were and are still being performed in that impressive building. People have very fond memories of weddings and joyous church celebrations as well as sombre occasions such as funerals. All the Catholics in this great city revere this old and historical church.

That day Fr. Yohanna was celebrating the High Mass, which was the final mass of the morning. This particular mass was very special to everyone, not because the priest was young and good looking but because his preaching was guaranteed to be a cracker, something that will touch every heart and soul! He talked about things which affected the average man, woman and child. When he spoke everyone listened and thought and acted or reacted! Oh yes, he was guaranteed to capture your attention!

It was Sunday the 3rd of June 2000. The weather as always was very warm. The church was packed to overflowing. Most people were dressed in their finest and were sitting on the beautifully carved mahogany benches. The fans hanging from long supports were appropriately placed and dotted round the perimeter of the church's lower tier ceiling underneath the balconies. These ceiling fans which were nearly as old as the church were kept in good working order and hung low over the benches to give people maximum benefit. Today they were all full blast on, because the weather was so warm. The inside of the church has all the beautiful paintings of Jesus, Mary, and Joseph; the twelve disciples, angels, cherubs and saints. Some pictures depict some aspects and stories in the Holy Bible. The church also has upper level seats. All these were filled to capacity today.

People were unaware that at times especially when faced with challenges, Fr. Yohanna tended to seek God's sanctuary, comfort and wisdom by fasting for two or three consecutive days. Today was the third day of his fasting. He has tasted no food or drink for three days. He was seeking

God's wisdom to address his congregation on a very contentious issue: The issue of Leadership.

Fr. Yohanna stood tall and straight in front of his congregation who were all ears to hear what he was going to say. He did not like standing in the pulpit. He liked to stand in the middle of the church, quite close to the front benches and at a touching distance from his congregation. He had to use the microphone so that the people who were standing outside could also hear.

He began his homily . . .
"Good morning to you all. It pleases me to see so many people here in the House of The Lord. This shows that we are all seeking the word of wisdom from God our Creator and rightly so, ladies and gentlemen. We are passing through a very difficult time in our Country's history.

When I was born, I was told that I used to cry a lot when the weather changes to either hot or cold. I used to object and scream incessantly when I was hungry or needed attention until I got what I wanted. I was a bad tempered greedy child". Some people smiled knowingly.

"People never realised how loud and big mouthed I was going to be. It was by a coincidence that I was called John or Yohanna. As I was about six years, the lady who used to call herself my mother took me to the local priest to be baptised. She said "This boy has a big mouth but he says some things which makes me wonder if he is a prophet or a *conjurer!*"

"The priest said 'I will call him John the Baptist' which is a translation from *Yohanna El Mamadan.* John the Baptist was as loud and irritating to people as your son is.'

At that time I was young but I knew what I wanted. In those days when people got baptised they had to take a Saint's name. This practice is now discouraged and people are baptised under any name.

"Call me Yohanna. I said quickly. I do not want to be called 'John', like the boy who lives over there who has lice all over his hair". Laughter . . .

"I also wanted to be called Yohanna because it is such a different and cool sounding name. No one in the whole school was known by that name.

So Yohanna became my name. As I grew up I used to get in a lot of fights in school. I used to play horrible tricks on older boys and beat up younger boys. I was known as a rascal and when I went home and played tricks on the women who used to sell doughnuts I was referred to as *walad haram*."

This brought a loud laughter from the congregation who were given a rare view into the priest's carefully hidden childhood history.

"One day" continued Fr. Yohanna "I said to one of these women; but I was not around when I was being conceived, so it can't be my fault!

I used to get on everybody's nerves and under people's skins. It is a good thing I chose a job which does not allow me to marry because can you imagine how I would be with my in-laws?

Unfortunately in this world I will still be able to annoy and harass other people who do not happen to be my in-laws. Today I am going to speak about "responsibility and leadership". I may annoy some people sitting right here in this very church!"

Father Yohanna looked at the congregation up and down the church and asked, "Is there anyone in this church from age seven onwards who does not know the story of the Good Shepherd in the Bible? Please be frank because it is very important for people to know what I want to talk about". The church fell silent.

"Well, I am glad that we all know about today's Gospel. Today's Gospel is about leadership. What a leader should be. How a leader should be.

This parable about 'The Good Shepherd' is one parable that should hang from the wall of every leader's house; man or woman in the South of Sudan, to remind them of their duties and responsibilities to this nation. This is a nation that have suffered like no other nation; a nation that has been slaughtered like no other nation; a nation that has known nothing but humiliation, degradation and empty promises as no other nation."

Fr. Yohanna paused a few seconds. Everyone was silent. Some even stopped fanning themselves.

Vroom, vroom, vroom was the only sound of the motor of the rotating fans.

"I tell you this, everyone who will lead this nation of South Sudan at this time will be chosen by God; whether it is a woman or a man, of this tribe or the other, educated or illiterate. A person that becomes a leader of God's people has to follow His word. That person has to obey His rules. A leader has to make sacrifices.

God's word is clear. His rule is simple: '*look after my people*'. Looking after people is not saying 'hello' to them once a year via the TV screen. Looking after people means feeding them, clothing them, offering them shelter and giving them respect and dignity every single day. If you cannot do this to this nation then do not take this job."

Suddenly he raised his voice so loud that many people jumped from their seats

"If you don't want to obey God, then do not take this task. Let others who can, do it".

Father Yohanna then moved on one side and pointed up to the dome of the church which had the painting of Jesus Christ with a little lamb on his shoulder.

"Let our leaders look carefully at this picture. Who is carrying who? Is Jesus sitting on the back of the lamb or is the lamb sitting across Jesus' shoulder? Unfortunately today our leaders are doing the opposite of what Jesus is doing. They are riding on our backs. They are stripping us of our dignity, of our basic needs which is food and shelter. They are robbing us of basic services, while they are living in palaces, amassing great wealth at the cost of toils and rights of this nation; forgetting their promises to God when they took the oath by placing their right hand on the Holy Bible. Our leaders are used as a scourge to whip this nation and humiliate them. You hear of leaders changing their religion, changing their identities, leading other people astray.

Jesus described himself as the 'Good Shepherd' because a good shepherd is humble and gentle. At the same time a good shepherd is strong and courageous. If he is looking after one hundred sheep and one gets lost, he will lay down his life and look for the lost one. He knows that he can get attacked by wild animals and can lose his life when he goes out there but he will not be put off until he finds the one that is lost. Can our leaders do that for us? Our leaders are now partying, eating, drinking, thinking that they have reached the finishing line. They are wealthy. Their wives and women friends are covered in gold. Their children go to private schools abroad. Woe to those leaders. They will pay back every single item which they have taken that does not belong to them. God will make them pay seven times for seven generations."

Some people moved restlessly in their seats.

"I did not say this. It is there in the bible. Those who have eyes let them see and read. Those who have brains let them use it. Those who have ears let them hear.

If I was God I will change the rule. Instead of taking from those failed leaders seven times I will take seventy seven times. Instead of cursing them for four generation, I will curse them for forty four generations.

Our leaders have allowed themselves to be marked on the flesh; a mark of slavery, a sign of bondage to Satan. They have become everlasting enemies of God and of this nation. Woe to them. They have sold their souls to the devil.

My message to these leaders is this: Our God is a God of Faith, a God of Love and a God of Hope. He is the Alpha and He is the Omega.

You can deceive everyone but you cannot deceive God the Almighty. God not only created us but reads our minds even before we form our thoughts;

even before we were born. But, God is great. He has created us in his own image and gave us the knowledge and discernment to differentiate between the good and the bad; between what he wants us to do and what he does not want us to do. He asks us to choose. When we choose a wrong turning and come back to him he will forgive us. If we continue to take the wrong turning you all know what will happen to us ladies and gentlemen. We will end up in a wrong place or in a ditch or a hole or even worse.

Vroom, vroom, vroom, vroom . . . You can hear a pin drop.

"No one so far has come into power because of their muscles or because of their bravery or because of their own design and will. Every leader that has stood up in any community whether here, in the South or anywhere else in the world is chosen by God the Almighty. God is that power. He is the power of his people; the will of his people, the voice of his people; these people that he has created and breathed into the breath of wisdom and knowledge.

He is a God that does not blink and does not sleep. He does not forget. So listen carefully you leaders: God is watching. He is watching you day and night, from early dawn to dusk, every year, every month, every day, every hour, every minute and every second. He is everywhere. He is in your Continent, in your country, in your town, road, house and room".

Fr. Yohanna nodded gently three times to emphasise what he said then paused.

"To those shepherds, God says 'Feed my sheep'. But what are these leaders doing? They are feeding themselves and forgetting their sheep. How can God forgive such leaders who take the food from the mouths of the orphans and widows and fill their own bellies? Some have acquired such big bellies that they are now ready to pop!"

"Throughout the bible in the Old and New Testament, God has specifically and strongly asked us all and by all I mean you, me and everyone in this planet to look after the orphans and widows that live among us. This war has created millions of orphans and widows. Have our leaders ever mentioned these people? Do they know that such people exist? Did they make any provisions for them?

God's way is not our way. The way He thinks is not how we think. He can forgive but he will never forget.

Our Leaders have placed a high barrier between themselves and the people they are supposed to look after. Even in God's own house, the church which is a place where people are all equal, those leaders have set themselves apart. My message to them is this:

"The church is God's house—A place, where you show humility and respect to God the Almighty. Turn away from your empty pride and pomp and do what every Christian does in the church: Kneel down on your knees, bow down your head and worship and pay homage to your Maker. You will see wisdom; you will receive God's blessings . . ."

"That was a very strong and passionate sermon." said Lucinda later to Marianna as people were filing out of the church. They were staying for two days with Marianna's in laws in Omdurman, one of the three towns of the capital, Khartoum. St Mathew's church is easy to travel to from Omdurman than from Jebel Awlia which is seventeen miles away.

"I will be careful if I were Fr. Yohanna. These politicians don't like to be criticised" answered Marianna.

"Well, all the things Father said were true. If he does not speak for us and remind our leaders of what they should do then who will speak up?"

"Politics and religion should not be mixed. Each should be separate." Since Kennedy's death Marianna has become paranoid and distrustful of all the politicians. She felt that when things get tough the politicians tend to turn against their own people so that they can survive. Marianna as a widow never received help or recognition from the Southern politicians in Khartoum. She would have been left there in the sun to dry if it was not for her family's kindness and generosity.

"Politics is the other face of religion. The church should not stand by and let our leaders do what they want, especially when they are abusing their power and leading corrupt lives. The Church has a duty to us in front of God to stand by us and help us as well as direct our leaders. I think Fr. Yohanna is very brave. He does not care whether they imprison him or even kill him. He is a true leader. He is *Our Good Shepherd.*"

As an apple tree among the trees of the orchard,
so is my Beloved among the young men.
In his longed-for shade I am seated
And his fruit sweet to my taste,
He has taken me to his banquet hall,
And the banner he raises over me is love.

The Song of Songs 2:12

Twenty Two

Norah was forty six years and she was suffering from a number of conditions such as arthritis, high blood pressure and mild asthma. These were not life threatening conditions but could potentially be so if complicated with other endemic illnesses such as malaria and typhoid. Drinking water was not clean but Norah always boiled and filtered their water for drinking. In spite of all these precautions, they would sometimes get caught out every now and then.

She came from school with a very high temperature. "Malaria!" she said to herself. Most people in South Sudan just know the symptoms of malaria because it is so endemic. Many do not even bother to go to the hospital and will go straight to the market to get medicines. Normally they will not be issued medicines over the counter of the local pharmacy without a prescription. There were virtually no medicines in the hospital. Yambio Hospital was running on disjointed help from some aid organizations. If you want medicines then you will have to hit the black market.

Norah had a box full of medication. She took out the box and looked for anti malaria tablets. Take four initially and two daily for the following three days was the instructions. She took four. There were people in the house so they gave her some juice and she went to bed. Nadi soon arrived from the school and tiptoed to her mum's room. She found her sleeping. In the evening Norah went to sit outside. Nadi offered her food but she said that she did not feel like eating. A minute later Norah started to throw up violently. Nadi helped her inside the house and took off the dress she was wearing. She asked for some water to be warmed. She then brought a big basin and helped her to wash and change into a comfortable night dress. Nadi knew that this illness was quite serious and they needed help. Norah was shaking and said that she was feeling cold. Nadi covered her with blankets. Nadi went next door and asked them to call the medical assistant from his house. The medical assistant lived about three miles away and Nadi had to ride the bike to reach him quickly. She gave her bike to the neighbour's son to go instead as she wanted to stay with her mother.

"Please go quickly, and tell him that my mum is very sick" she called out to the boy.

Nadi felt like crying. She always panicked whenever her mother became ill. Her father died suddenly and she will never forget that nightmare. She did not want her mother to go the same way. It will be too cruel. Her brother and two sisters were studying in Uganda. She was here looking after her mother. What will she do if her mother was to die? She will be left all alone. Her uncles don't help them much. Her mother was a very strong and hard working lady. This is why she has managed to get to her present position and build this big house. Both her grandparents died last year within three months of each other.

As she went into the room, she saw her mother on the bed covered with blankets, shaking with fever. She knelt down and held her mum's hand and whispered to her that she has called the medic who will help her very soon. She will be alright.

After a short while the boy came back gasping for breath as he had to run with the bike at full speed. The boy said that the medical assistant has gone to Nzara to see his dad who was also sick.

"Oh ", cried Nadi in desperation and frustration. Then she suddenly had an idea.

Gai

Oh God, aren't you great! In her fluster over her mother's condition she forgot Doctor Gai. Perhaps he was the best person in town to treat her mother. He is the doctor! She could have cried out with relief.

She asked one of the women who lived in the house to sit by her mum while she goes and calls the doctor.

She then stopped short in her tracks. Where does he live? Oh no. Why didn't she ask? There were several buildings belonging to different Organisations. Which was his? An idea came to her; run to David. She started running and found David eating his meal in the shade.

"Nadi, what is wrong, why are you running like this?" said David's mother.

"It is my mum. She is very ill" said Nadi, not able to hide her tears anymore.

"David" cried his mother. Get up quickly and help Nadi find the doctor."

Twenty minutes later Nadi, Gai and David were entering Norah's room. Norah was delirious by now and Nadi thought that for sure something dreadful was going to happen.

Gai tried to see if Norah was conscious, telling her who he was but she did not recognise him. He examined her thoroughly and opened his briefcase which contained an array of medicines. He gave her two injections as she could not take anything by mouth at this stage and he inserted a drip in her left arm. He suspended the drip by pinning its holder on the wall. After about two hours the shaking subsided and Norah slowly drifted into a deep sleep. Norah woke up about two hours later and was given some more medicines and went back to sleep.

Finally around midnight after her temperature dropped Norah seemed to have stabilised. Gai and David bade Nadi goodnight and went away to rest for the next day.

Early next day Gai came back, before starting his clinic. He gave Nadi some medicines to give Norah and wrote in a piece of paper when each should be taken. Later on he came after the clinic closed to check on his patient. Nadi looked very tired and upset. He advised her to try to eat and sleep to be able to look after her mother. He said to her that her mother was now out of danger and will be able to sit up and eat in a few days. Norah had another drip before Gai left.

He came to see Norah every day after shutting the clinic. Nadi discovered that he was very caring and a natural with kids. There were four young boys in the house. Their mums who live in the house are distant cousins of Norah's. Gai made the boys chase him and he chased them around the compound and played football and other children games with them. Nadi and the women would just smile and shake their heads at this distinguished doctor who was so down to earth. He didn't mind if the kids pushed him on the floor. He would get up and brush the dust from his clothes laughing. He made Nadi laugh a lot. She started to understand his language more. He taught her how to pronounce some words and gave her two story books to read. He would then ask her what she thought about each character. He was indirectly teaching her. He smiled at the serious way she took the task. He was at least winning as a teacher. As a lover, he was not doing as well. His other problem was that there was not a single moment when they were left alone. There was always someone in the room or in the courtyard with them.

Norah was getting much better as she could sit up and eat some porridge and soup. Nadi's worries were now getting less and less.

One day Gai came as usual at about quarter to six. He sat on the chair next to Norah and was talking to her and making her laugh as he usually did when he spoke in Arabic. Nadi was not in the house. She came at around six. She said that she has been to her friend's child's ceremony. In the Zande culture when a child is born, it is kept inside the room for three or four days depending on whether it is a girl or boy. After that time the child will be brought out to be blessed by the elders and given a name. This is an intimate but important occasion and certain foods are usually cooked. The occasion is usually attended by close relatives and friends only.

"Is this the time when your parties here in Yambio finish?" Gai teased.

"It was not 'a party' Doctor!" She teased him back.

"Oh don't try and cover up. I know that here in Yambio you guys go to bed at six o'clock. If you deny that then go back to that house. You will find them all snoring in bed!"

Norah laughed.

"I can't go back now! Look, it is six o'clock and we have not gone to bed yet." Said Nadi.

"It is me that is keeping you awake!"

They kept on teasing each other. Norah knew for sure that these two liked each other very much. It is a shame that he was not "one of them".

Nadi usually wore maxi dresses or skirts but today she was wearing a light yellow cotton dress reaching only up to her knees, exposing well shaped long legs. She took off her high heels and kicked them under Norah's bed. She said she couldn't wait to take the pests off as her feet were sore. She slipped on one of her mother's slippers and sat on the two seater couch near the window.

"Nadi, please make tea for the doctor" said Norah.

"Please call me Gai"

Norah would say ok, but will always "forget" and call him "doctor" out of respect.

After serving tea, Nadi put on some music. An enchanting Zairian melody started to flow softly into the room. The record player was powered by batteries. Norah liked music.

Gai was telling Norah about his travels and Nadi was relaxing on the couch and listening to him.

Nadi had a nightmare last night and was not able to sleep afterwards. The nightmare was a big snake chasing her in the forest. The snake was black with shocking pink saucer eyes. When she woke up screaming, she could feel and hear its ragged breathing as it chased her. Sweat was dripping from her body.

"Oh, this is very cosy" Nadi said to herself "Oh yes it is". She smiled and put her right arm around the cushion burying her head further in the chair.

Then she froze. What is this warm air against her forehead? Then she thought she smelt the faint smell of that all familiar *old spice*. Where was she?

What?

She sat up bolt upright as if an electric shock went through her spine. She blinked several times at Gai who had a big smile on his face. She frowned and looked at Norah's bed which was empty.

She was speechless. She pointed to the bed.

"She has gone to have a bath."

As Norah and Gai were talking earlier on, one of the women came to say that hot water was ready for her in the bathroom. As she got up Norah said something to Nadi. Nadi looked as if she was reading her book but has just dozed off finally after trying her best to hide the fact that she was fighting the mighty power of sleep. Gai was right after all. They do sleep at around six o'clock in Yambio!

Thanks be to God. For a moment she had a sickening feeling, which she could not form in her mind . . .

She blinked again. What was in that tea?

"When I saw you dozing, I came and sat near you to prop up your head like this so that you don't break your neck"

171

And he showed her how, which meant that he had his arm around her and her head was on his shoulder for at least ten minutes or even more! She felt very embarrassed. In fact it was less than five minutes!

"Why didn't you wake me up?" She said severely

"I tried to but you were deep in sleep. You looked like an angel."

She stood up abruptly and nearly fell backwards. He caught her and stood up. Unable to resist it, held her tightly.

"Stop it "she hissed, alarmed in case her mother suddenly materialises in the room and catches them embracing, especially after the warning Nadi received yesterday!

He moved away and thought to himself:

I will catch you one day you little witch and you will know the full force of my love and desire.

"I will have to get going" he said picking up his briefcase. She accompanied him up to his car which was parked in the compound. Everybody seemed to have retired for the night.

He held her hand for a while as he was getting into the car. He raised it to his lips. She did not pull it away. She was surprised at herself!

"Goodnight"

Her fragrance was still in his nostrils and the feel of her soft skin against his body played havoc with his mind as he drove away. Nadi once explained that they soak the sweet smelling bark of particular trees and spices in water for a few days and boil the contents with oil until all the water evaporates. They then mix the oil with a small quantity of beeswax to give it a certain thick and creamy texture. They use it as hair and skin oil. The oil is a cost effective essential beauty product. Gai totally agreed, but he did not agree with the rest of the things he was thinking about. He did not agree to this play acting and stupid charade. Why is she acting as if she has never been touched by a man, and why is he helping her in this silly act? By now they should be in a strong relationship and she should be going with him to his bungalow instead of acting like an innocent virgin. He hit the steering wheel with his hand in frustration and swore loudly. He couldn't understand why women make men's lives so difficult.

'Bone of my bone' indeed. If God knew what was going to happen to man, he would have left his bones well alone!

Well, he relented; she had a bad experience, didn't she? Those animals that have molested her. Of all things to happen! He cursed again. Why did it have to be her? And then that fool who had a child with her and left her. Why is he, Gai, now paying the price for those men's mistakes?

He has never been left dangling from the end of a stick like that by any woman before. A few months ago, if he was told this would happen to him in Yambio of all places, he would have laughed and laughed. Yambio is supposed to be a place where nothing happens. It is a place where you can come to have a peaceful retirement. Now he was not so sure. Many things seem to happen to him in Yambio. This haunting beauty and her secrets have occupied a big chunk of his thoughts. There was a possibility he will be rejected, something which he will fight hard to reverse. His clinic work was also quite draining and tiring. He has lost some weight. He could tell by the way some of his clothes feel.

Going back to her, in spite of the attack by those villains, she had a relationship after a year or so and even had a child. That means she must have recovered from the rape issue. The father of her child is a local man; a Zande or *something*. Who cares? He thought, but he was becoming more annoyed. The mere thought of another man in her life was making him very jealous and angry.

Gai was so jealous he did not want to know. He hoped that the man was *dead* and safely buried. A ghost in Yambio to haunt him was the last thing he needed right now.

An idea suddenly hit him smack in the face. Could it be because he was "different" that she did not want him? He was a Nuer and these Zande people do not like or trust Nilotics. He knows that because one of his uncles told him when he went to visit them in Malakal. God, these are black thoughts! He always thought of the Zande as friendly people. At the moment, he is in a bad mood! He never thought that his thoughts will ever go along these lines, being brought up in a totally different country. He is in a potentially tribal-biased situation. He always thought that tribalism is only for the narrow minded. He would not be drawn into any discussions about tribalism or any such negative views but the question which was presenting itself in his mind is: Was he being rejected because he was not a Zande? No, he thought Nadi was attracted to him in spite of his tribe as much as he was attracted to her. His daily visits to the house have given him plenty of indications but with her you can never be sure. She is a dark horse. She is so secretive and deep, you would never guess what was going on in that pretty head of hers. Oh God, if she was a Nuer girl or any other, he would most probably be home and dry by now. As it is, he had to be very careful not to put the wrong foot anywhere. He has to plan his steps very carefully because those Zande people can get upset at anything. It was hard sometimes to know what they want. If they were displeased they would not tell you that to your face, but by God they will make you *feel it*. They are a funny people but right now he needed them on his side to get Nadi. He thought that it was easy to have a relationship with Zande girls but he certainly came against a solid rock! Trust him to pick the most difficult one! Compared to her the other girls he met in the office and the church were easy to chat with and he was sure he would not find much difficulty striking a relationship with any of them. The exception is *her!* And she is the only one he wants. The other issue was that he perceived some reservation in her mother's attitude towards him during his last two visits. She must have noticed his admiration for Nadi and has gone a notch or two cooler. Norah does not seem to approve, he said to himself. Nothing seems to be going right for him!

Nadi felt that her resistance to this man was weakening. She needed to reinforce her energy to keep him at bay. She was not admitting even to herself that she has been looking forward to his daily visits. After school she would quickly go home, prepare the evening meal and take a long relaxing bath. She would then wear a nice outfit and rearrange her hair, oiling herself with the fragrant oil he liked. She would then sit on the sofa opposite her mother's bed and pretend to be busy marking the school books or reading. He would come and sit on the chair next to her mother's bed and ask Norah about her progress. Nadi would then make tea and bring it on a tray and then she would pretend she was busy doing other things. He would then converse with her mother, every now and then stealing long gazes at her. She knew that he knew that she knew that he was very interested! It seemed that each one was playing a game, trying to outsmart the other at the art of fencing.

Nadi sat down slowly on her bed. What will she do now? He certainly liked her and will want to have a relationship with her. He will insist. He has spelt it clearly now. Where will she run to? If it was not so dangerous she would go and live in her uncle's house in Tambura or even flee to Wau. There was nowhere to go and sooner or later she will have to face the music. Oh God, why was life so complicated? First of all, when she was young and innocent she got attacked and damaged forever by those savages. When she started to recover, her mum and Mazindo's mum who used to be friends put their heads together and arranged for Mazindo to marry her. She, Nadi never cared much for Mazindo. He used to go to a different school in a nearby village and was four years ahead of her and was average in everything. Not like Paul. Mazindo was working as a prison officer and was soon promoted and seemed to be doing well. He started to visit them regularly and gave her presents. It was clear what he wanted. The dowry was soon settled and she became his wife. She did that mainly to please her mum. She did it also to protect herself. She knew she was left vulnerable after she was raped. They lived with Mazindo's parents, while he was building their first house together. After they were married for five months, Mazindo disappeared. He wrote a small note to his father, saying that he has joined the SPLA. He did not leave her any message. She knew why. Mazindo knew she did not love him. She did her duties as a wife and helped his mother with the household chores. Mazindo started to drink and went out with other women. She never complained. She thought that her portion in life was bad luck. After his father made the contents of the note known, Nadi told her mother. Norah called for a meeting and demanded that her daughter should come back to her house. Mazindo's family argued that Nadi was married to their son and should stay where he left her. Norah insisted that since Mazindo wrote a note to his dad and omitted mentioning his own wife, then she will take it that he did not care about her. The argument went on and on. In the end it was agreed that

Nadi goes to stay with her mother until Mazindo comes back. Nadi was over the moon. Since living with her mum she has grown from strength to strength. She soon discovered that she was pregnant. Mazindo's parents were told. They were overjoyed. Mathew came and brightened their lives. When he died, part of her died with him. Mazindo's parents grew distant soon afterwards. Their visits stopped altogether. Nadi sensed that they did not want her to visit them either. They were polite but cold. She remembered the last visit. It was last Christmas. She went to them with some cakes which she baked. They refused to take it from her. His mother commented on Nadi's expensive dress and shoes, saying that if her son was here she would not have looked so good, it is a good thing he was gone (dead). That upset Nadi so much that she stood up and walked away. She vowed to herself that never will she let life treat her badly again. She will have nothing to do with any man or his family, ever again. She was soon going to be twenty five years of age. She was old enough and had enough experience to be independent and free. Mathew was dead. Mazindo was dead. What else do they want from her? Do they want her to die too?

Nadi wiped her tears which were overflowing by now.

She has accepted her portion in life and vowed to keep it so. She had her family and her job. She helped other people when they were ill or when they needed help with their children. She was a Christian and did all her Christian duties. So far she has been quite satisfied, until Gai came into her life.

He kept bothering her and was now trying his best to break the solid wall she has built around herself. If he came into her life earlier, who knows, things could have been much different? She liked him more than she could admit but that was beside the point. The point was: She did not want him to know about her past. She would rather die than tell him about the rape and later how she was abandoned by her husband. He thought that she was an innocent girl; untouched. It was a good thing he was a "Khawaja ". For her at least he, being the person who mattered most, thought of her as pure and innocent. It felt so good. She felt that he never looked at her as the other men did. That made what he felt for her seem to be engulfed in purity and myth. This is something she never had the chance to experience before. He will soon go and forget about her but she will never forget him. His best friends are David and David's brother, Samuel. They will not tell Gai about her murky, unpleasant past. This was her wish and no one should rob her of that. She will make sure that until Gai leaves Yambio, he will be none the wiser. She will also make sure that not Gai or any of her cousins will ever know about her true feelings for him. She knew that if David were to know, he will try and "help" and that would be a disaster. She will have to remind him next time she sees him not to tell Gai about her awful history at any cost! Otherwise she will never speak to him.

With that she slipped into a dreamless, unhappy sleep.

Norah who woke early in the morning the next day was turning in her bed and thinking

"Thanks be to God, I am getting better".

She will soon go back to her beloved school. She thought by now, the children and the other teachers and staff would have driven Mr. Tambura to destruction. Mr. Tambura was her deputy. He was a young and dynamic teacher. He was rapidly promoted to that post for his hard work and diligence.

Norah's thought went to her daughter Nadi. Nadi was taking far too much interest in this foreign doctor. Norah corrected herself: Sudanese but westernised which was as bad she told herself with satisfaction. If Gai was a Nuer from Sudan, she wouldn't have minded at all, but he was a foreigner, yes, a foreigner from Canada. This was what was bothering her. Trust the awkward girl to pick the most unsuitable man in town! It was not that there was anything wrong with the doctor. Oh no. He was very polite, seemed to come from a good family, unmarried, loaded with money (all doctors are, especially the foreign ones!) and young. The only problem was that he would make Nadi love him and then suddenly one day he will go away and leave her. This was what these foreign people do to our girls, she thought. This was what she, Norah, will not be able to take any more. Nadi has suffered enough. Why should Nadi get attached to a person who will definitely leave her one day? Worse still he could leave her with child! Norah shuddered and closed her eyes tightly at the thought. We have been through all this before! She thought. Why should a snake bite you twice from the same hole? Not that Gai was a snake.

Two days ago she managed to call her daughter and warn her. Norah was a person who did not beat around the bush and she certainly did not in this particular case. She called Nadi and told her about her fears. Nadi was annoyed and asked

"What makes you think that I have "anything" with the doctor just because I am polite to him? He is looking after your health, for God's sake mum. You should be grateful and stop accusing me".

"I am just trying to make you aware that you might make a mistake"

"No I will not make any mistakes" replied Nadi impatiently and walked out of the room.

You shall not covet your neighbour's house. You shall not covet your neighbour's wife, or his servant, man or woman, or his ox, or his donkey, or anything that is his.

Exodus 17

Twenty Three

Norah was one of the women in Yambio who you will have to be careful not to cross. She was well educated, well spoken and came from a good family. Everyone in Yambio and beyond knew the Bakata family. Norah refused to remarry after her husband's death. She started to work harder than ever in the school which had the best reputation in the whole district. She also worked hard to finish her big house where they were living at present. Her only problem was minor ailments and one or two more serious ones such as asthma, but she was generally keeping well and made sure that people in her household had decent meals and kept healthy. She was not going to marry again. Period. She wanted her children to get the best education. Mado, Gloria and Taban are all in Uganda in her cousin's house. At least they were safe and they were studying. Nadi managed to travel to Uganda last year and visit them. She told her mother that they were fine and were all in school. The house they were living in was overcrowded and food could be scarce at times, but at least they were safe and that was all that mattered.

Here of course they were relatively safe as they have all been recruited in the SPLA. There was of course the major threat of the Ambororo who could leave a lot of damage and devastation when they strike. The SPLA recruits were given guns and ammunition and were taught how to use the guns. Norah could defend herself and her daughter. Her parents died suddenly last year, one after the other. That was one of the biggest shocks of her life. She felt that there was nothing that she has not been through, perhaps only death. On a brighter side, there were her loving sisters Susan and Lucinda. Lino was also a good brother but they were so far away. She missed them every single day. What was the use of having brothers and sisters and ending up like this? Alone? There was a possibility they will never see each other again. Is there an afterlife? Can they have a chance to meet somewhere for a cup of tea and hug each other and tell each other how much they are loved? Norah sighed deeply. There was nothing but tears, only tears and very fond memories. Susan used to be like her twin sister. Oooooh!

She had to be strong. She had to be strong to face horrible people like Makawa; the Great Chief! She Norah did not care whether it was a chief or a slave when it came to one of her precious children. Makawa had his eyes on Nadi ever since he first saw her; just after she married Mazindo. Makawa was Mazindo's cousin. He used to study and work in Khartoum. His father the Great Chief Riwa The 19th died about six years ago and Makawa was inaugurated as the Great Chief Riwa the 20th in his place. Norah has never seen a more arrogant, boastful and disrespectful person as the new Great Chief. He thought that he was the best of the best and had a habit of humiliating and snubbing people. He also liked the ladies and thought that every woman who attracted his attention should be happy and thankful to God because he Makawa, the King of Kings has bestowed her with favour. He was married to one wife before he became the Great Chief but now he has acquired another two and please do not count "the others".

When Makawa came to Yambio, Mazindo, his young cousin became close to him. Norah was sure that Makawa was behind Mazindo's sudden decision to join the SPLA six years ago. When Mazindo went away, Makawa pretended to want to help Nadi. He was adamant that Nadi should stay either with Mazindo's parents or in his household. Norah was an intelligent woman. She was able to smell the rat from miles away. Norah insisted that her daughter should come to her house. She became angry and agitated in the meeting which was conducted over nearly three days. In the end the elders thought it best to compromise and allow Nadi to live with her mother until her husband returns. Makawa knew that he could not push it further. Whenever Makawa visited Nadi, Norah was always present and answered all questions on her daughter's behalf. Makawa understood Norah perfectly and hated her for her interference. Two years ago when Mathew died, Makawa renewed his interest in Nadi, thinking that now what tied Mazindo to Nadi was no longer there and

Mazindo was dead anyway, or so he hoped. In the Zande tradition, when a man dies, one of his brothers will redeem his widow by marrying her and raising children for the dead man to keep his name alive. Mazindo was not seen or heard of for more than six years. No woman should wait for her husband that long. Makawa started to chase Nadi in earnest, going as far as writing her love letters. He said that he loved Nadi the moment he saw her and he wanted to marry her now that his cousin has died. He will build her a separate mansion exactly the way she wanted and will give her anything she would ask for. Nadi did not show the letter to her mother for fear of a big bust up. He used to send for her to visit his house so that "she could help his wives with organizing food and entertainment for his distinguished guests" as Nadi was his cousin's wife. Nadi ignored his requests. It was not only Makawa who was interested in Nadi; many other young men felt that she was a single woman and available again and so tried to win her also. Makawa had his messengers and servants spy on Nadi. He was given reports as to who these interested suitors were. Makawa used to fly into a rage when he was told that someone who was showing interest dared to visit her house. He used to send death threats to people to put them off. People started to complain to Norah. Norah kept quiet and bid her time . . .

One day there was a marriage celebration. Nadi, Norah and all the family attended. The party was in the bride's parents'house and people sat outside celebrating. Nadi was sitting with her friends having a good time. Some people were dancing. Late in the night, many people left, including Norah. The bride and bridegroom also retired to their new home. Nadi said that she will return home later with David and his brother Sam. Nadi was chatting and laughing with her friends when suddenly she felt that everybody went quiet. One of the girls indicated to Nadi to turn around. When she turned, she saw Chief Makawa standing immediately behind her chair. She stood up and curtsied not quite knowing what to do. He took her hand and led her to the dance floor. He pulled her towards him and encircled her waist. He had his other arm around her shoulders, pulling her closer, with their chests touching. Nadi felt trapped, confused and embarrassed. He was intoxicated. She said to herself that she could pull this off gracefully by not struggling and attracting other people's attention. One of his wives started to hurl abuses at "girls that have no shame, trying to steal other people's husbands in broad daylight."

Nadi looked frantically to see where David and Sam were but they were nowhere to be seen.

Meanwhile Makawa was whispering in her ears that he wanted her as he has never wanted any other woman. He wanted to marry her. After all she was his 'right'. When Makawa unexpectedly slackened his grip, she quickly wriggled free and made a dash for it, running straight into the house. Her friends ran after her to protect her. By now, David who was having a romantic time with his fiancée was alerted. He took the shaken Nadi home. He could not say anything to Makawa as he was the Great Chief and Nadi's brother-in-law. Besides, Makawa was well in his forties. He had to show respect to an "elder". Norah will be able to sort out that 'kind of problem' later.

Norah was fuming when she was told about the incidence. She felt that Makawa was not going to leave her daughter in peace unless she, Norah did something about it.

Early the next day which happened to be a Monday, Norah sent word to Mr Tambura that she was going to be late by about an hour. She asked him to continue with school as normal. Norah then put on her full army uniform, complete with a revolver. She got on her bike and rode to Makawa's homestead which was about five miles from the town centre. Makawa had a large estate, inherited from his father the Great Chief Alexander Riwa the 19th. The front part of the compound was separate from the rest of the house which is the chief's residence. The two compounds joined by a big wooden gate with beautiful carvings of different animals and palm trees. The front part of the house was where the chief conducted his business which was mainly presiding over the Great Chief's Court. There was a long veranda supported by many pillars. In the central position was the Great Chiefs' high chair which was especially hand crafted, made from mahogany. A lion's head carved at the top. The arms of the chair were shaped like big lion paws and so were the legs. The seat of the chair was made of fine intricately woven cane strips. On top of that a soft cushion of black and white animal fur was placed. On each side of the chair there were four carved chairs for the council members to sit, all made of mahogany. Wooden benches were put in rows in front of the Chief's chair for people that present their cases and those who attend with them. The chief's throne was on an elevated platform together with his council. The floor of this magnificent throne was covered with animal skin; think of zebras and tigers. The walls were adorned with antique weaponry from the time of the Great Gbudwe and his Royal Army. There were also rifles captured from different wars. Eye catching artefacts such as bows and arrows and other hand crafted weapons of war were also displayed. Some were from the Iron Age which seemed to be the trademark of the Azande warriors and fighters. There were also different types of shields and spears. Everything arranged to show its full glory and to impress visitors. There were oil paintings of Gbudwe and other warriors and chiefs. Chief Yambio commanded a large vantage point and Makawa's photographs during his graduation from the prestigious Khartoum University and his inauguration as the Great Chief were also displayed. Makawa brought to Yambio the money he amassed in Khartoum and rebuilt the Great Chief's Homestead to this high level of dazzling sprawling mansion, complete with solar power. He made his money from buying and selling property in Khartoum and Uganda. Makawa used to wear his traditional Chief's attire whenever he was sitting in his court. He had fans put everywhere and instructed people to "have a good wash" before they attended his court, otherwise they will be "thrown out". He did not stomach the strong smell of sweat in his court. There was a saying in Yambio" wash yourself and change your clothes before you appear in front of Chief Makawa". He loved cars as he loved women. He kept at least three in this mansion. He had others in Ezo which he considered his holiday home. His workmen were mostly from Uganda. The whole compound was surrounded by fruit trees such as mangoes, bananas, palms, guava and orange. At one end he had a "flower garden, nearly two acres in size where different plants and flowers such as Jasmine, birds of paradise, camellia and azaleas flourished. There was also a wide variety of Rhododendrons and other wild varieties of carnations. He called the garden his "paradise "and used to spend most of his time there when meditating or when courting a new woman. Yes a chief can do what he wants in his own garden! Chief Makawa was a class apart from everyone else. He was up there while everyone was down here. Nearly half of the country side near Yambio belong to him. He had a big farm of sheep, goats and cows which he brought from Bahr El Ghazal. He recently introduced boars and hogs. He liked hunting and used to go out hunting with his henchmen and friends for days. He surely had it all and was a very shrewd businessman. Everyday all his possessions used to be counted from his herds of cattle up to his chickens. The figures were entered in a book and he looked and checked how much he has lost and amassed and why. He used to inspect his land every week and knew everything that happened anywhere. He was not one that sleeps and lets the servants do as they wanted.

But today Norah was not impressed. Not even the day before or the year before. Norah saw Makawa as no one else could see him. He was a blood sucker!

Makawa's Council used to sit very early in the morning, starting at seven. Norah suddenly appeared straight in front of Makawa as there were not many people as yet that have gathered for the first case.

"Here comes trouble on two legs" he thought to himself.

Makawa knew Norah well enough to sniff trouble. He gestured to his guard to ask Norah about the business that brought her. Norah said that she wanted a private word with The Great Chief "right now."

He asked the guard to take her to an inner room and tell her to wait there for him. Norah stood in the middle of the room with her arms akimbo, waiting.

"Mamma Nadi, Please sit down". In the Zande culture a man or a woman are not usually called by their names but by reference to their first born as a sign of respect.

"I have not come here to sit down. Call all your wives. I want them to hear what I have to say."

"Shouldn't you tell me first what this is all about?"

"You know what it is about" said Norah barely controlling her anger.

Makawa looked about him in alarm.

"Mamma Nadi, please talk to me if I have done anything to upset you. We can put it right, right here."

"Well, in this case I will stand in the yard and shout to everyone at the top of my voice" said Norah threateningly.

Makawa had no choice but to call his wives. Norah was still standing in the middle of the room.

"Look here all of you. You might be rich, kings and queens, but I Norah I am a commoner. Yes I am a commoner but I have rights. My right is to be respected. My right is to be left in peace. My right is to choose who I will talk with, eat with and marry. So is the right of all the people in my house.

If I give you respect it is not because you are a chief or a king or a queen but because you are a human being like me. If anyone wants anything to do with my daughter, let them come to me first. You Makawa if you want a woman in my household, come to me, Norah the daughter of Bakata. I am your size and your age. My daughter is young enough to be your daughter. If you say that you are The *Great Chief*, then behave like one. Stop running after girls half your age. Today I am standing here in the place of Nathana my husband. Do not think for one minute that Nadi is an easy prey because her father is dead. I am wearing his shoes and am ready to do battle with anyone who so much as hurts a hair on her head.

You wives of Makawa; I am giving you a warning; keep your husband well entertained in order to keep his hands off other people's daughters. If I hear any one of you insulting my daughter out of spite then you will know who you will be dealing with. I have never crossed words with anyone since I set foot here in Yambio but you lot have tried my patience to the limit."

One of the women got angry and started to shout at Norah. Makawa gave her a sound slap across the face and told her to "shut up". The rest took the hint. Makawa then asked them to leave the room.

He apologised to Norah. He said that he had a bit too much to drink on the wedding night and did not mean any harm. He was just joking with Nadi because she was his sister-in-law.

Norah walked out without another word.

Nice Day! Said Makawa to himself. The woman is a real devil. Her aggression is unprecedented. Zande women are not that aggressive. She can scare Satan himself! He could not imagine that lovely and gentle Nadi will one day become as aggressive and as hard as her mother. For a moment he thought that she was going to shoot them all! What did she think she was doing coming to his house dressed in a combat uniform and carrying a gun? He should have disarmed her, but she completely unnerved him by calling his wives. Today his youngest wife will give him a big headache. She was always jealous of Nadi. He will spend the night alone in his bedroom by the rose bush. He will be unavailable and in a bad mood.

He could have asked his servants to throw Norah out or "deal with her" as soon as she uttered her insults but he wanted what Norah had . . .

Nadi

If it was not for Nadi Norah would be six feet under by now for her disrespect of him and his authority. He will just have to wait.

A month later when things settled down Makawa paid a visit to his aunt and uncle: Mazindo's parents. He told them that they will have to consider the fact that their son might never return. Their grandson has died. Nadi might one day run away with another man and they will be the losers. He said that there were reports that Nadi was 'going around' with other men and he could not hold it against her as she was young. What they needed to do was to demand that Nadi should be redeemed by one of Mazindo's brothers to raise children for Mazindo. If she refuses then they will have to demand for the return of their dowry. Makawa thought that the dowry which he contributed towards, about £1000.00 will be too much for Norah to raise at this time of war and with her being cut off from the rest of her family who could otherwise help her. It will then be his golden chance to pounce by offering another£5000.00 and much more;

everything that Norah wanted and become the man to step in Mazindo's place and redeem Nadi. He, Makawa is a cunning fox. He was the best planner in the whole of the Zande land. He would never stand by and let that beautiful jewel slip from his hands. Every time he saw her, he desired her even more. Norah's bark was much more than her bite. He learnt a saying in Arabic while he was in Khartoum: "Even if a woman becomes an axe she will not be hard enough to break a man's head."

Well, Norah has proved that she was a good axe that can not only break but mince a man's head. She read her daughter's situation like a book and started saving money. Some of Nadi's dowry money was sent to the maternal uncles and used to buy her kitchen stuff for the new house when she married Mazindo. The rest was given to the paternal uncles. Norah started selling things such as the sweet smelling oil, jewellery etc and put the money aside. She also put some money from her husband's gratuity. Last year she was able to raise the thousand pounds. She hid it in the ceiling of the house in a place that no one will ever think of looking into.

When everyone assembled in her house and demanded that they wanted Nadi to be redeemed to raise children for Mazindo, Norah put her foot down. Nadi was called. When she was asked if she would consent to be redeemed, she said that she did not want to marry anyone. Makawa was angry at Norah for "giving the wrong advice to her daughter". He said that since Nadi did not want to comply, they had no other option but take their dowry back. Norah silently went out of the room as a great commotion broke out from Norah's representatives about the unfairness of the Chief. Will they be able to return Nadi's body to how it was before she was married?

Makawa replied with the spite of a venomous snake.

"Did Mazindo have to change anything from how it was?" Two or three relatives of Norah's wanted to lay hands on Makawa and break his bones but Norah urged for calm. It was a rat in a chief's clothes.

Norah then calmly laid the £1000.00 pound notes on a table.

Everyone was speechless.

"Take your money and go".

Makawa could not believe his eyes. He wanted to apologise and return the money but Norah signalled to him again to take the money and go.

David stopped everyone before they went and wrote out an affidavit to say that Mazindo's family have received such an amount as a return of the dowry and that meant that Nadi and Mazindo are no longer husband and wife. The document was then signed by everyone. That was the strangest happening and people spoke about it and debated that whatever was done Mazindo was still Nadi's husband. Nothing so shameful has ever happened in the Zande land. Why was the Great Chief entertaining the breakdown of his brother's house?

To Norah it was freedom from the family of Mazindo. Makawa has blighted her daughter's life and can cause her real grief. Nadi was now free. Free.

A year later, Makawa heard about the new doctor. He never laid eyes on the doctor before but thought that he was a foreigner and so did not give him much thought until one day when he saw Gai in a UN security meeting. Makawa as a chief played a great part in the security of the Zandeland. There was infiltration into the Zandeland by the Ambororo who are calttle herders that come through Western Sudan from Chad. They used to arm themselves up to the teeth and tended to kill and capture innocent civilians especially women and children taking them as slaves. These security meetings were conducted to brief people and make them aware of any impending dangers. Strategies are also thought about and implemented to protect civilians and property.

When Makawa was introduced to Gai, Makawa was completely taken aback.

"Doctor,I was told that you were a Khawaja".

Gai laughed.

"I seem to surprise many people when they see me for the first time. I am a South Sudanese but I grew up in Canada"

"But you don't look like a South Sudanese, which part of the country are you from?"

"Very rude" thought Gai to himself.

"From Upper Nile" said Gai shortly and walked away.

Later on Makawa learnt that the doctor was half Nuer and half Ethiopian.

As soon as he arrived home he called Kenge, his spy.

"Come here you son of a bitch and sit there on the floor." The Great Chief was in a mad rage. They were in the Chief's office. He ordered everyone outside except Kenge.

"What have I done now?" said Kenge totally at a loss at the sudden hurricane blowing in his face.

"What have you done or what have you not done, you stupid fool. Didn't I tell you to tell me about the men who visit Nadi? Why did you not tell me about this doctor?"

"But I told you, Chief. I told you that a Khawaja doctor visited Norah every day because she was very ill."

"Yes, you told me, you stupid dullard. Does he bloody look like a Khawaja to you?"

"But he speaks English all the time like all these Khawajat (plural) and does things like them. He could be from Uganda or Kenya, I do not know" said poor Kenge who felt hard done by.

"You are so stupid I do not know why I deal with someone like you. Did you think that I am paying you all this money so that you will come up with your foolish tales? This man has been going there to see Nadi not Norah. Doesn't that head of yours ever works? Why should he go every day to their house, even if Norah was ill? Who will go to see Norah everyday with that razor sharp tongue of hers?"

"But Norah was dying . . ." said Kenge not comprehending.

"Just get out of my face you idiot"

Correct your son and he will give you peace of mind:
He will delight your soul.

Proverbs 17

Twenty Four

S usan was a lady who was always on the go. She enrolled in local colleges, completing several courses in languages, food hygiene and finished a degree in Nursing. She later worked as a nurse in Manchester Royal Infirmary. Her husband, after finishing several courses, worked with the City Council.

Susan and her husband worked for several years and saved money to buy their new home. They bought a three bed room house in the outskirts of Manchester called Oldham. Susan and her husband never dreamt that one day they will own a lovely home in England of all places. They took a mortgage from a Building Society to buy the house. It was a terraced house with a large garden at the back where the boys used to play football. Susan and her husband worked very hard and they got their just rewards.

Susan, on hearing about the suffering of her people in Sudan decided to start a charity. She was inspired by the work of an Agency, OLS, which worked with suffering civilians in Eastern Equatoria and Upper Nile areas. One of their programmes was to restart school education for children who used to live in the SPLA rebel held areas.

Susan wrote to some agencies and charities that work overseas. She also invited all the South Sudanese women and men in Britain to a conference to discuss issues of the 'lost boys of South Sudan' and issues pertaining to child soldier and orphans of the war. She received a very positive response. The conference was well attended by Sudanese from the North and South and by other Africans and British citizens who have interest in Sudan or work with other children charities. The local MP was invited too, but he sent his representative as he had to travel abroad.

The main speakers were doctors and psychologists who spoke about human development and child Psychology, the importance of parenting and family structure and its devastating effects on the individual's interaction and relationship with others in later life if the structure is removed. Another speaker talked about nutrition and its effect on the normal growth and mental function of children. He also talked about the painful and irreversible effects of starvation on the body of a child. Another speaker from South Sudan highlighted the problems and impediments, mostly manmade and how the aid agencies were finding it difficult to distribute food to areas hit by famine. The main causes and complications were highlighted. Many people were shocked to discover that some of the problems were caused by armed forces from the indigenous South Sudanese people. The speaker detailed the dilemma of the lost boys or boy soldiers and its impact on society and the future of South Sudan. These boys were abducted or taken by force from their parents. Some of the boys were as young as seven. They were then used as slaves; fetching, carrying, cooking and were used to fight as soldiers. Some of the boys have grown to become the deadliest killing machines as they became dehumanized and disinhibited through the horrific things they were taught and told to do. Some boys ended up in places in Eastern Equatoria such as Palataka Secondary School ruins. The boys were spirited there and were used as slaves, looking after stolen herds of cows for high ranking SPLA leaders. Some people in the conference wept with raw emotion and feelings of helplessness.

After an interactive group work and discussions people had a glimmer of hope to help with the cause for the lost boys and girls which was "education". One of the aid workers who worked in South Sudan and Ethiopia made a moving speech about the work they have so far done in South Sudan, especially in Equatoria and Upper Nile; the schools that they have opened. A "school" mostly was nothing but a shade under the tree. Children loved their schools and some worked very hard and did well. They needed money to buy books, pencils etc. It was much more uplifting and people listened attentively.

Someone spoke and said that issues about children's education should be taken up with the SPLA leadership. The Leaders were sending their children to study in the neighbouring countries such as Kenya, Uganda and even Europe while forcing other people's children to work as their slaves.

Everything that was hidden under the bushel will be lifted high up on the tree tops.

God will one day reveal everything and woe to the perpetrators.

When Susan's turn came to speak, she reported that the focus of the Conference was to look for ways to make the World aware of child slavery in South Sudan. She said that the children were not bought or sold but taken from their parents by force and coercion. They were taken by the SPLA leaders to tend to their cattle, fetch and carry and do other jobs for them. They were also used as soldiers at an age when a child should be sleeping in the bosom of its parents. She said that this heinous act is one of the biggest blot in their country's history because by doing these deeds, those people have in effect destroyed the country's future generation.

Susan reported that some of the perpetrators of this crime send their own children to study abroad in expensive; private schools while using other people's children for free labour. She said that these people must be stupid because they should know that if you stop children from learning then you will end up with a worthless generation who will give a lot of headache to the children who have been educated in private schools! If you put "crap" into a child, you will get back nothing but "crap" and you will be the one to kneel down in order to mop it up!

She reported about the programme they were undertaking as a charity which is to raise money for organizations who work with children in South Sudan such as the OLS.

She ended her report by saying that the whole situation of "child soldiers" has stemmed from the bad attitude of certain group of people or tribes who think that they are better than others. She said that those people do not have to be so conceited because they are the very people who have suffered most in this conflict. She said that some of them have adopted the slogan:

We are born to rule and not to be ruled!!!!

Susan posed this question to people:

How can anybody rule a nation if they are uneducated, uncivilized, undisciplined, unprincipled, uncouth and unruly? Shouldn't they rectify all these problems first before "ruling" others?

Susan ended her report by quoting her own slogan

"We are born to rule **ourselves.**"

She earned a warm applause and a standing ovation.

If Yahweh does not build the house
in vain the masons toil:
If Yahweh does not guard the city,
In vain the sentries watch.

Psalm 127: 1

Twenty Five

Lucinda gave birth to twins Anthony and John; shortened Tony and Johnny one bright morning in November in Khartoum Teaching Hospital. It was the best time. It was winter. The temperatures can drop to 19 degrees C at night and that is cold by Khartoum standards where temperatures in the summer can reach up to 45 degrees or more!

Tony was slightly bigger than Johnny but they were identical, absolutely cute. Tony was born first. Marianna told the midwife to cut the thread on her right wrist which was black and put it round the baby's right wrist. After ten minutes Johnny came along. The white thread which was cut from Lucinda's left wrist was transferred onto his dainty wrist.

Peter was so proud and happy that he seemed to have increased at least three inches in height. He also seemed to have a permanent smile on his lips. Marianna left her children with her cousin and came soon to join Peter and Lucinda in the Hospital. She brought some porridge and soup in flasks for Lucinda. Lucinda could only drink black tea as she felt nauseous. After the babies were checked, they were discharged home.

Two months later the twins were baptized in the local church and the occasion was followed by a small family gathering. Peter thought that they could celebrate their children's Baptism in a special way. They will celebrate it with the school children. The children were not ordinary children. They were "displaced" children. They were *Naziheen*. These children might not have had a decent meal for months. What is the use of eating a good meal while teaching hungry, deprived children? For once they should share. He asked his beloved wife, who was so surprised and shocked at the idea that she started to laugh hysterically.

"No I am serious" said Peter as if he was saying "I am going to the market."

"These children have school meals made of beans. Right?"

"Right".

"We can improve the meal by giving the cook more onions and oil and tomatoes to make the beans taste nicer. We can then buy some cheese. We can also add another dish of meat. I will buy four big goats and their meat can be roasted or fried. We can then buy a big bag of rice to be eaten with the meat."

Lucinda started to get very excited! They planned the day to be Friday that same week. During lunch the Naziheen kids got the best surprise ever. They ate to their very full. Some were so happy that they composed a little song for the twins. They sang and sang and blessed the two boys who were the loveliest twins they have ever seen and may God give the headmaster three more twins! Lucinda gave her husband a sheepish look. He just looked at her and smiled. Marianna, who helped with the cooking and organizing, was very proud and brought her children as well who basked in the twins' glory. They were two little sisters, now they have two little brothers, younger than them, who they will boss about and love. Isn't everything just great?

Marianna has taken a teacher's post in the school. She had to get intensive training and has just started. The two girls will be looked after by Lucinda as she was now going to be at home for at least one year!

It was amazing how everything seemed to fit in nicely with Peter's family.

Peter's problem was not the family; it was their precarious position in this God forsaken place. He felt insecure at times. He wondered to himself what if something happens to them here. By the time they get help they will all be dead, if suddenly people around them attack them for whatever reason. His fear was for the children. The fact that they were not Muslims and that they have a school was in itself a big problem. There was a wrong perception that Christianity taught people hatred against Islam. Most of the villagers were quite friendly and wanted to keep themselves to themselves but some were curious and resentful to these "Southerners" who have infiltrated their society with their bad habits: brewing and drinking local beers, prostitution, diseases and God-knows-what. This was a belief which was drummed into every Northerner almost every day. "Do not approach them. They are filthy and dangerous. The best thing you can get out of them is money. Milk them until they are dry because this is your destiny; to be rich with the money of the *Kuffar*". Now what makes them think that the *Kuffar*'s money is not defiled as well? It comes out of their filthy promiscuous pockets, doesn't it? Hypocrisy; nothing but hypocrisy.

One day Peter was sitting in his office looking at the time table for the next week. It needed minor adjustments. He was working on it when he heard the children screaming and running out of the classes. The teachers were unable to control them and a great chaos ensued. When he ran out, he saw a scene which made his blood run cold. He saw an army jeep with at least six soldiers in full uniform carrying guns. Some of the children started running to their homes and some young ones ran towards him, hiding under his desk in total panic, fear and terror. The army officers did not seem to care about the absolute mayhem they caused or to show any remorse. They sauntered arrogantly towards the "Rakuba School" as they used to call it and demanded to talk to the headmaster. Peter accosted them at the gate and took an aggressive stance which made them pause.

"I am the headmaster. What do you want?"

One of them who seemed to be the leader said

"We thought of visiting the school to inspect it"

"Do you have any official documents?"

"No. We just thought that we want to visit the school".

Peter then spoke angrily

"Did you realise the damage that you have just done? These children have come from a war zone. They associate any military person holding a gun with all the bad things which happens in war. They thought you came here to murder them" The soldiers started to snigger and some laughed in Peter's face.

"I will tell you something. Pray to *Allah* that you will never experience war as we did. Since you have no warrant to search the school, please go back in peace. I have no gun to fight you. There was no need for you to come here with guns and cause this mayhem to innocent children who have just fled the war. We are unarmed and we happen to be citizens of this Country and so have the right to be treated with dignity and respect as everybody else in this Sudan, our country." He added sarcastically.

The soldiers expected to see someone who could not speak Arabic and who could be easily intimidated. To their consternation and horror they discovered that Peter's Arabic was not only fluent but showed that he was better educated than them. He seemed to have a much more superior knowledge of the rules and regulations of the Country compared to all of them. They went back to their car and drove away without further argument.

Immediately Peter asked the teachers to take anything of value and clear the premises in ten minutes. He told the children not to come tomorrow to the school until they were told that it was safe to do so.

Peter told the watchman to take his children and go to another location as there might be trouble tonight or any time soon. He locked the school compound and went home. When he told Lucinda what happened, she started to cry with fear. He held her in his arms and kissed her.

"My beloved, whatever God plans for us we will have to accept it. Remember, God would never bring us to this place if he was not going to look after us." He then smiled and started to sing the hymn

"If God is for us, who will be against, If the spirit of God has set us free!"

Lucinda soon joined him in the song and then they saw Marianna coming towards them. She embraced them both and they stood up singing. Marianna had a lovely soprano voice. She sang on and on, holding hands with her young daughters who looked up at her and smiled, thinking that they were just having a nice time, not realising the danger surrounding them.

A week ago before the school incidence, school results for children who sat exams to go to High School in North Sudan was announced over the radio and in the newspapers. Comboni Dar El Salam Mixed School did extremely well. In fact they were sitting pretty, right at the top of the list of local schools. The teachers were delirious and the euphoria and happiness was such that some of the parents came to the school to congratulate those children who did so well. That did not come from nothing. The teachers worked round the clock to improve the standard of the children sitting the exams and to coach and give them confidence. Each day they sat late in the school giving the pupils extra lessons. The classes were poorly lit by kerosene lamps. Lucinda and Marianna and some of the parents who had some money would make tea and food and bring it to the teachers and some of the poorest children. They kept the children focused on one thing and one thing only: Success. The children did succeed. Only a handful got marks below average. Peter thought everything was going well for him until the Minister of Education made a speech. In his speech he showed utter disgust at a local school in Jebel Awlia run by the Government. That school which was close to Peter's was a failing school which fell well below standard.

"You should be ashamed of yourselves" said the Minister in anger. "How can you allow "the rakuba school" to become better than your school? How can a *Naziheen* school beat you in your own language and pass exams that you have failed? You are a poor example to the rest of the North of Sudan."

It was quite clear what the Minister of Education was trying to do. He tried to cover the failings of one of his schools by pointing his finger to a *Naziheen* school which was doing better. As far as he was concerned, the Southerners should never be better than the Northerners. His challenge was: "What are you going to do about it?"

People started to take the hint and argue amongst themselves. The incidence of the army gate crush was not a "cordial or a chance visit". The message they wanted to give to the headmaster was: "We are armed and very, very dangerous and we can harm you and your rakuba school".

Peter was no fool. He got the message loud and clear. What he always feared was now being realised. It was just a matter of time.

Nothing happened the following day or the next or the next. People were as friendly as ever. Children started to attend the school again and soon everything became something of the past. Months passed. Peter thought he was being paranoid and then . . .

Boom!

Peter was sleeping with his arms around his wife when suddenly one of the twins started to cry. He got up as Lucinda was tired and did not sleep well during the night. The other twin was crying so she had to sit up until he drifted off to sleep in the early hours of the morning. Peter thought he heard someone hitting the gate of his house to attract his attention. He woke Lucinda and put his trousers and shirt on quickly. As he came out he saw two people at the gate.

"Now what?" He thought. His head was still fuzzy with sleep. As he approached the gate he saw that it was two parents from his school. He hurried to them.

"I hope everything is OK". He knew that everything was not OK.

"Our school has been broken" said one of them, looking scared.

"What do you mean, broken? Do you mean someone broke into it?" said Peter, the truth starting to sink in slowly.

"What I meant is that it has been flattened to the ground. Nothing is left".

Peter and the men ran to the school or what used to be a school. It was as flat as a car park without cars. What greeted him from a distance were pages and pages of ripped school books flying everywhere, school items such as broken rulers and pens. The chairs and tables and all the school furniture was looted. Nothing was left. The watchman was taken to the local Police Headquarters for being 'drunk and disorderly'. His wife fled with the children to 'location unknown'. Peter told the men to tell everyone not to come near the school area. He will go to Khartoum and speak to his employers: The church.

Peter went to the local police headquarters and reported the crime. From the Police attitude and lack of interest he knew they were not going to get anywhere. He reported the incidence in case in future they accuse him of anything.

He related the incidence to the Bishop who showed a lot of concern and sympathy. He was reassured that something will be done about the situation. The bishop wrote a letter of complaint to the Commissioner of Police and begged for peace and protection of innocent and poor people. Charities working in Sudan were alerted with the sad news of the school attack. Within a month money was raised and a new school was reconstructed, made of brick and mortar. Eighteen big classes were built with a water pump in the middle of the compound. The school fence was built very high with a secure solid metal gate. Peter could see that: "If God was with them, who could be against them?"

The school was renamed "Comboni Dar El Naeem Mixed School". It was a school with seven hundred capacity pupils aged between five and fifteen. The aid agencies did a lot of work in the school. Part of the school programme was to provide lunch for the children who were very poor. The school lunch including milk gave the children a chance of survival and education. The school was later divided into an all boys and a girls' school. The girls' school which had even better facilities was also built by aid agencies. The two schools provided jobs and hope to the local Naziheen community so they called the new girls school "Comboni Dar El Huda for Girls". God is indeed the provider and the protector.

As the Community grew, Lucinda thought that people needed better health service in the area. She contacted some of the aids agencies and asked if they could help the community to have a small health centre run by local people. Lucinda was advised to write a project with the help of another Sudanese lady based in Europe. In no time a health centre was built and staff recruited to run the project which included treating minor ailments, women health and vaccination for babies and school children. The project proved very successful and was the envy of all the surrounding districts.

There are six things that Yahweh hates,
seven that his soul abhors:
A haughty look, a lying tongue,
Hands that shed innocent blood,
A heart that weaves wicked plots,
Feet that hurry to do evil,
A false witness who lies with every breath,
a man who sows dissention among brothers.

Proverbs 6: 16-19

Twenty Six

N orah was back to her normal self. She has started to attend school. Mr Tambura was very pleased and relieved to see her come back and take some responsibilities from his hands. There were so many issues which drove him to distraction while trying to get solutions during the period that Norah was off sick. He was starting to appreciate how much Norah has been doing in the school. It was not a job for the faint hearted.

Mr Tambura was not a mere colleague of Norah's, he was also an in-law. He was Mazindo's cousin. Mr Tambura was going to let Norah into a secret. He had a lot of respect for Norah; otherwise he would not undertake such a big risk.

Norah was by herself in her small office when he knocked on the door.

"Come in Albert" said Norah, glad to have a little break from the task in her hand.

He walked in and sat on the chair facing Norah. Norah finished counting on the piece of paper she was scrutinising and smiled at the young man.

"I hope you are not having trouble with 'that' class again."

"No Norah. I came to talk to you about something. I saw Mazindo yesterday"

Norah stared at Albert for about five seconds.

"What?"

"He was at his parents' house" continued Mr Tambura.

Norah recovered enough to say

"When did he come? Why didn't he come to see us?"

Mr Tambura scratched his head.

"Mazindo has arrived about two days ago. He did not want anyone to see him, least Nadi."

"Why"

"He has changed so much. His hair has turned grey. He sustained some wounds one of which has made him limp on his left leg. He looks a total wreck. I helped him shave his beard and cut his hair. He looks much better now. He looks so different from that handsome Mazindo that we all knew. Nadi will get the shock of her life when she sees him."

Norah held her side and rocked herself with despair and anguish.

"Does he know about his son?"

"We told him. He was very angry."

"With who?" shouted Norah quite overcome with emotion.

"With the whole world. He said that the message should have been sent to him by his parents or Nadi"

"Did he tell Nadi where he was going in the first place? Did he leave us an address?" said Norah getting quite cross and upset.

"Does Mazindo know about the returned dowry? Did anybody tell him that his cousin, the "Great Chief" decided to take the dowry and in effect cancel his marriage to Nadi?"

"I do not know "said Mr Tambura evasively. He quickly excused himself after asking Norah to keep what he told her as a secret and not to mention that it was he who told her the news.

Norah is clear about one thing: There was trouble ahead!

Norah quickly called Nadi and told her. Nadi started to shake and cry.

"Why didn't he come to see us?"

"I do not know."

Mazindo was sitting on a comfortable chair talking to his parents on Sunday morning. No one, not even the neighbours knew that he was back in town. He had a shave and a hair cut yesterday and he put some new clothes on after taking a hot bath, but nothing can wash his bitterness and anger at Norah. As for Nadi . . .

He would have had a son. His son would have been five by now. He has been left with nothing. Nadi has run away to her mother as soon as he left. Her mother has left her to run around with other men. Her newest is this "doctor" who is seen every day at their house. Mazindo is a careful planner. He has to sit back and plan as to how to get his wife back. As for Norah, he shook his head. She will never see her daughter again. He will take Nadi very far away to punish Norah. Yes he has been six years away from Nadi but Nadi should have waited for him, even for ten years. Isn't she his wife?

His thoughts drifted back to the "doctor". He accompanied his cousin, Makawa, late in the evening yesterday. They stood behind some trees. Makawa pointed out the doctor from their hiding place as he left a nearby building and walked to the Red Cross compound. The doctor was said to be a Dinka or Nuer or "something or other". To him Mazindo, the doctor was nothing but a *jenge*. To Mazindo the doctor was nothing but a 'naked, ash covered *jenge*'. How could he forgive Nadi? How could Nadi do this to him, he Mazindo, the son of the Royal Avungara clan? How can his wife have an affair with a *jenge* of all people, while he was fighting in the war? He met with so many terrible things which he did not want to recollect. He was put in prison for mutiny and was wounded in battle. He has come home a broken man after his wife, yes his young beautiful Acholi wife died in childbirth. He told no one about this. At least that girl loved him more than Nadi has ever done. Nadi, the cold, cruel, silent tormentor. He thought she will learn to love him when they got married but no, she grew as cold as a water pot. He will bring her here by force and make her obey him. He will not tolerate her attitude and airs anymore. He has changed. He will beat her and shave her hair and then he will see if that doctor will still fancy her. As for 'that son of the naked, ash covered jenge . . .' Mazindo's lips curled into a wicked smile and his eyes shone with unmasked hatred and madness.

His mother said

"Son, eat your food. You have lost so much weight. I want you to look good before you go to see Nadi." She smiled. She was so happy that her beloved son has come back from the dead. He looked terrible when he knocked on their door late at night two days ago. She never thought that she will see him alive. They cried and cried when they saw him. She kept touching him to tell herself that it was indeed her Mazindo. He was so good looking. The girls used to sing his praises. Now he looked like an old man. He lost half his body weight and his hair has gone grey. He lost some of his teeth and his left leg is lame. When Alberto, her cousin's son gave Mazindo a haircut and a shave, his handsome features started to emerge again. She stopped crying only after he took a bath and changed his clothes. Give him two weeks, she said to herself and he will be as right as rain. When he is right he will be able to go to Nadi and claim her. It might be difficult in the beginning because Norah will say that they have reclaimed the dowry and annulled the marriage but they will repay the dowry and reclaim their wife back. As for that doctor, she does not think that Nadi will break her house for a foreigner. Anyway the foreigner might soon go. She was in fear of the day Mazindo learns about the dowry. There will be trouble.

Mazindo's dad was also thinking about the dowry. Why did he have to listen to that fool Makawa? Now they are all in trouble. He was just hoping that when Mazindo goes to Norah, she will be so overwhelmed that she will agree to let Nadi go with him without bringing the topic of the dowry, otherwise they will all be in the biggest trouble ever. When they claimed back the dowry money they were convinced that Mazindo has died and at that time they were angry after the death of their lovely grandson, who looked a picture of Mazindo. When the little boy died, they felt empty and thought it best to sever relations with Norah who has a tongue that can slice the skin off a man's back. Norah can be aggressive and nasty. She told them all sorts of hurtful things and said that their son has taken her daughter's youth and future. Nadi is a lovely, quiet girl. He has never heard anything wrongly said by her although she suffered the most. He wished that they never removed that dowry from Norah. Norah is a very proud woman. She can be embarrassingly direct and abrupt. People think twice before confronting her. Mazindo has always respected her. He hoped things will come to a good conclusion.

When evil men advance against me
To devour my flesh,
They, my opponents, my enemies,
Are the ones who stumble and fall.

The Psalm 27:2

Twenty Seven

Mazindo was sitting with his cousin Makawa *that* evening which was a Saturday. Tomorrow, he will officially announce himself to Norah and will demand to take his wife back. He will go alone, without any ceremony or fuss. He will be very brief and will demand that Nadi should come home with him or else . . .

He sensed that something was not quite right. He sensed it in his parents and in Makawa. It seemed that they were trying to hide something from him. He learnt to use his six senses to their maximum capacity as a combatant in the bush. Something here smells like a rotten fish . . .

He looked at his parents and studied each carefully. His dad was the same. He has never changed. He wept when he first recognised him. His mother had slightly aged. She did not stop crying since he arrived. She said that she used to pray for him every day. She did not believe that he will turn up alive and well. She wanted him to bring Nadi home. She thought that whatever has happened in the past Nadi was still his wife and will be the mother of his children. She has always loved and admired Nadi. Norah should have never taken Nadi away.

Makawa was another kettle of fish. He knew by instinct that Makawa wanted Nadi. According to the Zande tradition, Makawa would have been the most suitable person to redeem Nadi and raise children for him, Mazindo if he was to die. He did not have to ask his parents. He just knew. Makawa told him that the doctor visited Norah's house every day, for whatever reason; he Makawa was not sure. Makawa said that he heard that Norah was ill but later on he heard rumours that Nadi was having an affair

213

with the doctor. When Mazindo asked his parents, they denied that there was such an affair, fearing that Mazindo might do something regrettable. They were quite angry with Makawa for stirring trouble. Mazindo instead kept quiet but asked to stretch his legs when it went dark. He wanted Makawa to accompany him outside.

He asked Makawa to take him and show him where the doctor lived. To their utter luck, Gai has just finished some late work in the clinic. He was accompanied by two guards. His tall and well built frame could easily be identified from a distance. Makawa and Mazindo stood behind a big tree, well hidden across the road from the clinic. Makawa pointed Gai to his cousin. At a certain point they came close enough as they were passing back into the compound. Mazindo was able to pick Gai's looks and the colour of his clothing.

After some time they stepped from behind the tree and walked silently home. Neither mentioned Gai or Nadi again.

On Sunday morning Nadi went to church, dressed in a pink light cotton dress, with a matching head band. She looked stunning and several heads turned as she walked to the front row. She was part of the big choir. It was the High Mass celebrated by the Archbishop. The prayers usually took about three hours or more and the mass was celebrated outside the church under giant trees due to the big number of people.

Today of all days Gai made an effort to attend. He did not come immediately. He could pray for one hour at a stretch but three hours was just not the kind of thing he would do. In actual fact he wanted to pass a message to Nadi—an urgent one. There was no chance for them to speak in her house as there were always those women close by who he suspected were acting as "body guards" or their kids who seem to think he was visiting especially to play with them. Or worse still; Norah . . .

He needed to ask Nadi to come to his house. What happened between them two days ago was a trigger. Does she want him or not? He is a man. He can take any answer. No play acting anymore.

As for Nadi she was thinking about Mazindo. She was told yesterday that Mazindo has been in town for at least two days but has never come to see her or visit his son's grave. She was afraid. Mazindo has never been violent towards her. He was honest and kind. He was a good man and a good husband. Her only problem was that she never loved him. Everyone wanted her to marry him. Her mum encouraged him and he respected her. He used to shower Nadi with presents and used to write her poems. She thought she was lucky especially after the horrible experience . . .

For someone to love and cherish a girl who has been so damaged and defiled . . . Why can't she love him? She was the luckiest girl among all the five that went on that fateful journey. She thought she will love her husband when they get married but as time went by she could not stand him to touch her. She just grew cold and unresponsive and unhappy. This caused Mazindo to become bewildered, confused and angry. Her nightmares would come at times and she would plunge into depression for a week or two. Mazindo was at his wits end. He went for advice to his friend and cousin Makawa.

After sometime, Mazindo started to go out with other women. Makawa told him that as a chief's son, Mazindo could marry another woman who will treat him better and show him more respect. After a marriage that lasted only five months Mazindo disappeared.

After mass, Nadi was talking to the church elders when she noticed Gai leaning against his car with his arms crossed over his chest, looking very bored. She quickly looked about her and walked towards him. He looked as if he was waiting for her. She guessed right.

"Hello doctor!" she said breathlessly with that smile of hers "I didn't know you attend church."

"You are right. I do not know how you guys pray for all that time. I came to see you. I thought to myself: where will I find her? Where will I find her?" He tapped his forehead with his fingers as if thinking, then snapped them "church"

She giggled.

He smiled.

"I want you to come to me today."

"Huh?!" Her eyes grew larger.

"That's right. I want you to come to my house later so that we can discuss 'our situation'." She knew exactly what he meant.

She looked surreptitiously around her as if to see if someone was listening or looking at them.

"I do not know whether I should go."

"Listen, girl" he said losing patience "I am sick and tired of playing games. I need to talk to you. Make it two o'clock. I will be waiting" He added quickly under his breath as he saw a group of her friends approaching.

Before she replied her friends came and joined them. They giggled shyly and said "Hello doctor Gai" to the good looking doctor. Nadi is a lucky girl, they thought. He had eyes for no one but her.

After chatting to them for a short while, he got into his car without directly speaking to her and drove away. He has already told her the message loud and clear. If she does not turn up at his bungalow at two he will go to her house. Nadi knew that. She could run but cannot hide. She would happily go to his bungalow but Mazindo has come back from the dead. She was going to tell him that, when they were interrupted. If Mazindo sniffs the fact that Gai was interested in her, he will be very angry and there might be serious trouble. Oh God. Why was her life so complicated? She did not want Mazindo. She wanted Gai. He has awakened in her such a flood of emotions. She was almost always breathless when she spoke to him. Did he notice? It was because her heart always raced or missed a beat or somersaulted or did something whenever he came near her or looked at her.

Mazindo did not go to church, but heard that Nadi went to church. He gave her time to return home. He was going to pay a visit to his wife. He quickly ate his breakfast and went to see Nadi.

216

Nadi half expected to see Mazindo today. Something told her that he will appear today. True enough there he was. He was much thinner and part of his hair turned grey. His eyes were sad but cautious. She was afraid that he was going to hug or kiss her but he simply held out his hand to her as well as to her mum. They acted as complete strangers. He sat in the big chair. Nadi sat by her mum.

"Nadi, please bring tea" said Norah.

"Do not trouble yourself Norah. I came to take my wife home" He never used to call Norah by her first name. He always referred to her as *Nina* meaning "mum" in the Zande language.

The battle line was drawn.

"Didn't your family explain to you what happened?"

"No. Did anything happen?"

"Yes" replied Norah.

"Nonsense" said Mazindo, getting angry. "I want my wife"

"I am no longer your wife. Your family have annulled the marriage" replied Nadi.

"Listen Nadi. You are the cause of all my troubles. You should have never removed from the house when I left in the first place. Keep your mouth shut or I will shut it for you".

"Do not speak to my daughter like this in my own house. Before you went off to save the world, did you think that you had a wife? You turn up after six years; six bloody years and demand to take 'your wife' home? If it was one of these other Zande girls she would have been married by now to another man, with six children. Your cousin the Big Chief, your mother, your father and other people came here and demanded that we pay them back the dowry money. I laid the money you paid as a dowry right here on this very table. They took it and went away".

"What?" shouted Mazindo, standing in the middle of the room menacingly.

Norah quickly called the two women to sit with Nadi while she went out of the room. She came back with the signed copy of the document which stated the return of the dowry to Mazindo's family. Mazindo took the letter and read it. He was incensed. He ripped the letter to shreds and said to Nadi.

"You are my wife no matter what. The filthy money cannot annul our marriage. Our marriage was a vow in front of the elders. Money cannot change that."

"Where are the elders? They are the ones who annulled the marriage. They said that you were dead and the child was dead. They said that I have brought them nothing but bad luck" said Nadi.

Norah said "I think that we need to sit down again and talk properly about everything". She was feeling tired of fighting every one every single day. First, it was Makawa and then Mazindo's family and now Mazindo. She just felt drained and completely shattered.

"No mother. It is my life. It is about time someone gave heed to what I want. I do not want to sit down again with anybody. I have heard enough insults and enough blame. Leave me alone. I do not want to go home with you Mazindo. I do not love you. You cannot force me to go anywhere with you."

"Look who is speaking! So you have grown up in the few years I went away!" said Mazindo with contempt, then continued "Nadi, I know what you have been doing. Sleeping around with men, haven't you? Do you think I do not know? Your jenge doctor visits you here and your mother encouraging you? What kind of a family is this? I am going to beat you in front of your mum if you do not obey me. I am telling you to come home with me now!"

Nadi fled. By now some of the neighbours came, after hearing the raised voices. They stood their ground and said that they had a right as neighbours to protect Norah and her family. They asked Mazindo to leave peacefully.

Mazindo was in a wild rage. He went quickly to his parent's home and did not answer their anxious queries. They could see that things have gone awry in Norah's house. He went into his room. He was shaking with fury. His mind was like a torrent of lava. He could not contain his anger and madness. Instinctively he put his arm under the bed. His parents hovered anxiously near the door. He walked swiftly towards the door and slammed it shut on their horrified faces. His mother moved away sobbing. His father looked totally bewildered.

"Go away. I want to be left alone!" Mazindo shouted.

His father knew not to say anything. His son has changed. He thought "May God put a curse on the SPLA from here up to the Dinka land. I have lost my son." He also broke into bitter tears for the first time since Mazindo arrived. His son has never shouted at him or disrespected him before today.

Meanwhile Mazindo had one thing in his mind. He reached quickly under his bed and brought out "his friends"; An AK-47 assault rifle and a mean looking knife, tied to the gun. The knife was in its sheath. He inspected the gun briefly. Yes it was loaded. He knew it was loaded because he cleaned it and checked it every day. It came to him as a habit to check his gun whenever he wanted to use it. He quickly wrapped the rifle in a blanket and a small mat that was lying on the floor. He unsheathed the knife and held it in his hand for a minute or two.

He had a flash back. Those bulging scared eyes of his victim, who very nearly killed him. He, Mazindo was quicker. A sudden instinctive movement and the tables were turned. From a victim *he* became the assailant. Mazindo quickly over powered him and slashed his throat in one smooth thrust . . .

How he would love to do the same to the *Jenge* but no, this time he wanted to finish the job fast and from a distance. He threw the knife back in the wrap and kicked it under the bed.

He marched out, carrying his wrapped up "friend" which to anyone else looked like a small bedding.

He made for the Red Cross compound. He stood for a while and saw the old man Tomazo. He asked him about the doctor.

"He has just gone to that building to get something. Today is Sunday so they do not work. What is it that you want?"

"I was asked to give him a letter from one of the nurses in the hospital"

"You can go to him in this next building" said Tomazo pointing to the building next to their compound.

Mazindo went quickly round the building and waited behind a tree.

He could hear other voices. So the doctor was not alone. After about ten minutes, Mazindo saw two armed guards holding cases in their hands going towards the main building. When they disappeared round the corner, Mazindo waited and listened carefully. No one was about. It was about one o'clock.

During that time as the area was under the SPLA jurisdiction, the aid agencies used to hire armed guards from the SPLA soldiers to guard their buildings and staff. The aid agencies and the SPLA leadership used to negotiate those deals and so create jobs for some soldiers who were in dire need of cash.

The two guards with Gai were from the SPLA.

NOW the doctor was alone.

Mazindo took out his rifle and slowly approached the building in a stealth move. The guards shut the door behind them as they were going but the window was open. Mazindo could see the figure of a person moving in the room. When the two guards were going towards the Red Cross building, they were accosted by another member of staff, so they stopped and started chatting. At that point Mazindo thought they were already in the Red Cross compound and therefore out of sight.

Unbeknown to Mazindo one of the guards was standing facing directly the building where the clinic was and saw the figure of a man approaching the building in a combat style with a rifle pointing towards the office they have just left. The guard was baffled and made the others turn round and look.

Gai who was picking some notes from a shelf, was not aware how exposed he was to his predator. He moved back to his desk which was in the corner of the room. Suddenly he tripped over some wiring and fell on the floor, cursing loudly. At the same time a hail of four or five shots were fired through the window nearly deafening him. He lay down dazed and bewildered. His survival instinct kicked in. He quickly crawled under the massive desk.

What the hell was happening? Where are the guards?

Again a quick burst of bullets through the open window.

He was a dead man. It will happen anytime now.

He then heard shots from different directions and loud shouting and commotion.

The sound of running feet and then silence.

Gai kept in his position, wondering how he was still alive.

He then heard voices and a bigger commotion.

"Doctor, are you there?" He recognised the voice of one of the guards. He did not immediately answer.

"Oh no! Do you think he got shot?" There was genuine concern in the voice. They stood at the door peering anxiously and calling his name.

They found him standing in the middle of the room, in a dazed state. Other people came rushing in. One of the guards spoke sternly "Everyone stay out. We need this building cleared in one minute."

A car was quickly brought round and Gai was taken to his bungalow.

He was examined by one of the senior nurses. He was fine apart from grazes on his elbows and knees.

He was shaken but not stirred.

He was given a glass of sherry. That helped him regroup.

He wanted to know why someone wanted to shoot at him. Was it a case of mistaken identity?

Straight away armed guards were deployed round the perimeter of the building. No one from outside was to be admitted inside the compound. One of the drivers later came with the news that it was rumoured that the culprit was called Mazindo, Norah's son-in-law and the son of Lewis Badi one of the local chiefs.

Gai now knew that it was not a case of mistaken identity.

He wanted to go and see Nadi. He was advised by the coordinator of the Red Cross and the other workers to stay put as he was in grave danger. Gai did not care. He needed to see Nadi now and nobody could stop him. In the end he was given guards to accompany him, one of them driving the car. When they arrived at Norah's house they found the house locked up and there was no sign of anyone inside. One of the neighbours told Gai that Norah, Nadi and all the family went to stay at Norah's cousin's house about five miles out of Yambio. He would not elaborate on the reason why they went.

One of the UN officials interviewed Gai about the incidence. The Red Cross coordinator radioed their headquarters in Lokichoggio (shortened Loki) in Kenya. Gai was advised to leave Yambio immediately for his own safety. Another doctor will replace him. He will swap places with that doctor.

The next day David told him that Nadi and her mother went to a relative's house as Mazindo went to their house yesterday and demanded to take his wife. Norah could not immediately let Nadi go with Mazindo.

"Why?" said Gai pretending not to show any interest.

"Norah refused saying that she needed the elders to meet in order to sort out some problems before allowing Nadi to go with him."

Gai was very quiet. He eventually asked.

"How do you know that Norah wanted a meeting?"

"She told me so when I visited her".

"What about Nadi?"

"Well she was very upset but of course in our culture you have to go with what the elders say. I think eventually they will sort out their problems. I visited Mazindo in hospital. He has been shot in the leg by the guards before being captured. Did you know that?"

I wish he was shot in the head thought Gai.

"Yes" he said shortly.

"I do not know why he accused you of having an affair with Nadi. Probably it was Chief Makawa who stirred all this trouble. He wants Nadi for himself."

It was that rude, inquisitive chief! Things are now clearer. What a tangle!

"Mazindo was relieved when he heard that you are leaving Yambio. He said that he is planning to get his wife home as quickly as can be arranged" David was completely unaware of his friend's anguish. He went on, "I explained your connection with Norah's family and that it was a total misunderstanding. I said to him that you used to visit because Norah was seriously ill and that it was I who introduced you to the family. Mazindo was sorry and said that it was the chief who gave him the wrong information."

"Tell him that I accept his apology" said Gai sarcastically but it was lost on David who had no idea about the strong feelings between Nadi and Gai.

In the evening David visited Norah. They came home after hearing that Mazindo was safely in the hospital and under two armed guards.

David told Norah and Nadi about the attack on Gai by Mazindo. Nadi tried her best not to show emotion although she was shaking and felt faint when she heard how close Mazindo was to killing Gai.

The bombshell fell when David said that Gai was travelling for good tomorrow morning. He was advised to relocate for his own safety. Nadi could not hide her emotions any longer. She stood up quickly and went inside the house. David looked with surprise at Norah but she said nothing. After sometime David went inside the house looking for Nadi. He found her lying face down on her bed, crying.

He stood for some time watching her from the door.

"Nadi, what is it?"

She turned her face to the wall.

"Are you upset about Gai?"

She shook her head from side to side and kept on weeping silently.

He came closer and touched her shoulder

"I am sorry my sister. I had no idea . . ."

When he went away that evening he wanted to kick himself. How did he miss that? So, these two love each other and he had no clue. He was preoccupied with Margaret, his fiancée. That dowry list was driving him crazy and he could not even raise half the amount of money needed.

Why were Nadi and Gai so secretive? No wonder Gai was so quiet when he talked to him about Nadi and Mazindo. How could he, David be so stupid? To be fair, they never gave him any indication that there was something going on between them, apart from the way Gai liked teasing Nadi and how she laughed a lot at the silly things he used to say to her. He, David did not read anything into that.

Let him kiss me with the kisses of his mouth.
Your love is more delightful than wine.

The Song of Songs 1:1

Twenty Eight

The next day Nadi rose very early in the morning; at about five o'clock. She hardly slept the whole night. The thought of Gai travelling tomorrow was shattering for her. Things have moved so fast that in a few hours Gai was going to walk away from her life forever. What was most upsetting for her was that she might never see him again. She was told that Gai's compound was now encircled by armed guards and no one from the locals was allowed to enter. The doctor will be under escort until he finally boards a plane, probably to Kenya or Uganda. She, Nadi will be left with nothing but heartache and scandalous gossip. Everyone was now convinced that she had an affair with Gai and that the whole thing was a love triangle which has turned nasty by the resurfacing of her husband Mazindo from the SPLA.

She sat down on the bed and thought what to do? Everyone was still asleep. She could sneak out now and try and see Gai, if they will let her enter the compound. These aid planes land very early so she better hurry up. She hurriedly slipped on her pink cotton dress which she wore when she last went to church. It was the nearest thing that her hand fell on; she dared not put on the lamp in case someone wakes up. She took a light square piece of cloth and covered her head and quickly slipped soundlessly outside. Their house was about two miles away so she started to walk quickly, running part of the way.

After about twenty minutes, she could see the walls of the compound. She slowed down and took a deep breath. One of the old slippers she was wearing got caught by a small stone and its strap came loose. She threw them into the bushes and walked bare footed. Her feet became muddied from the rain puddles and started to ache and the bottom of her skirt became soiled with the red mud water. She did not care. All she cared about was to see Gai.

On approaching the compound, she saw two armed guards standing near the gate. She was so frightened; she wanted to retrace her steps. She mustered her strength and came near the gate. She saw Tomazo walking past.

She shouted to him "Uncle" in the Zande dialect. He turned round surprised. When he saw her he approached the gate which was locked with a chain and a big padlock.

"Nadi" there was concern in his eyes. "What brings you here so early in the morning my daughter? Is your mum OK?"

An idea came to Nadi.

"Yes, she is but she needs a vital medication which Dr Gai promised her but did not give it to her yet. I heard that Dr Gai is leaving this morning so I came to collect the medicine"

"Stay where you are because no one is allowed in. I will go and tell the Doctor."

After some time which Nadi thought was eternity, Tomazo appeared with another guard. The guard called Nadi to come closer and state what she wanted. Nadi explained to him in English what she told Tomazo. He told her to wait for him. He went back to talk to the doctor.

Gai asked him "What does she look like?" He did not want to take any risks in case it was someone else.

"She is that tall and is wearing a pink dress" said the guard pointing to just below his head. He was unsure as to what to say.

"Pale skin, big eyes?" prompted Gai

The guard was relieved "Yes, yes and pretty". He smiled slyly, suspecting something more between these two than a mere doctor-patient relationship. He drew an imaginary hourglass with his hands in the air.

Gai fixed him with a cold stare.

"Let her come".

The guard went to fetch Nadi and led her to Gai's bungalow.

Gai came out and the guard went away. Nadi was shocked when she saw Gai. He was always well groomed, wearing casual but quite expensive clothes from what she could gather. He was wearing light grey pyjamas with thin darker stripes and looked "rough". His eyes were blood shot, later she discovered that he was drinking nearly the whole night. His thick afro hair was unkempt and he needed a shave.

She tried to smile at him but his face was so hard set that her smile froze and the things she wanted to say disappeared from her tongue.

He indicated to her to sit on one of the chairs in the lounge and quickly went inside the bedroom. She could hear the sound of water splashing.

He was not expecting anyone at this time of the morning, least of all Nadi. She caught him in the worst time and he was in a foul mood anyway. He brushed his teeth quickly, washed his face with cold water and poured more cold water on his head. He came out with a towel in his hand still drying his hair. After drying his hair he threw the towel carelessly on one of the chairs and went to switch on the kettle in the kitchenette opposite the lounge chairs where Nadi was sitting.

"Tea or coffee?" he asked her shortly.

"Thank you. I am not having either".

What the hell has she come for? He was irritated at her calm and unruffled expression as if she was sitting in the queen's salon, waiting for tea. God, he was nearly killed by that crazy husband of hers and she seemed not in the least concerned. Her duplicity, her manipulation and temptation has nearly cost him his life. Since she came to him out of her own accord he will not let her go until she told him everything.

He quickly made himself black coffee in a big mug took it and sat down opposite her.

"What brings you here?"

"I came because David said that you are travelling this morning. Is it true?"

"Yes" he said shortly.

He seemed so unfriendly and not at all pleased to see her that she wondered if it was a good idea to have paid him this visit after all.

"Does your husband know that you are coming here?" he demanded softly.

She now started to realise that Gai was displeased with her and was blaming her for the attack by Mazindo.

"Mazindo is not my husband" she answered, shaken.

"Really?!!" His question was full of sarcasm. "Let me think, does this make him your 'brother' then? Nadi, Nadi . . . Ever since I have known you, you have been very secretive and evasive with your past as far as I am concerned. You gave me the wrong picture about yourself. You do not have to tell me the whole of your life story but why pretend that you were never married?"

Nadi's lips started to quiver. That would have been a clear warning of a gathering storm to someone who knows her well but Gai, unaware did not take heed and went on

"Tell me, do you enjoy it when men fight over you? I was told that many poor men were left dangling after you and you were the cause of many fights. My dear girl, you better watch out because if you continue like this, one day you might just get seriously hurt".

Gai wanted to hurt her as much as he has been hurt. He felt angry because he did not as much as touch this witch and he found himself being accused right, left and centre. He felt that Nadi was deliberately refusing to clarify things to her husband and others. If he had an affair with her he would not have minded whatever was thrown at him. He came to realise that the real reason she refused his advances in the first place was because she was waiting for her husband. She was just playing with him and that really hurt.

"I never lied to you about anything. You never asked me if I was married or not. My life has been so horrible; I am ashamed to talk to anyone about it, least of all you. Mazindo has stopped to be my husband a long time ago." Her voice broke "Oh . . ." She stood up and held her chest as if in real physical pain. She could not believe that one day Gai of all people would speak to her with so much anger and disgust. She felt as if she was going to faint.

In a quick movement, she pulled the chair back and started to run towards the door.

"Wow, wow, where do you think you are going?" Totally unprepared, Gai stood up quickly and caught up with her as she was exiting through the door. He gently turned her around and all he could see was a flood of tears covering her face. She started to push him away to free herself but she could not match his strength. He held her to him and she started to sob loudly.

"I am sorry my darling. I am sorry my sweetheart" he kept saying to her over and over.

He bent and kissed her forehead and as if they could not help themselves, their lips met in a kiss that wiped all the agony, the frustration, the anguish and longing. After some time he held her hand and led her towards where they were sitting. He sat down and made her sit on his knees.

231

He was mortified and felt ashamed at his outburst. He did not know what got into his head. He did not tell her how elated he felt when she walked through the door to see him. His anger came as a side effect of his pent up emotion and uncertainty for not being able to know exactly what she wanted. Does she want him or does she want to return to her husband?

"I am sorry for being such a pig just now. Please forgive me. I was angry at the situation I found myself in. I wanted to know if you two are going to be man and wife again. I was so frustrated. I went to your house but no one was there. I wanted to ask you if you care about me. I was told by one of the neighbours that you went to your uncle's house. I thought that if you really cared you would have come to me yesterday, but I waited in vain. David later came and said that the elders are planning to get you and your husband back together. Can you imagine how I felt? In the end it seemed to me that you have decided to return to him. I was surprised to see you this morning."

"Mazindo came to our house as soon as I arrived home from church. When you came to the church and asked me to come to your house, I wanted to tell you that Mazindo has come back but the girls were coming to talk to us. He demanded that I should go home with him straight away or he will beat me in front of my mum. He accused me of having an affair with you. My mum said to him that the dowry was returned to his family and that I am no longer his wife. She explained to him that the dowry was returned after a big meeting and that they all signed some papers. My mother showed him the signed document. He took it, read it and ripped it to pieces and said that whatever was done was done without his will. He just wanted me back. I had to run away and hide in a neighbour's house. He then went away. We left the house because we were not sure what he will do next. All the people in our house went to my uncle's house which is about five miles from here. We rode on bikes through the forest. It was only the next day after hearing that Mazindo was in hospital under armed guards that my uncle let us come home. Late last night David came to see us and told me that he nearly killed you and that your compound is guarded day and night. When he told me that you were travelling for good I was beside myself. I wanted only to come and see you and tell you how sorry I am".

Poor Tomazo who wanted to come and ask Dr Gai about the clothes which was promised to him, received the shock of his life when he saw Nadi and Gai in the veranda. He was carrying a garden tool in his hand. It dropped with a loud "clonk" on the floor as the shock was registered in his brain. His jaw dropped and his eyes bulged from his head.

"In the name of Mary, the mother of Jesus, what is Nadi doing sitting on the doctor's knees in that scandalous fashion?" Tomazo looked nervously around him to see if there was another witness to this "shameful behaviour". As far as he was concerned, Nadi was married to Mazindo. The day before yesterday the doctor was attacked by Mazindo who everyone thought was mad to accuse the doctor, but now he has witnessed the affair with his own eyes. Oh God if he knew what she was up to, he wouldn't have helped her to get into the compound. And Dr Gai, he always seemed the perfect gentleman. He is so polite and respectful to everybody. Tomazo would never have believed that Dr Gai of all people will resort to having an affair with someone else's wife. This shows you that the world is coming to an end. He started to walk away deflated and kept thinking: Perhaps he should tell Norah about her daughter's bad behaviour. He was very disappointed in Nadi who he always praised to his wife and nieces. He was deep in thought that he nearly passed his own little hut near the gate.

"To-ma-zo-o-o"

"A, Na-a-a" meaning "yes madam" in Zande.

"Are you becoming blind as well as deaf? Where do you think you are going?"

Meanwhile Nadi and Gai were so wrapped up in themselves that they were totally oblivious to Tomazo's injured sensibility and pride.

Nadi wrapped her arm around Gai's neck and he had his arm around her waist.

They looked so happy and so different from the two people who sat down an hour ago.

233

Gai turned Nadi's face so that he was looking into her eyes and slowly asked

"Nadi, I have just got over an hour to go to the airport. Do you want to come with me to Kenya?"

It took Nadi few seconds to register what he was implying. Gai noticed her eyes registering surprise and then they suddenly clouded over. She took her arm off his shoulder and stood up.

She let out a deep sigh. Gai's face fell and he stood up facing her.

"I am sorry. I knew you might say no, but it was worth asking" He sounded deflated.

"No, Gai. You do not understand. You were right when you said that I have been hiding things from you."

She looked as if she was going to start crying again, but she controlled herself and continued

"My life has been a disaster, Gai. You do not want to tie yourself to someone like me. I am nothing but a rubbish heap. No one that knows what happened to me would want to associate with me. I am not fit for someone like you. If you knew what has happened to me you will not want to see me again."

By now she was sobbing again and turned away from Gai. This time he did not make an attempt to touch her.

"Are you talking about the things that happened to you when you were captured by the rebels?" She swung around so quickly that she nearly lost her balance. Her eyes looked like saucers with surprise.

"How did you know?" and then something dawned on her "Who told you?"

"Is it important for you to know who told me? I knew right from the day I first met you"

"Then why didn't you say something?"

"Why should I? I was told that you do not want me to know."

"Oh" she said quite put out by the fact that people were talking about her behind her back. She will speak to David, the two faced tale teller, as soon as she sees him. She knew it was him and she was very cross.

Gai took this chance, gathered her in his arms and gave her a long lingering kiss, hoping to recapture the dreamy, magical moment again.

"I do not care what happened to you in the past. When I first saw you, you completely blew me away with your beauty. To me you are beautiful inside and out. I want you to be mine and I promise you that whatever happened in your past will be kept there; in the past. We are both young and we have a whole lifetime in front of us. Our love will be enough to help us in our journey."

"Ohhhhh, no one has ever said such nice things to me. Are you sure you are from this world or am I dreaming?" He sat down and she sat close to him, with her head on his shoulder. He put his arm around her and played with her hair for a while.

"Yes you are dreaming girl, because if you do not wake up quickly we are going to miss our flight".

"Gai, are you sure you want me to come with you?"

"Nadi," he mimicked her "I really, truly, honestly want you to come with me. Do you have travel documents?"

"I think so"

"So you are not sure"

"I will have to go home and look for it. I used it last year to travel to Uganda to see my brother and sisters"

"Go to Tomazo to take you to any one of the drivers so that they can give you a lift. Get the documents and go straight to the airport. I will meet you there. Do not delay. Do you think Norah will allow you to travel with me?"

"Of course she will. I am not a child anymore. She will not be able to stop me."

Twenty Nine

―――――――――――――

When Nadi went home, Norah was beside herself with worry looking for her daughter.

"Where have you been? I nearly raised the alarm, thinking that Mazindo's friends have abducted you".

"I went to see Gai. I am travelling with him to Kenya in an hour".

"What?" shouted Norah. She looked as if she suddenly saw Nadi growing another head.

Nadi started to look for her documents which she easily located in her mum's wardrobe. She checked it. Everything was fine. She took her handbag and carefully put them in.

"Mum, Gai loves me and I love him. He asked me to go with him. Please do not be angry. He was put under armed guard in case someone tries to attack him. He was told not to go anywhere except the airport and under guard, so he cannot come here to explain things to you and ask your permission. He promised that he will take good care of me. Please mum let me go."

"My child, I will never stand in the way of your happiness. You are old enough to make your own choices and decisions. I know that you love him and I know that he loves you. You have always been an obedient and good daughter. I can't hold you back. I hope and wish that one day I see you happy in your own home."

Nadi ran to her mother and hugged her and cried. They both knew that they might not see each other again.

Nadi then said that she was going to the airport. It was about eight. They had to be at the airport at half past eight.

"Are you going to Nairobi by plane looking like that?" asked Norah pointing to Nadi as she started to say her goodbyes.

"Yes. Why are you asking?"

"Did you see how you are looking like?" She held Nadi by the hand and made her stand before the full length mirror built in the wardrobe. Nadi herself had second thoughts when she saw her image. Her hair looked as if she was dragged through the bushes. Her eyes were red and puffy from the crying and sobbing she did this morning. Her pink dress was crumpled as if she used it as a night gown. The hem of her dress was soiled and her feet were dirty. She looked at her mum helplessly.

"There is plenty of hot water on the fire outside. If I were you I would hurry up and take a good wash."

One of the women quickly prepared warm water and put it in the bathroom. Nadi quickly scrubbed herself until her skin shone. When she went back to the room, she saw her Ethiopian dress spread on her bed. It was made of pure soft cotton, embroidered with bluish green and black boarder round the neck and down the middle, stopping half way. A beautiful design of a small cross was attached to a larger cross beneath it, just above the hem. The crosses were made of a number of smaller intricate crosses which lent the whole design a magical and highly artistic look. A bluish green boarder, framed in black ran just above the hem of the dress. The colour of the dress was off white and it had a gauze matching *netela* or shawl with matching bluish green boarders at both ends. She remembered that it was one of two dresses which was sent to her mum as a present by Auntie Susan when she went to Ethiopia for a conference. The other dress was made of different shades of red, yellow and green. The white dress was smaller and was meant for Nadi but she was not interested to wear it at the time because it looked too "fussy" and unfamiliar for the type of normal wear in Yambio. Everyone could not deny how beautiful the dress was. Nadi asked her mum to look after it for her and forgot about it. She dried herself and put plenty of that oil which has fascinated Gai with its natural perfume. Norah helped her in the dress which looked as if it was made for her. The hem reached up to her ankles. She then put some oil on her hair until it shone and rearranged it; pinning it on the left side with a clip, while leaving the other side to fall over the right side of her face. The Kohl was her only make up. After treating her eyes, she looked the complete opposite of the girl she was half an hour ago. Her eyes looked huge and dreamy and she could not help feeling quite pleased with herself. She slipped on her white slippers which was one of the products smuggled from Zaire by local traders. Her mother then brought a black pouch and opened it to reveal the most exquisite silver jewellery set Nadi has ever seen. Her mum explained to her that Susan sent it with the dresses but Nadi did not see it as her mum never wore those things. How could Norah wear such expensive and flashy jewellery in this terrible time? The set was Ethiopian, made of large diamond shaped earrings with small bluish stones. The necklace, made of a thick but very smooth intricately woven chain, had a matching diamond shaped pendant reaching the level of Nadi's pointed breasts. The bracelet had a matching diamond shaped centrepiece with four fine chains at the sides. She put the scarf halfway over her head. When Nadi was ready she looked like a bride.

Norah then gave Nadi five hundred Kenyan Shillings the remainder of money she acquired when she went to Kenya for a short course. Nadi said that Gai asked her not to take anything as he will buy her everything she needed, but Norah insisted that she should not go to Gai penniless.

"I will miss the plane" cried Nadi

"If he loves you he will wait for you. I will give you a piece of advice my daughter; never go to a man's house looking like a beggar because one day he will remind you of how you came to him. Trust me. If you have nothing, wash yourself, oil your skin and put on your best rags."

Norah then asked for some water to be brought and asked Nadi to stand near the door leading to the veranda. She took some water in her mouth and sprayed Nadi. This is a Zande custom of blessing by the elders. This ritual is performed as a blessing and cleansing of the souls. The Zande elders believe that the cold water will wash away all the heated words, curses etc. uttered in the past. This will then allow the person to travel in peace and safety.

As Nadi got into the car with her small hold all with few of her belongings on Norah's insistence, the Red Cross plane was circling over Yambio.

They arrived at the airport after fifteen minutes. Nadi breathed a big sigh of relief when she saw the plane.

Gai went to the airport at about eight. When Nadi left him, he was in seventh heaven. He could not believe how his luck has turned. Everything seemed so gloomy for him and now he can safely say that he was the happiest man not only in Yambio but in the whole wide World. He could not believe that Nadi is actually his and that Mazindo will rot in hospital or prison. He was humming some crazy songs when he shaved and took bath. Everything was absolutely fabulous.

He dressed quickly and gathered his bags. It was ten to eight. He went and said good bye to the rest of the team and asked the driver to take him to the airport. A guard had to accompany him.

He jumped out of the car when he arrived at the airport but left his bags. His driver and the guard jumped out as well. The guard taking his stance not far away from Gai. He had a gun. It was quarter past eight. Doubts started to assail him.

What if she does not turn up? His elation started to turn into agony with every minute of the clock. By the time it was half past eight his fingers were racking his hair. People who know him well have noted this as a sign when things are not going well for him. The plane suddenly appeared and touched down. Other travellers were standing there watching the plane taxi and come to a halt. He told the pilot that he expected "someone else" to travel with him. The pilot said that he was already on a busy schedule and will not delay more than the thirty minutes allocated.

Gai moved away from the man before he committed murder after stating clearly that he will not travel without that "someone else". The pilot guessed what was going on but kept his mouth shut.

Just as Gai was giving up the land rover with the Red Cross sign suddenly materialised from among the trees. Gai tried very hard to crane his neck and strain his eyes to see if Nadi was in the car. For a moment he felt faint as he could not see her. He knew that Norah will be the stumbling block. He felt sick and turned away, nearly bumping into the pilot who was reading some notes held in his hand.

The car stopped a few feet from him and when he turned round the most eye catching picture presented itself. Nadi was standing there bang in front of him, a distance of about ten meters. When their eyes met, she gave him that half smile, exactly like the one when they first met. Her eyes smiled more than her lips. She looked like a bride or a queen or something regal and dazzling. She looked surreal in this war torn, rugged part of the globe.

Gai and the pilot were now standing side by side and both could not help gaping at the remarkable picture in front of them.

"Wow" said the pilot." This is certainly something worth waiting for."

Gai collected his wits and came towards her.

"You look like the queen of Sheba, my love." He smiled down at her and took her hand, walking with her towards the pilot.

"Meet Nadi, my fiancée. Captain Brown, our pilot."

Gai took Nadi's hand and started to lead her to the plane.

"Not so speedy Dr Casanova Gonzales. I need to look at her documents."

After checking the documents the luggage was loaded on the plane and they were soon airborne.

"What does the queen of Sheba look like?" she wanted to know, looking up at him through her amazingly long and thick eyelashes.

Gai winked and gave her a crooked smile.

"Like you" He whispered softly in her ear.

> *"Wherever you go, I will go,*
> *Wherever you live, I will live.*
> *Your people shall be my people,*
> *And your God, my God.*
> *Wherever you die, I will die*
> *And there I will be buried.*
> *May Yahweh do this thing to me*
> *And more also,*
> *If even death should come between us."*

Ruth 1:16-17

Acknowledgements

I would like to thank Retired Lieutenant General Joseph Lagu Yanga for his part in laying the foundation for the Independence of South Sudan. Without his solid foundation we wouldn't be here today.

Gillian Jones, Lucia Raymondo Tambura, Victor Vuni Joseph, Damien Obringer and Nasir Atanasio Surur.

My children; Andrew, Cynthia and Patrick. Their support has helped to keep me focused and motivated.

My biggest thanks to all the unsung heroes of the Sudanese civil war: men, women and children who have inspired me to bare my feelings and write their story.

Without my husband's assistance, inspiration and guidance I would have found it hard to break the taboo and finish writing the book.